Praise for

One Bad Apple

"There is a delightful charm to this small-town regional cozy . . . Sheila Connolly provides a fascinating whodunit filled with surprises." —*The Mystery Gazette*

"An example of everything that is right with the cozy mystery . . . Sheila Connolly has written a winner." —*Lesa's Book Critiques*

"A warm, very satisfying read." —*Romantic Times* (4 stars)

"The premise and plot are solid, and Meg seems a perfect fit for her role." —*Publishers Weekly*

"Antique apple trees and historic houses—what's not to like about Sheila Connolly's *One Bad Apple*? It's a delightful look at small town New England, with an intriguing puzzle thrown in."

—JoAnna Carl,
author of the Chocoholic Mysteries

"A fun start to a promising new mystery series. Thoroughly enjoyable . . . I can't wait for the next book and a chance to spend more time with Meg and the good people of Granford."

—Sammi Carter,
author of the Candy Shop Mysteries

Berkley Prime Crime titles by Sheila Connolly

ONE BAD APPLE
ROTTEN TO THE CORE

Rotten to the Core

Sheila Connolly

BERKLEY PRIME CRIME, NEW YORK

THE BERKLEY PUBLISHING GROUP
Published by the Penguin Group
Penguin Group (USA) Inc.
375 Hudson Street, New York, New York 10014, USA

Penguin Group (Canada), 90 Eglinton Avenue East, Suite 700, Toronto, Ontario M4P 2Y3, Canada
(a division of Pearson Penguin Canada Inc.)
Penguin Books Ltd., 80 Strand, London WC2R 0RL, England
Penguin Books Ireland, 25 St. Stephen's Green, Dublin 2, Ireland (a division of Penguin Books Ltd.)
Penguin Group (Australia), 250 Camberwell Road, Camberwell, Victoria 3124, Australia
(a division of Pearson Australia Group Pty. Ltd.)
Penguin Books India Pvt. Ltd., 11 Community Centre, Panchsheel Park, New Delhi—110 017, India
Penguin Group (NZ), 67 Apollo Drive, Rosedale, North Shore 0632, New Zealand
(a division of Pearson New Zealand Ltd.)
Penguin Books (South Africa) (Pty.) Ltd., 24 Sturdee Avenue, Rosebank, Johannesburg 2196,
South Africa

Penguin Books Ltd., Registered Offices: 80 Strand, London WC2R 0RL, England

This is a work of fiction. Names, characters, places, and incidents either are the product of the author's imagination or are used fictitiously, and any resemblance to actual persons, living or dead, business establishments, events, or locales is entirely coincidental. The publisher does not have any control over and does not assume any responsibility for author or third-party websites or their content.

PUBLISHER'S NOTE: The recipes contained in this book are to be followed exactly as written. The publisher is not responsible for your specific health or allergy needs that may require medical supervision. The publisher is not responsible for any adverse reactions to the recipes contained in this book.

ROTTEN TO THE CORE

A Berkley Prime Crime Book / published by arrangement with the author

PRINTING HISTORY
Berkley Prime Crime mass-market edition / July 2009

Copyright © 2009 by Sheila Connolly.
Cover illustration by Mary Ann Lasher.
Interior text design by Laura K. Corless.

ISBN: 978-0-425-22876-0

BERKLEY® PRIME CRIME
Berkley Prime Crime Books are published by The Berkley Publishing Group,
a division of Penguin Group (USA) Inc.,
375 Hudson Street, New York, New York 10014.
BERKLEY® PRIME CRIME and the PRIME CRIME logo are trademarks of Penguin Group (USA) Inc.

PRINTED IN THE UNITED STATES OF AMERICA

10 9 8 7 6 5 4 3 2 1

Acknowledgments

Once again, I have reaped the benefits of the information and advice from a wonderful group of people in bringing this book to fruition. Thanks go to my agent, Jacky Sach, of BookEnds, and my editor, Shannon Jamieson Vazquez, who never fails to make my words better. And as always, Sisters in Crime and the very talented Guppies provided bottomless support (and even titles).

Duane W. Greene, Department of Plant, Soil and Insect Sciences at the University of Massachusetts, and director of the University's Cold Spring Orchard, inspired this book when he said that pesticide issues could possibly drive someone to murder. Marvina and Jon Brook of Muddy Brook Farm in Granby have kept me up-to-date on the status of the surviving apple trees on the former Warner property. Christie Higginbottom, research historian and horticulture and landscape specialist at Old Sturbridge Village, offered wonderful information on historical orchards and heirloom apples. And Mother Nature came through again, with yet another wonderful apple crop.

Finally, I need to thank my entomologist husband, who first made me aware of integrated pest management, and my daughter, who continues to serve as my apple-bearer, taste-tester, and critic.

1

Striding up the hill toward the apple orchard, Meg Corey inhaled the spring air that smelled of damp and growing things. Maybe the weather was just teasing her: after all, it was only March, and New England winters were notoriously unpredictable. For all she knew, it could snow tomorrow. But she didn't care: she was going to enjoy the moment.

At the top of the rise she paused to look back at the house. The winter had been kind to it, from what she could see. The curling shingles were still more or less intact, and the peeling paint was still clinging to the old wood. She would look into getting a new roof and a paint job when the weather warmed up for good. At least the creaky furnace had limped through the winter without failing, and her new septic system was working just fine—ever since the body had been removed.

No, she wasn't going to think about that. Right now she wanted to take a look at the orchard. She had been auditing a class on orchard management at the University of Massachusetts for a couple of weeks now, and she wanted to see if she could apply what she'd learned to real trees.

She had plenty. Her fifteen acres of trees stretched a quarter mile to the highway to the west (she was proud that she now knew her local directions) and ran in a narrow strip up over the rise toward the north, ending at the adjoining Chapin property. To an ignorant eye, the trees looked dead, but Meg knew otherwise. *Silver tip, green tip, then half-inch green*, she recited silently to herself. She couldn't wait until the trees began to bloom, although Christopher Ramsdell, the UMass professor who had been advising her, and Briona Stewart, her soon-to-be orchard manager, had told her that full bloom was still a month off. But there was plenty to be done between now and then, as Meg was fast learning.

She turned back again to look past the house toward the Great Meadow beyond. Maybe she was being overly optimistic, but wasn't there a hint of green among the trees on the far side? Spring was coming, and Meg was looking forward to it eagerly.

She wandered through her trees, looking critically at them. She still had trouble distinguishing between the varieties, especially before leaves and fruit appeared, although Christopher had informed her that she had at least twenty varieties, many of them now considered heirloom. She savored the names: the standards like Baldwin, Russet, Winesap, and the more archaic names like Cornish Gilliflower, Hubbardston Nonesuch, Pink Pearl. So much to learn, and she had just started. And was enjoying every minute of it.

She reached the midpoint and looked down the neat rows. Christopher and his staff, plus a few university students, had done a good job of clearing out the lingering weeds and the deadwood. Branches were pruned neatly, and the brush had been removed. Even the fringes of the orchard lot had been cleared of weeds, which Christopher had told her could harbor harmful pests. It looked good to her—ready for the coming season. She breathed deeply once again, savoring the air, with just a tinge of apple from the last deadfalls.

And something else. Something that smelled . . . rotten? Meg sniffed again. She was new enough to country living to realize that there were lots of smells she didn't know. Plus, there were sheep and cows in the neighborhood, so that meant manure.

But this didn't smell like manure. More like a dead animal—a deer?—which was certainly a possibility, although she didn't see anything like that. Of course, whatever it was could have been there for a while, frozen under the snow, and was just now warming up enough to decay. But surely Christopher and his crew would have noticed before now and cleaned up that kind of thing. Whatever it was must be fairly recent.

She sniffed, moved, sniffed again. Definitely coming from the north and the odor was getting stronger. She followed her nose along the row of trees and realized she was approaching the springhouse. When she had first seen the springhouse, she had had to ask what it was: it looked like a roof planted in the ground. Christopher had explained that it had been built to protect a spring that burbled up at that spot, but even he had no idea how long the structure had been there. To Meg's eye it looked old, but that could mean anything from twenty to two hundred years.

As she drew closer she could tell that the smell was definitely emanating from the springhouse. The two triangular ends were faced with vertical boards, but the center of the rooflike structure was open, with a few additional boards tacked across to prevent animals from falling in, Meg assumed. Apparently they hadn't worked. Approaching the opening, Meg peered into the dark interior. She could see water and rocks and some floating boards. And a body.

Meg's legs failed her, and she dropped down onto the damp ground under the nearest tree, leaning against the trunk for support. She shut her eyes, but when she opened them, she could still see the soles of a pair of boot-clad feet facing out of the opening. *Damn!* She had gotten through thirty years without ever seeing, much less finding, a body, and now in the space of months she had discovered two. It wasn't fair.

And why hadn't she noticed him before? The trees had blocked her view of the springhouse from within the orchard, but surely she could have seen him from the house, at least from an upstairs window? Not that she spent much time admiring the view of the orchard—there was too much else to do in the house. But still . . .

She waited for her mind to stop spinning and then stared at the feet. From what little she had seen, the body appeared to be male, lying facedown in the water inside the springhouse. Drowned? But why here? The man wore a coat, blue jeans, and black rubber boots with red soles, appropriate for mucking about muddy fields in spring. He lay neatly, not sprawled. That was all she could tell from where she sat, and she had no desire to get any closer. She looked around her: everything else seemed the same— the waiting trees, a few vehicles passing by on the highway not far away. Somewhere she heard a bird. All nice and normal, except for the body in the springhouse.

With a sigh, Meg fished in her pocket for her cell phone and called the police department. Why bother with 911 when she had friends—well, acquaintances anyway—in high places? When someone answered, she said, "Can I talk to the chief? It's Meg Corey."

The voice on the other end replied, "Oh, hi, Meg. Yeah, he's just come back from lunch. Hang on while I transfer you."

While she waited, Meg wondered if she knew the person at the desk, who obviously knew her. Well, after her last adventure with murder, half the town knew who she was, even if she'd only lived here since the beginning of the year. This round would probably reach the other half.

"Hi, Meg," Art Preston said cheerfully. "What's up? You aren't going to tell me you've got another body, are you?" Meg couldn't find an answer to that before he went on. "You're kidding. Aren't you?"

"Unfortunately, no. I've just found . . . someone dead in my springhouse."

"Ah," he said. Meg heard the sound of papers shuffling. "Okay, give me the details. Where's your springhouse?"

"In the middle of the orchard. You can see it from the main road, if you look."

"Anyone you know?"

"I don't think so. Of course, I've only seen the back of him. And his feet. I didn't get too close."

"Ah, Meg, Meg . . ." Art sighed. "I'll be right over. And I guess I'll call the state police guys in Northampton."

"You do what you have to do. I'll wait here."

After she'd hung up, Meg leaned against the tree again. Nice that Art was a friend now, because the lead detective in the Northampton office of the state police certainly wasn't, even though she'd solved his last murder for him. Nothing to be done about that now.

Last time, she'd known the dead man. This time it seemed unlikely. Too bad she hadn't noticed him earlier, because whoever this was had been here long enough to begin to decompose, to put it politely. When was the last time anyone had visited the orchard? Christopher was often around, with or without his students. The class occasionally met in the orchard on Friday. This was Monday. She tried to remember the last time she had noticed the UMass van pass by, and failed. Had Briona had time to walk the orchard recently? Meg didn't know.

Two murders in the last hundred and whatever years in peaceful little Granford, Massachusetts, and she was right on the spot for both of them—and both on her property. What were the odds of that? At least she didn't think she had anything to do with this one, but she'd learned never to assume anything. She'd just have to wait until somebody turned the dead man over and figured out who he was.

She pulled her coat more closely around her, tried to ignore the damp seeping through the seat of her jeans, and settled back to wait for Art.

2

 Meg watched Art's police car approach the orchard along the main highway and slow down before speeding up to come around to her driveway. He couldn't approach directly because of the fence. Christopher had explained why she needed a fence along the road: to keep people out, the eager tourists who seemed to think that an apple hanging on a tree was fair game for anyone who could reach it. The fence wasn't high enough to discourage the local deer, and the smaller critters could climb through or burrow under. Still, it didn't go all the way around the orchard; it was open on the side nearest the house, and the side toward the adjoining Chapin property.

She stood up and brushed off dead grass and leaves from her jeans. She waited until the chief of police clambered up the hill, huffing a bit. Too much time at his desk? "Hi, Art."

"Hi, Meg. Okay, let's get this over with. Where's the body this time?"

"Not in the plumbing, thank goodness. He's in the springhouse there."

Art turned and methodically surveyed the orchard in all directions, then zeroed in on the springhouse. He walked toward it, approaching obliquely, staring at the ground, and then continuing carefully around the small building. Finally he approached the body and looked down at it for several seconds. "Been here a day or two. You didn't notice anything?"

"Nope. I don't get up here every day, and I can't see it from the house, except from certain rooms. The crew from the university hasn't been around since Friday—at least, that I know of. I'm not always here when they are—they have my permission to be there. You remember Christopher, right?"

"Who?"

"Christopher Ramsdell. He's part of the IPM Department at the university." At Art's blank look, she added, "That's integrated pest management. It's one approach to pest control for crops, minimizing pesticide use. You remember—you met him when . . ."

Art nodded. "Oh, right, older guy, English accent."

Meg went on. "I've hired someone to help with the orchard—she's a student, named Briona Stewart, but she hasn't really started yet. And I didn't see any lights at night, either, or hear partying. You think maybe this was an accident?" She wanted to hold on to a little hope.

"Can't say. You'd think if he hit his head he'd fall face up. Unless somebody hit it for him."

Murder? Meg wasn't ready to think about that. "You going to turn him over?" she asked.

Art studied the scene. "Don't think so. I'll let the pros handle that. I don't want to mess up any evidence, if there is any. Ground's still pretty much frozen. But I think I can get to his pocket, see if he's got any ID on him." He matched his actions to his words, hunkering down next to the body and reaching into a back pocket of the dead man's jeans. He managed to pull out a wallet, molded by long use to the shape of the man's body and worn at the edges. "Got it."

He walked back to Meg's side before opening it and reaching into it to pull out a driver's license. He squinted at it. "Looks like . . . Jason Miller, age 27. Comes from the eastern part of the state, outside Boston. He's got a UMass ID here, too—probably a student."

"A grad student, given his age," Meg said absently.

"You know him?" Art asked.

Meg shook her head vigorously. "I do not, thank goodness! Well, maybe if I see his face—I've been auditing a class at UMass, but I haven't really talked to anyone there. And there's Christopher's class—they're over here maybe every other week. But I'm not sure I'd recognize anybody from that group." She was swamped with relief: Jason Miller had nothing to do with her, save that his mortal remains had ended up in her orchard.

Art scanned the road. "I called the state police before I set out, and Marcus said he'd contact the medical examiner. So I guess we just wait for them to show up. You want to wait in the house? I can handle things here."

Meg shrugged. She wasn't cold, and she didn't want the detective from the state police team back in her house again if she could help it. "I'm okay. He's going to want to talk to me, so I might as well wait." She fumbled for a neutral topic, keeping her eyes away from the body. "So, looks like the development project's moving along well. They've already cleared the trees and torn down the buildings along the highway toward town."

"Yeah, it's looking good. Course, they can't pour footings until the ground thaws, but they're going to be ready to go. I hear Seth Chapin's moving his plumbing shop into your barn?"

"He's renting space from me. Heck, I'm not using it.

Well, I will need some place to hold the apples when we harvest, but Seth said he'd help me put that together—there's plenty of space in the barn. It's handy having a plumber around."

"Nice to see the place being used. I hate to see the old barns just fall down. Or worse, these builders who think that old barn boards are just great for their new McMansions and buy 'em up for the lumber. So, you said you've hired a manager?"

"I did. Christopher found her for me, and he recommended her. She's only part-time right now, because she's finishing up her course work, but she'll be full-time when she graduates."

They carried on a perfunctory conversation for the twenty minutes it took for Detective Lieutenant William Marcus and his crew to arrive from Northampton. He pulled into the driveway behind Art's car, and then the group made its way up the hill to where they waited. Art stayed by her side, and Meg guessed he wasn't any more eager than she was to greet the detective.

Marcus was a big man, inflated further by his own self-importance. "Ms. Corey, Preston. What've we got this time?"

Art pointed toward the feet sticking out. "Young guy named Jason Miller, or at least that's what his ID says."

Marcus eyed Meg with distaste. "When did you notice you had another body?"

Meg straightened her shoulders. "Less than an hour ago. I smelled him first, then I saw him. I haven't been up to the orchard for a couple of days."

"You know him?" The detective's voice was cold.

"No." Meg took great satisfaction in being able to say that.

"Uh-huh." Marcus appeared skeptical. "You get a look at his face?"

Meg shook her head. "I didn't touch him. That's the way I found him."

"I pulled his wallet out," Art volunteered. "Seems to be a student."

"The ME'll be here soon enough, and we can get a look at him. Who else has been through here lately?" The detective cast an eye around the orchard, its grass winter dry.

"Me, Christopher Ramsdell from the university, some of his students, and my new orchard manager, Briona Stewart," Meg answered.

"I'll want to talk to them all, find out if they saw anything," Detective Marcus said. "You can give me a list of names and contact info, right?"

"Of course," Meg said, squashing the urge to add something sarcastic. "Well, I can for Christopher and Briona, but not for the students. Christopher can give you that." She watched as what she recognized as the medical examiner's van pulled into the already crowded driveway. They stood silently until the ME made his way up the hill, an assistant trailing behind him.

"Well, well," he puffed when he arrived, stopping ten feet short of the springhouse. "Didn't expect to come back here again. What, or should I say, *who* have you got this time?"

Marcus pointed silently. The ME nodded, then approached the body. "Dead, all right. Partially submerged, which might throw off the timeline a bit. I'll get his temp when we get him out. Been dead at least twenty-four hours, maybe more. It's been above freezing for a couple of days now. Any ID?"

"In his pocket. Looks like a university student."

"Ah. Too bad. Any idea how he got here?"

Meg thought it was time to step in. "None. I don't know him, and I don't know what he was doing here. Can you tell how he died?"

"Give me a few minutes and I'll have a better idea." The ME gestured to his companion, who pulled out a camera and snapped a number of pictures. Then he looked at Marcus. "You guys want to do your thing?"

"You mean, process the scene?" Marcus replied stiffly. Meg wondered if he and the ME had butted heads in the past. "Yes, before your crew tramples the place. Dillon, you want to get pictures now?"

Meg stepped back and watched as Marcus's team shifted gears and started snapping pictures and pulling out evidence bags.

Marcus, apparently too senior to get his hands dirty with such mundane tasks, turned back to Meg. "So, as far as you know, a dozen or more people have tramped through here in the last few days, including you, and you didn't notice anybody leaving a body behind."

Why did he always sound as though he expected her to lie? "That's right."

"And they all could have dumped God knows what while they were strolling around." He looked disgusted.

"Not exactly. One of the class's tasks is to clean up the dead plant litter and any other debris up here—that's good orchard management, or so I'm told. So it should all be pretty clean."

"Huh," Marcus replied, keeping his eye on his team.

It took under an hour to make a full sweep of the area, with little to show for it. The man named Dillon said, "Not much to see. Ground's frozen, didn't take any prints. No trash. Can't exactly fingerprint the old wood there." He nodded at the springhouse. "Did find evidence that somebody vomited recently, so we collected that."

"Get that to the lab, ASAP. Eastman, you can take over now."

The medical examiner gestured toward his assistant, and between them they managed to lift the body and pull it out, before turning the man over and laying him on his back on a large piece of plastic.

Meg was torn between fear at what she might see— would his face have been damaged?—and an unexpected need to be sure she didn't recognize him. Curiosity won, and she forced her eyes to the man's face. No blood, no obvious damage. He definitely looked dead, but intact. His face was dusky blue, and his eyes were slightly open, as was his mouth. Meg tried to visualize the face in life. He looked younger than his twenty-seven years: dark curly hair, badly cut; dark brows; nondescript clothes, wet but not particularly dirty, not new. Just an ordinary man, except he was too young to be dead.

As the ME and his assistant bundled up the body into a zippered body bag and began transporting him down the hill to the waiting vehicle, Meg stopped him. "Can you tell me now how he died?"

Eastman glanced briefly at Marcus. "Sorry, no, not yet. You'll have to wait for the autopsy."

Meg, Art, and the detective watched the procession and waited until the van had departed. Meg broke the silence. "What now? Do you have all you need here?"

Marcus looked at her for several seconds before he answered. "We're done with the site—not much here. I'll need your statement, but I guess that can wait. Stop by my office."

Dismissing Meg, he turned to Art. "I'm going to check the guy out, see if he's who his ID says he is. I'll want to talk to you then, Preston." He nodded to Art, then left without further niceties.

"Well, I suppose that could have been worse," Meg said dubiously, watching him go.

"He can't pin this one on you, Meg. That must be some small comfort," Art said sympathetically.

"I guess. But why leave a body here? Someone has a grudge against me?"

Art shrugged. "Too early to guess. I'll ask around town, see if anyone noticed anything. You haven't seen a car sitting anywhere it shouldn't be for a couple of days?"

Meg shook her head. "Not that I remember. Maybe he came alone, on foot?"

"Could be, but it's a good hike from Amherst. Doesn't help much."

"I know what you mean. I wonder how he died? I don't see how someone could just wander into my orchard and drown in the springhouse. I mean, the water's not very deep. But I didn't see any blood or anything."

"Nope. So no gunshot or knife wounds, and his head wasn't bashed in."

"Suicide, maybe? Although why pick here? There have to be better, more private places around. And he's not even all the way in the springhouse. Did he want to be found sooner rather than later?"

"Meg, I just don't know. We'll know more once we find out more about him. But don't you worry—you're in the clear."

"Gee, thanks. I'm so glad you're on the job." When Art's face fell, she added, "I didn't mean that the way it sounded. I just don't like my place being used as a dumping ground for bodies. Especially not my orchard. I'm getting rather fond of it."

"No offense taken. I'll be on my way, then. Can I walk you down the hill?"

"Sure." The wind had picked up, the sun was sinking, and Meg didn't feel like being alone in the orchard now, even though the body had been taken away. She shivered. "Let's go."

3

Meg hadn't even had time to close her front door after Art's departure when Seth Chapin's van pulled into the driveway. The van had begun life as a mobile supply unit for Chapin Brothers plumbing business, but now that Seth's brother Stephen was no longer involved in the family business, Seth had seized the opportunity to move in a different direction, to take on more of the renovation and preservation work that he loved. Seth had asked to rent space in Meg's tumbledown barn because the previous site of his plumbing business, once part of the Chapin family farm north of Meg's property, was destined to become parking for Granford Grange, the new commercial strip along the highway. Meg had happily agreed. She hoped that Seth could keep the barn standing at least. In fact, he had much bigger plans for it: he intended to combine his business office with storage for the architectural salvage he collected, which involved upgrading the barn's electrical supply and adding minimal plumbing facilities. And there was an added bonus: as part of the rental agreement he was going to help Meg install a temperature-controlled storage area to hold her apples. All in all, Meg was thrilled that the old barn and attached buildings would see new life.

Seth jumped down from the van and came over. "Hey, Meg—was that Art's car?"

Meg nodded. "Yup. And guess what?"

Seth studied her face, searching for a clue. "Do I want to hear this?"

"Probably not. I found another body. In the orchard." It sounded ridiculous when she said it like that, but it was true. *Another body.* Last time around Seth had been the lucky one to find the corpse, shoved into her septic tank.

"You're not kidding, are you? Oh, Meg, I'm sorry."

Meg shrugged. "At least I didn't know him this time."

Seth showed a comforting lack of curiosity about the dead man. "Are you all right? Listen, you look cold. Why don't we go inside? How about some tea?"

Meg smiled. "I'm not a fragile flower, you know." But when he looked disappointed, she relented. "Tea sounds lovely, Seth, and thank you for suggesting it. Come on in."

She led the way through the back door into the kitchen. Filling the teakettle from the tap, she looked out the window and studied the van. "I see you got the van painted. It looks good. I like your new logo."

Seth came up behind her and followed her gaze. "If I can't afford a new van, I can at least handle a new paint job. It *does* look good, doesn't it?"

He looked inordinately proud of himself. Meg knew that he had been thinking about branching into old-house renovation for a while, but it had taken the events of the previous months to push him to make the change. Maybe, Meg thought, it was a classic example of a silver lining. Or of Seth's ability to make lemonade out of the sourest of circumstances.

"Excuse me." She slipped past him to put the kettle on

the stove. "We might get that tea faster if I actually boil the water. Why don't you sit down?"

Seth didn't move. "Meg, you really are something, you know? You stumble over a body and you just keep right on going."

"Maybe it hasn't really sunk in yet. Although I do dearly wish that people would find someplace else to die. Or to leave the remains." Meg clamped down on her sudden anger. Maybe she was more upset than she'd realized. She should be, shouldn't she? A man was dead. A young man, cut down in his prime. She felt tears sting her eyes.

Seth was quick to notice. "Sit. I'll make the tea."

He knew the kitchen well and had things assembled by the time the water boiled. Meg sat obediently, thinking of nothing. Seth set the teapot, cups, spoons, sugar, and milk on the table, then sat across from her. "You want to talk about it?"

Meg shrugged. "Not really."

He gave her one more searching look before he changed the subject. "You want me to bring you up to speed on what I'm planning for the barn?"

"Sure. Have you changed things around again?" Seth had been acting like a kid in a toy shop, making and discarding plans almost daily. Meg had to admit his enthusiasm was infectious.

"Sort of. Here, let me sketch it out for you." He pulled a paper napkin from the holder on the table and fished a pencil out of his pocket. "Okay, here's the basic ground plan, right?"

Meg looked on as he produced a rough sketch. It had never occurred to her to take a bird's-eye view of the place. Her mother had inherited the property decades earlier from their distant aunts Lula and Nettie Warren, and had ignored it ever since, content to collect rent. Meg had been living here for only a few months—after she'd lost her banking job in Boston, her mother had decided that Meg could use her "spare time" to renovate the house. But the brutal New England winter hadn't inspired Meg to do much exploring—and she had had more than enough to do to make the house livable, and so much to learn about the orchard, that she hadn't had time to consider the broader layout of the buildings. Of which there were a surprising number, or at least their remnants. As Seth sketched, her house appeared, with the driveway running alongside. Then the roughly framed addition where she parked occasionally, which was connected to the kitchen. Beyond that, at an odd angle, lay what Seth had informed her was the nineteenth-century carpenter's shop, then finally, perpendicular to that, the old barn facing the house. To her eye, the barn was no more than two stories of splintered wood and patches, but apparently Seth saw a lot of potential in it.

As he warmed to the subject, Meg zoned out, studying him, bent over his diagrams. She had to admit he was pleasant to look at: real New England stock, sandy haired, gray eyed, with a sturdy body and capable hands. And she could tell that he really enjoyed his work: give him a problem to solve, and he'd come up with six ways to do it, then find the people who could make it happen. The people of Granford had acknowledged that when they elected him selectman in his relatively young thirties, and he hadn't let them down. That infectious enthusiasm made him a great business partner—and friend. She wasn't sure how she would have made it through the last couple of months without him, and she probably wouldn't be sitting here figuring out what to do with tons of apples without his help. He was warm and strong and sweet, just like her cup of tea.

Oh, ick. The aftermath of the shock of finding the body, plus the warmth of the kitchen, were rapidly putting her to sleep, and she was getting mushy. Not that Seth wasn't an entirely suitable candidate, if she were in the market. But she had too much on her plate at the moment, between the house and the orchard, to think about romance.

"Seth," she broke in, "could we maybe wait until tomorrow to talk about all this? Briona's going to be here then, and you'd just have to repeat it all. And you need her input about the apple storage part. For that matter, she may have some good ideas herself. So why don't we just save it for then?"

Seth tore himself away from his increasingly elaborate drawing, now bristling with lines and arrows. "Oh, right, Briona's your new orchard manager. You want me to swing by tomorrow sometime?"

"I told her to come over in the afternoon—I've got a class in the morning. She's going to stay in the room over the kitchen—I've moved into the front bedroom—and she said she had some stuff to move in. Why don't you plan to stay for supper tomorrow? That'll give us plenty of time."

"Sounds good. So, what's she like?"

Meg considered, choosing her words with care. "She's young, around twenty-one. Smart. Very focused. Seems a little prickly. I told you she was Jamaican, didn't I?"

"A lot of the pickers around here are Jamaican—that's been true for years. Makes sense," Seth commented.

"I didn't make the connection with the pickers. Briona was born here, from what I can tell—since I'll be paying her, I had to do the paperwork on her. And we're still wrestling with what to do about health insurance—that's one reason I threw in a free room, to save her money. Anyway, I think she believes she's got a lot to prove, but she certainly knows more than I do—not that it would be hard—and we've got Christopher as a backup if we get stuck on something. It'll be a new experience, at least. I've never done anything like this."

A month ago she had been planning to look for a job in municipal finance while getting the house ready to sell, and it hadn't been easy to wrap her head around the idea of not only keeping the house and living in it, but also managing an orchard and trying to make a profit at it. Scary stuff, but exciting. She realized now that maybe she had been naïve, but she was learning fast, auditing a course on orchard management at UMass and reading everything she could lay her hands on. Thank goodness Christopher had found Briona to help her.

Seth stood up, folding the napkin drawing neatly and putting it in his pocket. "You sure you'll be all right alone tonight?"

"Don't worry, I'll be fine. See you tomorrow, then."

Meg watched as Seth took one more look at the barn, then climbed into his van and drove off. As he drove out of site, Meg carefully locked the back door and went to check the front door as well. Maybe the dead man in the orchard had nothing to do with her, but she didn't want to take any chances.

4

Meg turned on all the lights downstairs. It wasn't that she was afraid of the ghost of that poor man haunting her. After all, he'd been dead for a day or two without stopping by to bother her. And she refused to give in to an irrational fear of being alone. Still, she was new to living in the country, accustomed instead to city sounds—cars, horns, fire and police sirens. In Boston it was never really totally quiet. Here in Granford the silence was sometimes unnerving—although now, she realized, there was a new element: the peepers in the adjacent wetlands had awakened with the warmer weather and provided a shrill chorus. As for the "alone" part, she was used to that, although Briona's arrival would change that to some extent.

The sound of a vehicle entering her still-unpaved driveway interrupted her increasingly gloomy thoughts, and when she looked out the dining room window she was absurdly pleased to see Seth's sister Rachel climbing out of her van with a basket that looked heavy. Rachel seldom arrived without food, and Meg realized she was hungry. Rachel saw her watching and pointed toward the back door. Meg hurried to the kitchen to let her in.

Rachel entered the kitchen, dropped the basket on the floor, and flung her arms around Meg. "You poor baby. Seth told me about the body. Are you all right?"

"I think so. You didn't need to come all the way over here just to check on me."

Rachel finally released Meg. "Of course I did. I couldn't stand the idea of you moping around here all by yourself. And I'll bet you haven't eaten anything. Right?"

"Guilty. But I was going to do something about that shortly. You didn't have to—"

Rachel cut her off. "Shut up. That's what friends do around here. Besides, the kids were arguing over homework, so I let Noah take over. And this is stuff I had made and stuck in the freezer for an occasion just like this. Point me to your microwave."

"You stockpile food for murders?" Meg asked.

"You know what I mean." Rachel unwrapped a casserole dish and pushed it into the microwave, studied the controls for a few seconds, then punched some buttons. "There. Now we've got a few minutes. And you look like you could use a drink. You have wine?"

"In the fridge," Meg replied. "You don't need to . . ."

Too late. Rachel had already found glasses, extricated the bottle from the refrigerator, and set them all on the table. "I'll have one, and only one, since I'm driving. But you go right ahead. Sit!"

Meg sat. Rachel threw herself into a chair across from her. "Okay, what's the story?"

Meg poured herself a glass of wine and sipped. It did taste good. She felt her shoulders loosening. "I went up to take a look around the orchard this afternoon, and there was a dead guy stuffed in the springhouse."

"So he just wandered into your orchard and decided to drop dead?"

Meg shrugged. "I don't know anything different. I'm in and out all the time, with errands and stuff, and, no, I didn't notice any weirdness going on in my orchard. Is there any religion that makes sacrifices at the spring equinox?"

Rachel smiled. "I don't know of any, but nothing would surprise me in this area. You have no idea what some folks get into. You have a name for him?"

"His ID said Jason Miller."

"Jason Miller, Jason Miller . . . why does that sound familiar?" The microwave beeped, and Rachel bounced out of her chair, rotated the dish inside, then started it again. She leaned against the counter to face Meg. "Ah! Got it. He's the front man for GreenGrow."

"GreenGrow?"

"A group of organic farming zealots in Amherst. They seem to do a lot of protesting of one thing or another. Jason got the most face time. You haven't heard of them?"

"I don't think so, but I haven't been around here that long. I wonder why he was here in my orchard."

The microwave beeped again, and Rachel retrieved the casserole, set it on a pad on the table, then hunted down plates and silverware. Meg watched with amusement: Rachel had made herself right at home in Meg's kitchen, just as her brother Seth had. Finally Rachel sat down and dished up, setting a laden plate in front of Meg. "There, eat. But you can keep talking. The big questions are, did he die here? And did he do it himself, or did someone else?"

Meg forked up some food, chewed, and swallowed before answering. "Hey, this is great. Anyway, the ME didn't or couldn't say. The body was found with his face underwater."

Rachel looked stricken. "I'm sorry—is it too gross to talk about this while you're eating? You can tell me to shut up if you want. So how're Seth's plans coming along?"

Meg was grateful that Rachel had changed the subject.

"You mean for the barn? I'd say just fine, except they seem to change all the time. But he appears to be enjoying the process. Tell me, how upset is he about losing the old space? He doesn't say much."

"Seth doesn't worry about the stuff he can't change, and that's history now. He's really a glass-half-full type, you know? He's happy that the town is going to get some new life. He's excited about making this shift into renovation. And he loves to have new projects to work on. He's got a lot of energy."

"So I've noticed. You keep pretty busy yourself, with the kids and the B and B."

"Maybe it just runs in the family. And you'd better get used to it, once the work in the orchard picks up. You came in at the slowest point, but just wait. You'll see."

"I suppose I will. And I should probably try to get as much done as possible with the house before I get really busy."

"What's your next project?"

"I'm still thinking it over. There's a lot of woodwork that needs to be stripped, but I'm waiting until I can open the windows to tackle that so I don't asphyxiate myself. And I don't want to wallpaper until I get the stripping done, because I don't know what the wood will look like and whether I'll have to paint it again. And I've been thinking about doing the floor in here."

Rachel looked down. "Not a bad idea. The stuff on it now has lived a hard life, and it was probably cheap to begin with. But they usually used glue that will outlive us all, so it won't be easy to get it off."

"Noted," Meg answered.

Rachel checked her watch. "Well, I suppose I should get back and face the music. There are some cookies and some muffins in the basket, too. I don't know any problem that some good carbohydrates and sugar can't improve."

"Rachel, you're a wonder, and I think I agree with you. Why don't you leave the dishes and I'll bring them back to you tomorrow? I've got a class in the morning anyway."

"Deal. If I'm not around, just leave the stuff by the back door."

Rachel grabbed her coat, and Meg held the door open for her. Watching her go, Meg marveled at her good luck: a neighbor like Seth, now a sort-of business partner, who came with a sister like Rachel.

Before she shut the door she stood listening for a moment. The peepers were still going strong, and Meg could discern a range of voices. Spring was almost here; her new life was going to get a lot busier very quickly.

5

 Briona Stewart arrived just past three the next afternoon. When she rapped on the back door, Meg hurried to let her in. "Hi, Briona! Come on in. Have you got much stuff?" Meg looked past her to a dilapidated four-door sedan piled with boxes.

"Not much. I've still got the dorm room, but I brought over what I don't need right now. Uh, thanks for letting me use the room." The words came out reluctantly.

"Hey, with the pathetic salary I'm offering you, I'll do whatever I can to sweeten the deal. Can I help you carry anything?"

Briona shrugged. "I can handle it." Without waiting for an answer, she went back to the car. Meg watched her as she wrestled a box out of the backseat. She was stronger than her slight frame suggested, which probably wasn't surprising, given what little Meg knew about the demands of any agricultural pursuit. She was also lovely—skin the color of butterscotch, long dark hair bunched up with a clip.

When Briona clomped back to the door lugging a box that appeared to be full of books, Meg stepped back to let her pass. "You know where you're going?"

Briona nodded her head toward the ceiling. "The room over this one, right?"

"Yes. I forgot to tell you, there's a back stairway. Here, let me show you." Meg headed for the back end of the kitchen and opened a door to reveal a narrow staircase. "I'm not quite sure why it's here, but at least you can come and go without worrying about disturbing me. And you can park in the shed, or whatever you call it here, once I clean out some of the junk." Meg ended on a dubious note. She felt as though she had been clearing out stuff ever since she had arrived in January, but more always seemed to accumulate, and for the moment it was heaped in the open space: jumbles of trash, random construction materials, and plain old junk. "I'll talk to Seth about it."

Briona was halfway up the stairs with her box, but she tossed back over her shoulder, "Seth?"

"Seth Chapin. He's a neighbor, and he's renting part of the barn and the connecting link for his business, which is mostly plumbing now, but he wants to get into building restoration . . ." By the time Meg had finished her rambling sentence, Briona had disappeared up the stairs and was out of earshot. Meg trailed after her and caught up with her in the bedroom. "It's not fancy, but it's fairly private."

"It's fine," Briona said.

"I'm sorry there's only the one bath up here, but I was talking to Seth about putting in another one."

"I said it's fine," Briona repeated. "I've been living in student housing for the last four years, and this is way better. Plenty of room."

"Well, good. Listen, why don't you shift the rest of your stuff, and then we can sit down and figure out a schedule, what we need to do next, that kind of thing?"

"Fine," Briona said again, and went back down the stairs.

Not the friendliest person in the world, Meg reflected. Still, Meg wasn't looking for a new best friend, just someone who could do whatever was needed to keep the orchard healthy and productive. Someone who possessed all the agricultural knowledge Meg lacked. Orchard management was not something you really learned from books, Meg had found quickly. Briona was her best hope for the moment, not to mention the only person she could afford until she figured out what she was doing.

When Briona had finished hauling boxes up the stairs, she came back to the kitchen and hovered uncertainly in the doorway. Meg gestured her into the room. "You want something to drink, Briona? Oh, and can you stay for dinner? I asked Seth to come over. I thought you two should get acquainted, since you'll probably be crossing paths a lot. And he said he'd build the fruit storage areas I'll need in the barn, and he could use your input on that."

"I guess. You want to go up the hill now, and I can tell you what I'm thinking? And . . ." Briona hesitated.

"What?" Meg asked.

"Could you call me Bree? Briona is what my auntie calls me when she's mad."

Meg laughed. "Sure, no problem." She checked the clock. Only a couple of hours of light left, and dinner was already simmering on the stove. "Okay, let's go. But I warn you: you'll probably just have to repeat most of what you tell me later. It's all pretty new to me."

"No problem." Bree flashed a brief smile.

"Oh, before I forget, I had some keys made for you." Meg handed her a clutch of keys on a chain. "This one's the front door, this one's the kitchen door, and this one's the padlock to the barn. Although I think anybody could get in there with a rusty nail, so it's probably more symbolic than practical."

"Okay." Bree pocketed the key ring.

Meg retrieved her coat, and they set off up the hill. Bree seemed more at ease outside, loping easily up the slope. At the top she stopped, waiting for Meg to catch up, and Meg could have sworn Bree looked on the rows of trees with a kind of proprietary pride. Meg could understand that, since she'd caught herself doing the same lately. At least Bree cared about her work.

"Okay, where do we start?" Meg asked.

Bree scanned the orchard, then launched into a checklist of tasks that stretched on and on, ticking them off on her ungloved fingers.

"Okay, now. The pruning's done—Professor Ramsdell and his class took care of that. The dead stuff is gone—that's good. Bloom's still a ways off, but there's some spraying that needs to be done before then. We'll have to check what insects are emerging, keep an eye on them."

Meg listened with half an ear. Right now she was more interested in getting a feel for her new employee's personal and working style. So far she was impressed, at least by the latter. Bree talked a good line, and if Christopher had endorsed her, she must know her stuff.

They spent a productive hour walking from one end of the orchard to the other, and by the time they were done, the sun was sinking and there was a chill in the air. But Meg felt good. The more time she spent in the orchard, the more secure she became in her ownership of it. It was an odd feeling, possessing a large and living entity, especially one whose history stretched back more than two centuries, and though it sounded silly, Meg didn't want to let the orchard down.

Still, the nonstop flow of Bree's information was a little much to absorb all at once. "Can we call it a day now? Because I've got to process everything you've told me so far, and my toes are getting cold. Let's head back down the hill," Meg suggested.

"I guess," Bree said, looking disappointed. Silently they set off toward the house.

Once they were back in the warm and steamy kitchen, Meg shucked off her coat and poked at the large pot of stew she had left on the stove. "You don't have any, uh, eating restrictions?" Meg asked Bree, who was prowling around the kitchen studying things. Heaven forbid she should turn out to be a vegetarian.

"What? Oh, no, I eat about anything. That smells good." She nodded toward the simmering pot.

"Thanks. I'm not used to cooking for more than just me, so I'm kind of making it up as I go. But it's fun. I can't believe how many new things I'm learning, and all at once. Like house renovation."

"I like this place. It's a good house. Strong." Bree ran her hand over a door molding.

"I hope so. It needs to be—it's been pretty neglected for a while. I've got a list of things to do as long as my arm, and that doesn't even include the orchard."

"At least your trees haven't been neglected—they're in good shape. How old is the orchard, do you know?"

"Around 250 years, I think, in one form or another. It's mentioned in the town records as early as 1760," Meg said proudly. "The house was built by the Warren family, before the Revolution. In fact, Seth told me once that the intersection there used to be known as Warren's Grove, until the nineteenth century. I'm related to the Warrens somehow—my mother could explain how, but I've never been interested in that kind of thing until recently. Anyway, as you probably know, Christopher's been overseeing it for years."

"Sure," Bree nodded. "Orchards were a big part of life in the colonies. Back in the early days, every house had apples. Professor Ramsdell knows what he's doing. You know anything about what's been done with your apple crop?"

"Not really. I think the people here before—renters—just sold the whole crop to whoever asked first. A local co-op? Something like that."

Bree nodded. "Yeah, I know some of those folks." She hesitated a moment before asking, "Can I do anything to help with dinner?"

"I hate to ask you to peel potatoes, but that's what comes next with the stew."

"No, please, I'd rather be keeping busy. I'm . . . not real good with just talking."

Meg smiled. Maybe Bree *was* shy. "Great. Here." Meg handed her a bag of supermarket potatoes and a peeler. "Go for it."

Bree took the peeler and wielded it as if she knew what to do with it, digging into the potatoes with enthusiasm. "Garbage disposal or septic?" she asked as the pile of peels mounted.

"Septic." Meg grimaced. "I didn't think college kids knew much about cooking. You said you lived in a dorm? Do they allow you to cook there?"

Bree shook her head, her eyes still on her task, her hands moving efficiently. "No, but I've been cooking for a long time. My auntie—I lived with her when I was growing up—she worked full-time, so I just started fixing dinner for her, had it ready when she came home."

"That's a nice thing to do. It never hurts to know how to cook." Meg wondered if it was too soon to ask Bree personal questions, and searched for something neutral. "Where did you grow up?"

"Around here. Mostly Chicopee." Bree gave Meg a sideways glance. "Me, I was born here, grew up here. I'm American. But my parents are Jamaican."

"Oh. So your aunt raised you?" Meg wasn't sure whether this was a sensitive subject, and she wanted to avoid any land mines. On the other hand, if they were going to work together, it was bound to come up sometime.

"She did, mostly. My parents, they went back and forth." Bree kept peeling, quickening her pace. "You don't come from around here, do you?" When Meg shook her head, Bree continued. "Most of the pickers around here, they come from Jamaica. Not migrants, though. Seasonals. They come every year, the same people, to the same orchards. It's a skilled job, you know—you have to handle apples carefully. They get bruised, they lose value real fast."

"I assume Christopher has had some regular process for hiring pickers?"

"Sure. But if you're running this place as a business, you should take it over."

Just what she needed—another problem to investigate and deal with. But she'd asked for it, so she had to deal with it. "You'll help me out, won't you?"

Bree bristled. "Just because my folks are Jamaican doesn't mean I know how to deal with pickers."

Had she put her foot in it again? Meg wondered. "It's not a personal thing. If you're the orchard manager, you have to deal with the business side, right? Hiring? Selling the crop?"

"Oh. Right. Sorry." Bree hesitated before adding, "I guess I'm kind of sensitive about it all, maybe too much. I mean, I've been to Jamaica all of twice in my life, to visit my grandparents. But the pickers—I don't know how they'll treat me, you know? I'm one of them but I'm not, kind of. And I'm a woman, which doesn't make it any easier."

"Well, I guess we'll just have to work it out together. Look, Bree, I hired you because Christopher said you were one of the most accomplished and hardworking students he's ever had."

"Not just because I come cheap?" Bree kept her eyes on the potatoes she was peeling.

"That's part of it. But I need your help to make this work, and I'm happy to give you a chance. I know it's going to be hard, for both of us. And if you see me heading off in the wrong direction, give me a kick. You think you can handle that?"

Bree smiled reluctantly. "I think so."

"Then we're good." Meg was surprised to see that Bree had finished peeling the mound of potatoes. If nothing else, she was good at multitasking. "Can you cut those up so I can add them to the stew?"

"Sure." Bree turned her attention to quartering the potatoes, her hands moving competently.

With a start Meg realized she hadn't mentioned the dead man to Bree, even though they had walked right by the springhouse. Should she mention it now? No, she decided. She wanted one night to get to know Bree, to make her feel comfortable here, before throwing something like that at her. Meg had no idea how Bree would react, and she wasn't ready to deal with it yet. And since Bree hadn't brought it up, maybe she didn't know—and Meg didn't want to be the one to tell her.

6

Seth arrived at the back door after dark. Meg let him in, and he inhaled appreciatively. "Sorry I'm so late—I got hung up at a job. Old pipes. That smells great! Stew?"

"Hang up your coat. Yes, it's all-American beef stew."

Seth dutifully hung up his coat. "That old stove doesn't look very dependable. I can get you a good deal on a new one, you know," he began.

Meg held up a hand to stop him. "I'm sure you can, but there are a lot of things on the shopping list ahead of the stove. I'll manage, as long as the thing doesn't blow up on me. Let me introduce you to my orchard manager."

Bree was hovering in the background, nervously drying her already-dry hands on a kitchen towel. At Meg's urging, she stepped forward and extended a hand. "Bree Stewart."

Seth shook her hand and smiled. "Seth Chapin. I live over the hill, up that way, and I'm going to be working out of Meg's barn. Good to meet you. You've got a big job ahead of you."

"I know."

When Bree didn't volunteer any additional comments, Seth prompted her. "You'll be moving in here?"

Bree nodded. "After classes are done."

"Oh, that's right, you're still in school. But you'll be spending time here, right? Spraying, stuff like that?"

"Of course."

When Bree fell silent yet again, Seth apparently gave up trying to elicit conversation and turned back to Meg. "Did you get a chance to tell Bree about the barn plans?"

Meg laughed. "Not exactly. Why don't we sit down and eat, and you can describe it all again, so Bree can hear it, too."

"Deal. I'm a pushover, aren't I? Feed me and I'll tell you anything you want to know."

They had nearly finished the meal, and Seth had warmed to his subject, sketching on yet another napkin more ambitious plans for the barn. He had finally succeeded in engaging Bree, who was offering suggestions and pointing out details on the sketch.

Bree leaned back in her chair. "Okay, so if you're going to hold your apples for a couple of months, let them ripen, you need to control both temperature and the mix of oxygen and carbon dioxide in the storage area. And you've got to bring your apples down to the right temperature fast, like within twenty-four hours."

"So I'm going to have to deal with refrigeration and atmospheric control?"

"Exactly." Bree nodded vigorously. She went on to expound on the virtues of air-cooled versus mechanical refrigeration, types of refrigerants, compressors, condensers, and expansion coils, and Seth followed eagerly, making an occasional note on his napkin.

The phone rang, and Meg rose to answer; they didn't

even notice. When she picked up the receiver, she was surprised to hear Art's voice. "Meg, I've got the first round of results from the ME's office."

"All right," Meg said cautiously. "Am I not supposed to talk about it?"

"Well, you didn't hear it from me, and don't spread it around, okay?"

"Okay. But Seth's here, and my orchard manager."

"Well, keep it to yourselves, but it looks like Miller was poisoned."

"With what?" Meg had a bad feeling in the pit of her stomach.

"The full tox screen won't be back for a week or two, so I can't say. But the ME said everything else looked normal—no heart attack, no stroke, no wounds. They did a preliminary analysis and didn't find any alcohol in his system, or any of the standard drugs. The more specialized tests take longer, and there are still a lot of possibilities."

The bad feeling worsened. "No way of knowing whether he took the stuff himself, right?"

"Sorry, no," Art replied. "But nothing to suggest he was restrained—no bruises or anything."

Meg sighed. "Thanks for letting me know, Art. And keep me up-to-date, will you?"

"I'll do that. Say hi to Seth." Art hung up, leaving Meg bewildered. She wondered again about Bree's apparent ignorance of the event: she would have guessed that whatever gossip grapevine existed at UMass would have been quick to spread the word. But it was a large campus with thousands of people. Meg had avoided checking the morning paper to see what, if anything, had been reported, and in any case, Bree might not have read the paper, or watched the television news. She walked slowly back to the table and sat down.

Seth picked up her unease. "What?"

"That was Art." She caught Seth's eye, then she turned

to Bree: she was going to have to tell her. "Bree, did you hear about the body that was found yesterday?"

Bree looked blank. "No. Why do you ask?"

Meg sighed. "Because the body was found here on my property. In the orchard, in fact. In the springhouse." Meg watched Bree anxiously. Would she refuse to work at a place where a body had been found? "Is that going to be a problem?"

Bree considered briefly, then said, "Did you kill the guy?"

"No!" Meg realized Bree was pulling her leg. "I didn't even know him. He was apparently a UMass grad student named Jason Miller."

Meg wasn't prepared for Bree's reaction: she stood up abruptly, nearly knocking over her chair. "I've got to go," she said in a strangled voice.

Meg and Seth stood as well. "Okay. When will you be back?" Meg asked.

Bree was already pulling on her coat. "I don't know. I'll call you." She was out the back door before Meg could frame another question. She heard the car start up with a clatter, then pull out of the driveway.

Meg turned to Seth. "What was that all about?"

"Got me. At a guess, I'd say she knew the guy."

Meg's bad feeling deepened even further. "I suppose that shouldn't be a surprise. He was a student, and maybe they were in the same department. And Rachel said he was an organic activist of some sort. Damn. I hope this doesn't put her off this job. I really need her."

"There are other managers, aren't there?" Seth asked.

"Probably, but we're already coming into the first active part of the apple cycle, and it's kind of late to go hunting for someone."

"We don't even know what happened yet, right? What did Art say?"

She started pacing around the kitchen. "That there were no obvious physical causes, so it may be poison. But they don't know how, or what he took—or was given—and it's going to take a while to find out. Shoot—I didn't get a chance to ask Art if Miller died here or somewhere else. But why pick here?"

Seth shook his head. "I have no idea, but there's not much to be done about it. Listen, I have to get going—I've got a job in Hadley tomorrow, and I need to get started early. Thanks for dinner, Meg. And try not to worry, will you?"

"Sure, no problem," she said without conviction. "Let me know when you want to walk through the barn with me—you've got the key, right? Have you put much of your salvage in it yet?"

"Some, but I've never known anybody who wanted to steal antique sinks. Even if we keep it locked, I don't think that padlock is good for much."

"You have a point there. I didn't give much thought to replacing it because there wasn't anything important in there, but I suppose I need to consider it now. Good night, then."

Meg shut the door behind Seth. He was right: there was no point in worrying until she had more information. And tomorrow she would hunt down Christopher on campus and see what he could tell her about the late Jason Miller.

7

A night's sleep didn't bring any startling insights. Given their recent history, she didn't expect Detective Marcus to share anything with her, but at least Art was willing to pass on scraps. Still, it rankled, and Meg worried about her new livelihood. Would anyone want work at an orchard where a body had been discovered? Or even buy the apples? One more thing Meg had no answer for.

And what about Bree's strange reaction the night before? From what little she had seen, the younger woman was fairly abrupt, lacking in social polish. Maybe she had remembered something she had to get done last night. Maybe it wasn't the mention of Jason Miller's name that had sent her into a tizzy. Maybe, maybe, maybe . . . Meg had to know more.

She needed to get to the UMass campus and talk to Christopher. She wondered if Detective Marcus had already tracked him down, and if the professor had provided any useful information. It was likely he had known Jason Miller, and there was one way to find out.

She worried over her list of issues as she drove toward Amherst. There was no way she could run the orchard, much less make any money at it, without some outside help. The settlement she had received when she had been downsized out of her job in Boston a few months earlier had been generous, but that was all she had to keep her going until she produced and sold her first crop, which was months away yet. On top of that, she still had a lot of expensive repairs to do on the long-neglected house—a new roof, repointing the foundation, painting the exterior . . . *Shut up, Meg!* she scolded herself. Such fretting served no purpose other than to depress her.

Midday parking on campus was hard to find, and she settled for a distant visitor's short-term slot, then trekked across campus to the Life Sciences Building where Christopher's office was located. She wasn't sure whether he would be teaching a class or in his office, or somewhere else altogether. The only thing she knew for sure was that he wasn't scheduled to be at her place today, although he had been known to pop in unexpectedly. He really was very attached to her orchard.

Meg made her way to the faculty offices on the third floor. A schedule posted next to Christopher's door indicated that he ought to have just finished teaching his undergraduate class on integrated pest management and should be on his way back. Meg decided she might as well wait a few minutes and see if he appeared. If not, she could leave him a note. She scanned the unlit hallway: nowhere to sit. She leaned against the wall and looked over the required reading list for the next few sessions of her orchard class. After ten minutes she was rewarded by the sound of footsteps, followed by the sight of Christopher emerging from the stairwell. Despite his sixty-something years, he wasn't out of breath, and his silvery hair was unruffled.

As usual, he looked extraordinarily cheerful. "Meg, my dear, what a pleasure to see you here. Did you need to speak to me?"

Meg nodded. "I wanted to ask you about Jason Miller."

Christopher's face fell. "Of course. What a tragic thing."

"You knew him? Did you hear he was found in the springhouse in my orchard?"

Christopher paled visibly and laid a hand on her arm. "Oh no. Oh, my dear, how awful. You must be devastated. That rather unpleasant detective spoke to me and asked if I knew Jason, but all he said was that his body had been found in Granford. If he had mentioned where . . . but he seemed more interested in whether Jason had appeared to be suicidal, and I couldn't tell him much. Please, come in, sit down, tell me what I can do." He unlocked his door and ushered her into his small office, flipping on the overhead light. The room was crammed floor to ceiling with papers, posters, models, and what appeared to be a glass case with a tarantula in it. A live one. "Please, sit down, Meg."

Meg moved a pile of papers and sat. "I'm doing all right, but I have a lot of questions. I understand that Miller was a student here at the university?"

Christopher sat back in his chair. "Indeed he was. He was working toward a graduate degree in this department, as I told the detective yesterday. In fact, he asked me to identify Jason—from a picture." He broke off what he was saying and looked furtively around the office. "Meg, perhaps we would do better to take this out of the building. Shall we go into town and have lunch?"

Mystified, Meg said, "Sure, I'd like that. Do you have any other classes scheduled?"

"Nothing until two, which should be ample time to . . . well, you'll see. Shall we go?"

Christopher said nothing more about the late Mr. Miller as they left the building and walked toward the parking lot where Meg had left her car. "Are you enjoying your class?" he asked.

"Yes, at least most of the time. I can't remember the last time I took a biology course, and a lot of the material is going right over my head, but it's interesting, and I think I'm learning something. Or at least learning what I need to learn. I guess I hadn't realized what I was taking on."

"Don't let it intimidate you, my dear. I have faith in your abilities. Tell me, how is the barn coming along?"

They chatted about mundane details as they drove the mile or two into the center of Amherst, with Christopher providing directions to a midsize restaurant down a flight of stairs. Miraculously Meg found a parking space on the street in front of it, and they entered the dim and noisy place and seated themselves at a table in a corner. Meg managed to contain her curiosity until they'd placed their orders, and then she turned to Christopher. "Okay, why all the mystery? Why are we here instead of in your office?"

Christopher sighed. "I hate to speak ill of the dead, but Jason Miller was not particularly beloved by our department, and it will take some time to provide you with the history. I know it is unkind to say so, but I don't think Jason will be much missed."

"Well, you've got my full attention. What's the story?"

The waitress dumped their sandwiches on the table and retreated. Christopher began cautiously. "Jason was first an undergraduate at the university, then stayed on to pursue his doctorate. Unfortunately he was perilously close to wearing out his welcome."

"What do you mean?" Meg asked, taking a large bite of her club sandwich.

"The university has guidelines about the length of time one may take to complete a degree program, and Jason was pushing the limits."

"What was the problem? Poor performance? He couldn't

finish his thesis? He was scared of testing the job market?"

"A bit of all of those, but there was one overriding factor that interfered with his academic commitments. Are you familiar with the GreenGrow organization?"

"Barely," Meg said. "Rachel Chapin—Seth's sister—mentioned it the other day, but that was the first I'd heard of it. Please enlighten me."

Christopher took a substantial bite of his sandwich and sat back in his chair before answering. "GreenGrow is a regional activist group dedicated to organic farming and the complete suppression of all pesticide use. Jason Miller was a founding member and perhaps its most vocal proponent."

"Why did that get him in trouble with the university?" Meg ate a handful of potato chips.

"GreenGrow siphoned quite a bit of time from Jason's academic pursuits. Don't misunderstand me: our department supports the concept of organic farming. We even offer a few courses devoted to it, as well as to the public policy issues surrounding pesticide use. GreenGrow was a problem only because Jason had become increasingly confrontational over the past year or two. I think he came to regard organic purity as a holy mission of some sort, and he could be very self-righteous about it. Mind you, that alone would not have created trouble within the department, but he was in fact neglecting his responsibilities. You see, to obtain a doctoral degree, a student must submit and defend a thesis within six years of beginning the program, and this spring marks the end of his sixth year. He petitioned for an extension, but the director of the graduate program declined to grant it, and quite frankly, I don't think it was warranted. However, Jason took it rather amiss. He claimed that the department was out to discredit him because of his outspoken opinions about pesticide use."

"Was he any good? I mean, academically?"

"I'd say yes. He was an intelligent young man, he did well in his course work, and the drafts I had seen of his thesis were sound, if somewhat careless."

"You were his thesis advisor?"

"I'm afraid I was. I urged him to apply himself to completing the degree requirements before pursuing his other interests, but his attention was elsewhere far too much of the time."

"How did he take that?"

"He told me I was a stooge of the administration and was conspiring with them to silence him."

Based on what she knew of Christopher's character, Meg found this laughable. "He sounds a bit paranoid. Unless, of course, it was just thesis anxiety. Some people have trouble finishing things."

Christopher sighed. "I know. I've seen it before. But I think Jason's trouble went beyond that. He was obsessed with his cause and found the trappings of academia increasingly irrelevant. The department had no choice but to issue an ultimatum: finish the thesis or withdraw from the program."

"What did he decide?"

"I don't know. We were scheduled to meet this week, which probably would have resulted in his termination. As I told that unpleasant Detective Marcus."

Meg chose her next words carefully. "Christopher, do you think that Jason might have been depressed about being booted out of the university, and killed himself?"

Christopher regarded her steadily. "Heartless though it may sound, I think the young man was too full of himself to consider ending his life that way. Although if he did, I'm sure he *would* make it a political statement of some sort. Do you by any chance know how he died?"

Meg glanced around the room, where everyone, including the waitstaff, seemed to be ignoring them. She dropped her voice. "Art Preston said the ME has ruled out the most obvious causes, so he's thinking it was some form of poison, but it's going to take a while to figure out which one." Meg stopped because Christopher was staring blindly at a space over her head. "Christopher? What are you thinking?"

Slowly he brought his gaze back to her. "You might pass on the word that the medicos should look at pesticides."

Meg was startled. "Why? Do you know something?"

"No, not at all. But Jason was so . . . militant, you might say, about pesticide use. If—and I used that term deliberately—he ended his own life, he might have considered a pesticide the appropriate means. He would have had access to any number. As would many of his—I think 'enemies' is too strong a word, but there were those who disagreed strongly with him. He was on a crusade, and he managed to anger a number of people. Some of them no doubt have access to pesticides as well and could have used them unwisely, thinking it would be a fitting end. Jason could be considered a pest, if I may make a poor joke."

Meg wondered how she could find a way to pass on Christopher's suggestion to the medical examiner. "I'll see what I can do. How would pesticide poisoning work, in a human?"

"There is no single answer to that. It depends on the pesticide in question. But though they vary in their toxicity, they are undeniably effective if the dose is large enough. Although there remains the issue of how to administer them. Do you have any idea *when* Jason died?"

Meg shook her head. "No, Art just gave me the bare bones, and he was probably breaking a slew of rules to do that much. The ME originally guessed around twenty-four hours before I found him, on Monday. And it's still not clear where he died."

"Well, what happens now?" Christopher's eyes were warm with concern.

"You mean with the orchard? The police are done with it—there really wasn't much to find there. You know, I've been wondering about the springhouse. What's it doing in the middle of the orchard?"

Christopher looked pleased to have a safe topic to discuss. "Natural springs arise where they choose—there might be a cleft in the underlying rock there, or a vein of clay. You can tell it's not very active, since there is no runoff down the hill. But at some point in time it must have served a purpose, whether for drinking water or to water the trees. That's probably as much as we'll ever know. Nonetheless, it might serve you well if you wish to install an irrigation system for the orchard."

"Will I need one? You know, there's a well in the basement of the house. It's still open. That's part of what got me wondering—isn't the water table down there, not a hundred feet up the hill?"

"As I said, it's a spring, and they may pop up in the most unexpected places." Christopher checked his watch. "Well, my dear, I suppose I must return and prepare for my class, if you will be so kind as to drop me back?"

"Of course. Oh, one other thing: do you know if Bree knew Jason?"

Christopher paused for a moment. "Not to my knowledge, but I'm not privy to the personal lives of most of my students. I believe Jason was a teaching assistant at some point, although not lately, and they might have crossed paths. Otherwise the undergraduates and the graduate students have little contact. Why do you ask?"

"She was at the house yesterday, and apparently she hadn't heard about the murder." Which, as Meg thought about it, seemed strange. "Could she really be that oblivious?"

"Ah, Meg, were you never a student at a large university? We are our own little universe here, and it is possible to shut out the rest of the world, if one so chooses.

The students in particular are singularly uninformed about external events."

"If you say so. I only brought it up because when I mentioned Jason's name, Bree reacted rather oddly. But that could have been in reaction to the murder, not to Jason specifically."

"I'm sorry I can't help you. You'll have to ask her yourself."

As they drove back toward campus, Meg asked, "Does the rest of the department know about Jason's death?"

Christopher turned toward her. "I suppose they may have seen it on the news, as I did. But in general we aren't exactly a gregarious bunch, and we tend to follow our own pursuits, so I don't know what has been discussed. Dear heavens, I suppose as his advisor it falls to me to post some kind of notice, or perhaps plan a small informal gathering in his memory. What do you think?"

Meg wasn't sure what custom dictated when the deceased was someone who had apparently alienated most of his colleagues, but a recognition of some sort seemed called for. "That would be nice. If you do, can you let me know when it will be? I'd like to pay my respects." *And see how some of the other faculty members act, under the circumstances*, she added to herself.

She didn't fool Christopher, who said with a smile, "A bit of sleuthing, eh? Still, I see no harm in that. And I'll extend the invitation to the graduate students of the department as well as the faculty members. An excellent plan."

What Christopher had told her about Jason suggested that he wasn't a very nice person and had probably annoyed any number of people. But being annoying was seldom enough reason for killing someone. If in fact he had been murdered, which wasn't established. Yet.

And she ought to do some research on the GreenGrow

people, whoever they were. Besides, if she was investigating the full spectrum of options for managing her orchard, she should educate herself about pesticides and the alternatives. Which would give her the perfect excuse to talk to them, if she could track them down.

It was a plan.

8

When Meg returned home, she found Bree sitting on the step outside her kitchen door, her jacket wrapped tightly around her. Bree stood up as Meg got out of her car.

"Why didn't you just let yourself in?" Meg asked as soon as she was in earshot. "You could have kept warm."

Bree shrugged. "Seemed kind of rude, with you not here. But I need to talk to you."

Meg fought off apprehension as she struggled with the stiff lock on the door. When the door finally opened, she led the way into the kitchen. "Do you want something to drink? Have you had lunch?" she asked, tossing her coat toward the hook on the wall.

Bree made a vague gesture with her hand. "Don't worry about that. There's something I've got to tell you."

Looking at Bree's expression, Meg felt something like pity for the girl. She seemed so young. Or maybe it was just that she made Meg feel old, though there wasn't much more than ten years between them. "Then let's sit down and you can tell me whatever it is." Meg pulled out a chair at the kitchen table and waited for Bree to follow suit.

Bree sat, her hands clasped tightly in front of her on the table, avoiding Meg's eyes. "You probably wondered why I left so fast last night," she began.

"I thought maybe you were upset by hearing about the body."

"Well, yes, but the thing is, I knew Jason." She stopped, apparently struggling for words.

"From the university?" Meg prompted.

"Yeah. He was my TA a couple of years ago." Bree looked away, uncomfortable.

Meg stood up. "I'm going to make some tea, but please go on." Maybe if Meg was looking at something else, Bree would relax. She filled the kettle with water and set it on the stove.

"There was more than that, I guess," Bree volunteered to Meg's back.

Meg bustled around looking for mugs and tea bags. "You knew him outside of class?"

"Yeah. We sort of dated for a while that year, but things got, I don't know, kind of messy."

Wasn't that frowned upon? Meg turned and faced Bree. "Is that allowed? Was he harassing you? Threatening your grade if you didn't go out with him?"

Bree looked disgusted. "No, nothing like that. I could have handled that, no problem. The university's pretty good about warning people about that kind of thing. And I don't think he was that much into the whole relationship thing."

Now Meg was mystified. "What, then?"

"You know anything about Jason?"

Meg debated briefly about filling Bree in on her conversation with Christopher and decided against it. "I never met him. What should I know?" She comforted herself that she hadn't lied outright.

Bree sat back, her nervous expression fading as she warmed to her subject. "He was smart, and he was a pretty good teacher, I guess. But he didn't much like rules, and he was kind of weird."

The kettle whistled, and Meg filled the mugs. "What do you mean, weird?"

"Like he was on a mission. He was really into this whole organic thing, like pesticides were evil, and God wanted us to keep the plants pure as He intended."

"That sounds kind of extreme. You'll have to fill me in: did he have a lot of support for his position?"

"Aren't you taking that orchard class?"

Meg carried the mugs to the table and sat down again. "I'm auditing it, but I'm kind of overwhelmed by all the material coming at me. Can you give me the short version?"

Bree stirred sugar into her tea. "Okay. So, there's this whole spectrum of approaches, see? And pure organic is at one end of the line, and the big corporate chemical companies who make pesticides are at the other end, and integrated pest management is somewhere in the middle. And there are different strategies for IPM. There's chemically based, where you wait until the losses to pest damage are greater than the cost of spraying, or biologically based, which lets the natural enemies have the first crack. And that's just a start. You with me so far?"

"I think so. Obviously Christopher advocates IPM, but we haven't gotten down to details yet or discussed what approach he's been using here at the orchard."

"Look, you know the apples you see in supermarkets? They're all shiny and perfect, right?"

"Yes. Why?"

"That kind of perfect apple doesn't happen in nature, and you're going to find out pretty fast how many pests and blights and stuff are looking to do a number on your apples. Until consumers are willing to accept less-than-perfect fruit, we're going to have to use pesticides. But we can use them only when needed, and pay attention to their overall impact, how they interact with other systems. For instance, bees, right?" Bree looked at Meg to be sure she was paying attention. "You need bees for pollination, of course, but you spray the wrong thing at the wrong time, you kill your bees, and there goes your crop. There's a whole lot of fine-tuning going on, all the time. You've got to watch your weather, how warm it gets, how much it rains. You've got to keep your eye on which insects show up, and when, and decide what you want or need to do about them. You've got to keep up with the literature, because there's new research coming out all the time, and new products. Natural products, too, like bioantagonists or the kaolin strategy. You've got to decide whether to treat prophylactically or to wait and see just how bad an infestation turns out to be in any given year."

Meg held up a hand. "Wait, please! That's why I hired you, because I don't know any of this stuff! I'm willing to learn, but it's going to take some time. I get the basics: some pesticides are necessary if you want to produce a marketable crop, and you have to use them carefully. But there are different opinions about what that really means, right?"

Bree nodded vigorously. "Exactly. And Jason was kind of fanatic about it. He thought all pesticides were evil, and there wasn't any arguing with him. What happened with us . . . Well, he wanted to get serious, but not about us. He wanted to convert me to his way of thinking, and I couldn't do that, because I have a corporate scholarship from a pesticide company, and that's the only way I could pay for college. He thought it would be a real coup for him if he could bring me over to his side, but he didn't stop to think what it would mean for me."

"And you didn't want to go along?" Meg suppressed a smile.

"No way. Look, maybe I was naïve, and for a while it

was cool that this grad student was interested in me. And he could be real charming if he wanted to. He did kind of attract people, you know? But after a while it got old. He was kind of one-note, always dragging this organic purity thing into every conversation and pushing it all the time. After a while I got sick of it, and I told him he should back off. And then he got all high and mighty and said he was disappointed in me and he'd really hoped that I was smart enough to see reason. *His* reason. When I didn't back down and kiss his feet, he got pissed at me. The end wasn't real pretty."

Meg wondered if she was telling the whole truth. "Did he have any other friends who shared his views?"

"You mean, like that GreenGrow bunch?" Bree snorted. "Mixed bag, I guess. Some of them are okay, but some are kind of out there, you know? I think their parents fed them a lot of crap about the sixties and all the great activism that went on then. You part of all that?"

Meg tried not to laugh. At thirty-two she was hardly old enough to have taken part in any activities in the sixties. "No, that was a bit before my time. But certainly I've heard about it, and it sounds as though some good things came out of activist movements in that era."

"Maybe. But GreenGrow has been all about the show, with no substance. They run around spouting rhetoric and posturing for the cameras, and Jason was right at the front of the pack. But they don't follow through. They're colorful and make a lot of noise, so they get news coverage, at least now and then, but they're giving responsible people like Christopher a bad name."

"How heavily was Jason involved?"

"He thought he was the star. Heck, he was one of the founders of the group, and he certainly kept it going. They've got maybe fifteen, twenty members, although I know a bunch of people who got involved and then burned out pretty quickly. The ones that're left, they've really bought into the whole package."

"You know any of them now?"

Bree shook her head. "Some, but mostly I've steered clear of Jason and his buddies. I don't have time for that crap anyway, and like I said, I needed the scholarship and I didn't want to jeopardize that."

Meg took a deep breath. "Bree, were you worried about telling me that you knew Jason?"

Bree looked down at the table. "Maybe. I thought maybe you'd think I had something to do with his death. Dumb, huh?"

"Not at all." Meg had more experience than she wanted in that arena. "Bree, I think you should tell the state police about your connection to Jason before somebody else does. I can put you in touch with the detective investigating the case—Detective Marcus."

"You want me to go to the state police and tell them that Jason and I hooked up for a little while two years ago and it's just a coincidence that he ends up murdered at the place I'm working?"

Stated like that, it did sound suspicious, but Meg persisted. "It would be better coming from you than from someone else. The fact that you're connected both to Jason and to this place is going to jump out at them."

Bree did not look convinced. "I'll think about it." She hesitated before going on. "So you don't think I'm an idiot because I was involved with him?"

Luckily Bree didn't know about Meg's track record with relationships. "Of course not. And I don't for a minute think you had anything to do with his death. Was that why you ran out of here yesterday?"

"Kind of. I wanted to think about the whole thing before I tried to explain it to you."

"Well, I'm glad you told me. Now I'll know what to say if someone asks me about your connection with him. And I think you should be proud that you saw through Jason's BS and you ended it."

Bree brightened. "Thanks, I guess. Look, I've got to get

back to campus, but I can come back tomorrow and bring you some stuff to read on pesticides. That okay?"

"Fine. My schedule's clear. And do think about talking to the detective, will you? It always looks better to give the police information than to wait until they come asking for it."

"Maybe. But let me do it my own way, okay?" Bree did not appear convinced. "See you tomorrow."

9

After Bree left, Meg wondered what she was supposed to do next. She hadn't realized that there were political agendas in orchard management: organic, chemical, or somewhere in between. Now that she knew about GreenGrow, she should find out more about them before they showed up on her doorstep demanding . . . what? Vengeance for their fallen comrade? A guarantee that she would eschew all toxic substances and produce only wormy, shriveled apples? Or was she being unfair to them? Meg decided the first thing she should do would be to collect some useful information. If Jason had been so outspoken, surely there was some record online. Any half-respectable organization with a public ax to grind should have a website, shouldn't it?

But before she had time to boot up her computer, Seth rapped on her back door, looking anything but cheerful, and she quailed inwardly. She wasn't sure she was prepared to deal with yet another crisis. "Hi. You coming in?"

He stepped in, then turned to face her. "We may have a problem," he said without preamble. "Can we sit?"

"Sure." She took a seat, and so did he. "What's wrong?"

"I've been clearing out the barn in fits and starts. I haven't really had the time to do it all at once, and there are generations of junk piled up in there."

"I know. That's why I've stayed out of it. Did you find something?"

He sighed. "Unfortunately, yes. When you said Art thought Jason might have been poisoned, I didn't put two and two together until after I'd left. And I still don't know if this is important. Anyway, last week I stumbled across an industrial-size container of pesticide stuck in a corner. I can't say how long it had been there, but it was way past its expiration date."

"Something used in the orchard? But why is that a problem?" Meg asked.

"Somebody probably used it, years ago. Not Christopher—it's got to predate his work with the orchard. But it's a toxic substance, past its expiration date, and improperly stored, so I got rid of it. What do you know about disposal of hazardous wastes?" When Meg looked blank, he went on. "It's usually handled by the local community government. As selectman, I set up a program for Granford about two years ago. The town posts a list of what substances they'll accept. You've got to have somebody monitoring it, checking IDs, because you don't want everyone in the state dumping their nasty stuff on you. Anyway, that's the drill. I knew the stuff I found in the barn was potentially toxic, and I couldn't in good conscience leave it sitting in your barn, so I figured I should turn it in. And I did, last Friday."

"But that was before Jason died, right? Seth, what are you trying to tell me?"

"I don't know that this has anything to do with Miller's death, but if he was poisoned by something, and there was a toxic substance here on the property, it's not a stretch to connect the two things. And Marcus will probably blow it all out of proportion."

Meg's mind went into overdrive. "When you found the container, did it look as though it had been disturbed any time recently?"

Seth shook his head. "I couldn't say. I wasn't paying a lot of attention."

"And you took it away the same day?"

"I did. In any case, it's gone now."

Meg smiled wryly. "If Marcus asks, I never knew it was there. As far as I recall I never saw the stuff. And you know as well as I do what a mess that barn is."

Seth smiled in response. "I do indeed." Then his expression sobered. "Let me ask you this—who has access to the barn, other than me?"

"Currently? I've got a key, and it's hanging right there by the door. I gave Bree one, but not until yesterday. Christopher might have a key, since he's been using this site for years. And who knows how many assistants he's had in that time? But to tell the truth, just about anyone who really wanted to could get into the barn with a butter knife. It's not exactly secure."

"I agree. But someone would have to have a reason to break in. Not just kids snooping around. You and I have been around a lot lately, coming and going, which limits the opportunities."

"Could some earlier tenant have left the stuff?"

"Maybe. But they wouldn't have any reason to use commercial-grade pesticide, would they?"

"I doubt it. So what are we saying? It was there, for who knows how long. It's been gone since last week. And a whole lot of people could have known about it. It's going to be hard to make the connection with Jason's death—and we still don't know how he died."

Seth rubbed his hands over his face. He looked tired. "I know. I agree with you. But I don't like the coincidence, and I feel as though I should say something to Marcus about it. Just in case. Especially since there's a public record that I got rid of it, and I'm sure he'd like to find that was evidence of something."

Meg almost laughed. She'd just lectured Bree on acting responsibly and talking to the detective, but this time it was different. She knew Marcus disliked Seth even more than he disliked Meg, for reasons that went back years, and the last murder investigation had done little to change that. No doubt he would seize upon this information and try to twist it somehow. She felt a brief flash of guilt. Ignorance was no excuse: it was her barn now, and she had a moral and legal obligation to know what was in it and to see that it was maintained—or, in this case, disposed of—properly.

"What?" Seth asked.

"What what?" she replied, stalling.

"You're worried about something."

"It's that obvious? I was just thinking about Bree. She stopped by this afternoon to explain why she bolted last night. It turns out she and Jason dated a couple of years ago. I told her she ought to tell Detective Marcus about it before someone else does, but I don't know if she will. The thing is, I don't really know her. I can't absolutely, positively say she's not involved somehow. Not that I believe she could or would have done it." *But I've been wrong before* . . .

"Slow down and take a deep breath," Seth said, not unkindly. "Right now there's a lot we don't know, starting with how, why, and where Jason Miller died. If it's any comfort, I have trouble imagining Bree as a killer, based on what I've seen of her. But let's not go asking for trouble, okay? Let's see what the authorities come up with."

"Then can I panic?" Meg answered lightly. Still, he had a point. There was no reason to assume the worst—yet. "So, are you going to talk to Marcus?"

"Maybe I'll talk to Art first, get a law-enforcement perspective. Sounds like I'm stalling, doesn't it?" Seth managed an unconvincing smile.

"I know how you feel. But look at it this way: if you report it officially, the ME can look for that specific pesticide, and maybe he can eliminate it as a cause of death and we won't have to worry about it anymore. And even if it is the same stuff, won't a lot of people around here have some on hand?"

He brightened. "Probably—I know it's still in use. I'm sorry I had to dump this on you, Meg, but I just thought you should know, in case it comes back to bite us."

"Thank you, I guess. Better than getting blindsided down the line. But I'm sure you did the correct thing in disposing of it, and you had no reason at the time to think it was suspicious. And maybe that'll be the end of it. By the way, what was it?"

"The generic name is methidathion. Why?"

"I could do some research, find out where this falls in the spectrum of pesticides. Maybe it's not all that toxic and you'd have to consume five pounds for it to have any effect on you. I mean, humans are a whole lot bigger than bugs, aren't they?"

"Maybe, but I won't assume anything. This just gets better and better, doesn't it?" Seth stood up. "I'd better be going. I'll see if I can talk to Art tonight and maybe swing by Northampton tomorrow, if need be."

"I guess I'll take your suggestion and hope for the best, at least until we know more. You want me to ask Christopher if he knows anything about the pesticide in the barn? He's supposed to be here tomorrow."

"You might as well. Bye now."

Seth let himself out, and Meg remained at the kitchen table, staring into space. She was disturbed by the presence of poison in her barn, and by the man who might have died of poison not far away. Were the two connected? If not, it was a peculiar coincidence. And then there was Bree ... Meg wanted to believe Bree wasn't involved, but her connection to Jason was yet another disturbing coincidence. And Meg didn't trust coincidences.

10

It was nearly ten Friday morning when Meg saw Christopher's UMass van turn into her orchard, and by the time she'd pulled on her rubber boots and her jacket and headed up the slope to intercept him, he had already moved into the midst of the trees with his gaggle of students and was in full lecture mode. When he noticed her approach, he smiled and waved without interrupting his spiel, and Meg came close enough to listen. After a few minutes, he waved the students off, and they scattered in pairs through the trees, looking for something. Christopher watched them critically for a moment, then turned to Meg.

"How are you, my dear? Any further fallout from your unpleasant discovery?"

Involuntarily Meg glanced at the low profile of the springhouse. "Nothing on what happened to Jason, but there's something else that might be related I need to ask you about."

He studied her face for a moment. "Something the students don't need to hear?"

"It doesn't concern them, if that's what you mean. You use some pesticides on this orchard, right?"

"Yes, of course. Are you concerned about what we've been using? Whether it's safe?"

Meg hadn't even considered that aspect. Would something sprayed on the orchard drift down to the house? Once again she felt the weight of her ignorance. "It wasn't that, although maybe you're telling me I should worry about that angle. No, this is about something Seth found in the barn when he was clearing it out. A container of pesticide—methidathion, he said. He guessed it had been there for a while, but he thought it was too old, so he disposed of it. Properly, of course," Meg rushed to add. "But he was worried . . . we still don't know how Jason died. Seth put two and two together and didn't like what he came up with. I said I'd ask you if it's something you might have left here. You've been using this orchard for quite a while, right?"

Christopher looked troubled. "Close to twenty years now. That particular chemical has been around since the 1960s, long before we came to an agreement for the use of this orchard. I am fairly sure we haven't used it recently—it's fairly toxic, although it has a short half-life after application, and is reasonably kind to the environment. But it's not my pesticide of choice. In any event, generally we bring all our materials and equipment with us when we treat your orchard. What's more, since there was a certain amount of turnover among the tenants here, I was reluctant to leave anything at all in the barn, much less something hazardous. And I never would have used an out-of-date formulation—that would be unprofessional and irresponsible." He hesitated a moment before asking, "Do I take it that you suspect that might have been used by or against Jason?"

"Christopher, I don't know enough even to guess. But I suppose it wouldn't hurt if you pulled together a list of the chemicals you have been using here, how they're handled, stuff like that. In case Marcus wants it."

"Of course. I keep that material on file." Christopher cast an eye over his scattered class and apparently satisfied, turned again to Meg. "Is there any hope that it will be cleared up quickly?"

"I have no idea. They did the autopsy fast, but it'll take a while for the toxicology results. It did occur to me that if we suggested a few possible toxins, it might speed up the process. But I'm kind of scared of pointing the ME in any direction."

Christopher glanced again at his scattered students. "You'd asked if there would be any, uh, recognition of Jason's passing at the university. I've arranged for an informal get-together, a kind of wake, perhaps, at five this evening, if you wish to attend. I don't expect a large gathering. He was not a popular young man. On the other hand, I have made it known that there will be refreshments, and that usually guarantees some attendance."

Meg was torn. "Would it be too weird if I did? My only connection with Jason was finding his body. But I would like to pay my respects and meet people who knew him. Maybe it would help me figure out who might have wanted him dead. Has there been any talk within the department?"

Christopher shook his head. "Sad to say, the overriding response is one of relief." He looked away and gestured toward his scattered flock, gathering them in. "So I'll see you later, Meg?"

"I'll be there." She turned and went back down the hill toward the house. But rather than going inside, she walked around the perimeter to the side by the driveway, looking critically at the house as she went. Painting the trim was definitely on her to-do list but still on hold for warmer weather. She had to get the driveway paved since the installation of her septic tank had chewed across it. Meg was cheered to see a few green shoots emerging from the beds around the house. She hadn't been here in the spring before, so she had no idea what was planted, and this was the first sign of life she had seen.

The sun was warm on her face, the air smelled of damp leaves, and she wasn't ready to tackle her list of chores. Instead she sat down on the broad granite slab that formed her back stoop, outside the kitchen. She leaned back on her arms and contemplated the view of the Great Meadow beyond the barn. Yes, there was a hint of green among the trees on the far side. Spring was coming—and with it a whole host of activities in the orchard, about which she still knew very little. She had to sit down with Bree and go over the schedule. From now on she was going to make sure she knew what was happening on her own property.

A flicker of movement near the barn caught her eye, and she turned to find a cat sauntering toward her across the muddy drive.

"Hello," Meg said tentatively. "Where'd you come from?"

The cat gave her a lazy look, then jumped up to the low step, sat down, and began a leisurely bath. Meg took stock of her new companion: a brown tabby with white vest and paws, fairly young looking. Clean, so most likely not an outdoor cat, but no collar. Unafraid of her, so probably a cat who was used to people. Male or female? She couldn't guess. Meg reached out a tentative hand. The cat contemplated it for a moment, then stood up and butted its head against it. Cautiously Meg scratched behind the cat's ears, which the cat accepted for a moment, and then, formal greetings completed, sat down and resumed her bath.

Meg smiled and looked back toward the meadow. This was nice. It actually felt homey. Should she leave some food out for the cat? It didn't look starved—it must belong to someone not far away. Would leaving food out keep the cat around? Did she *want* to keep the cat around? She'd never even considered a pet, since the apartments she'd lived in in Boston had not allowed them. But this was the country, wasn't it? And Meg was willing to bet that there were mice in the house, although she hadn't looked too closely. Maybe a cat was a good idea. If not this cat, then some cat. Something to think about.

Obscurely cheered, Meg stood up and went inside. The cat didn't budge.

After taking inventory of the paltry contents of her refrigerator and freezer, Meg decided to run a few errands. She made the rounds of the stores outside of town, then stopped at the small pharmacy that served as a general store on the green in downtown Granford for a few odds and ends. As she emerged from her car door, she heard someone call her name.

"Meg? Over here! Got a minute?" Gail Selden, head of the Granford Historical Society, was waving at her from across the green.

Meg checked quickly for traffic—nonexistent—then crossed over to the historical society's dilapidated building. "Hi, Gail. What's up?" She hoped, fleetingly, that Gail wouldn't want to pump her for information about the body in the orchard.

"Were you serious when you said you'd help us out with cataloging?"

Aha. Meg *had* volunteered to input information into a standardized database from the endless files that the understaffed society owned. "Sure. What do you need?"

"Wonderful! I hoped you'd say that, because I brought a couple of boxes with me. They're a real mess, just thrown together, but I picked stuff I thought might have information about the Warren farm, just to give you a little incentive. You can learn the data-entry ropes and learn about your home at the same time. Sound good?"

"I'd love to see the files, and I should have time, at least in the evenings. You said you could teach me how to catalog?"

"Piece of cake! I can show you what we've done so far." Gail grinned. "And there's no deadline—this stuff has been waiting for decades, so you can work on it when you want. You're a lifesaver! You have no idea how it bugs me, having all this wonderful historical material and not being able to make it available. You wouldn't want to do a little fund-raising for us, would you?"

Meg laughed. "Why don't you ask Seth? Nobody seems to be able to say no to him."

"I have. I think it's on his to-do list but behind a lot of other stuff, like paying for police salaries and ambulance service and school supplies."

"Well, I'm happy to help."

Gail cocked her head at Meg. "You have room in your trunk for a couple of file boxes?"

Gail helped Meg load four bulging boxes, papers sprouting from the loose lids, into the backseat of her car. As she drove home, Meg realized she was looking forward to delving into Granford's history. From what little she had seen, the jumbled papers and artifacts would probably tell her much more about her adopted town than reading any dry written summary.

Back at the house, she unloaded and stowed her groceries, then returned to the car for the file boxes, which she carried into the dining room. She fought the urge to dig into them immediately. If she was going to present herself at the university, she ought to clean up and get moving. The files had waited this long, and they could probably wait another day or two.

The parking lots at the university began to clear out at the end of the day, and Meg had no trouble finding a convenient parking space. She had forgotten to ask Christopher where the ad hoc event was to be held, so she checked his office, and finding it empty, followed the sound of muted conversation down the hall to a large classroom, where a mix of faculty members and students huddled in awkward clumps. The desk at the front of the room had been cleared and was spread with a couple of supermarket deli trays of cheese and cold cuts, plus a few bottles of inexpensive wine and soft drinks. The attendees were clustered around the food and held glasses of wine or soda while juggling paper plates of food.

Christopher noticed her hovering in the doorway and beckoned her over. "Welcome, my dear. I'm glad you could make it. Have you met my colleague John Finkel?"

Meg extended her hand. "No, I don't believe so. I'm not actually enrolled here—I'm just auditing a class, trying to get a handle on orchard management."

Finkel glanced quickly at Christopher, who leaned toward him to say quietly, "Yes, that was the place."

Finkel's face showed an odd mix of curiosity and sympathy. "Meg, is it? Sorry to hear about . . . that you . . ." He stopped, apparently struggling for an appropriate phrase.

Meg took pity on him. "That I found Jason? I didn't know him, you know."

"Oh, yes, right, well . . ." Finkel looked around desperately. "I should go talk to . . . excuse me." He retreated quickly to the other side of the room.

Christopher had watched the exchange with a glint of humor in his eye. When Finkel was out of earshot, he said to Meg, "Peculiar situation, don't you agree? Not covered by any etiquette books, if such things still exist. 'Proper condolences for those who discover corpses.' In any event, I'm glad to see a few faces here. Jason deserves some recognition for his contributions to this department."

She had to admire Christopher's diplomatic phrasing. "Christopher, will there be any . . . well, for want of a better word, eulogies?"

"I had thought I would say a few words. Let's wait a bit and see if anyone else arrives."

"Is there anyone else I should meet?" Meg asked. Most of the crowd appeared to be hungry graduate students, attracted, as Christopher had predicted, by the lure of free food and drink.

"I think, perhaps . . . Ah!"

At the sound of his exclamation, Meg followed his gaze to the door. There were two newcomers: a tall young man in his late twenties who needed a haircut, and a frumpy woman a few years younger, both wearing what Meg defined as grubby student clothes. Both seemed unsure of their welcome.

Christopher, playing the good host, went toward them to welcome them, and Meg drifted along behind him. "Michael, I'm glad you came. And Daphne, is it?" Michael reached out to shake Christopher's hand, and Daphne mumbled something. She looked as though she would rather be anywhere else, and hung on to Michael's arm, radiating hostility.

Christopher turned to Meg. "Meg, this is Michael Fisher. He was a colleague of Jason's at GreenGrow. Perhaps I've mentioned the group?" Christopher all but winked at her. "And Daphne? I'm afraid I don't know your last name."

"Lydon. Daphne Lydon." Daphne jammed her hands in her pockets, her shoulders slumping.

Meg stepped forward. "Why, yes, Christopher, I think you did. Michael, Daphne, I'm pleased to meet you. I'm very interested in the concepts behind organic farming. I've just taken over an orchard in Granford, and I have a lot to learn. Christopher has been helping me, but I gather that the philosophy behind the organic approach is somewhat different?" She stopped, trying to look sincere and eager for enlightenment.

Christopher laid a hand on her arm. "You'll have to excuse me. I need to have a word with Professor Delgado," he said and then retreated discreetly, leaving Meg with Michael and Daphne.

An awkward silence fell. "How did you know Jason? Was that through GreenGrow?" Meg ventured.

"Yeah," was Michael's reply. "We go back a ways."

"Were you a student here?"

He nodded without volunteering anything more.

Meg was beginning to feel frustrated by Michael's unwillingness to hold up his end of the conversation. "I understand he was very committed to organic farming."

"Yeah. Sure."

Michael was not going to make this easy for her. "Tell me about GreenGrow, then," she asked. "What do you do?"

He brightened slightly. "We work to eliminate the use of harmful chemicals that are destroying the earth and all its creatures."

To Meg's ear it sounded like a canned response, but she didn't want to judge too quickly. "How do you go about that? Do you have pamphlets I could look at? Or maybe you hold public meetings of some sort that I could attend?"

Michael looked uncomfortable. "Well, uh, things are kind of unsettled now, after Jason . . . Maybe we could set up a time, and I could give you our info packet. Maybe go over it with you."

"I'd really like that," Meg said. "I'm still very new to all this, and I can use all the help I can get. There's so much to think about. I didn't have any idea!" She knew she sounded like a babbling idiot, but Michael appeared oblivious to the falseness of her tone. Not so Daphne, apparently; the girl was staring at her speculatively, and the expression on her face wasn't exactly friendly.

"Do you want to set up a time now?" Meg hurried on. "I'm on campus a couple of days a week, for classes, or I could meet you somewhere here in Amherst. Maybe lunch? Tomorrow?"

Maybe it was the idea of another free meal, but Meg's offer spurred Michael into something resembling enthusiasm and he nodded.

"Good! My treat," she added, in case he had any doubts. "Where would you like to meet?"

"Um . . . you know the place across from the bookstore?"

"On the way to Emily Dickinson's house? Sure." Emily Dickinson's home, a block or so from the center of Amherst, was one of the town's most treasured landmarks, and even newcomer Meg knew where to find it. The restaurant was small and shabby, but Meg seemed to remember good sandwiches and coffee there.

"How about noon?"

"Great. I'll see you then."

"Michael?" Daphne tugged on his arm. "We should go."

"Oh. Right, yeah. Let's grab some food first, okay?" He gave a shy nod to Meg, and he and Daphne moved toward the impromptu buffet. Meg realized that Daphne had said almost nothing during the whole encounter. What was her problem? Just awkward? Overcome with grief? If she was devastated by Jason's death, it hadn't hurt her appetite any, Meg noted, watching her fill a paper plate with cheese, bread, and slices of ham and turkey.

She turned to find Christopher at her elbow. "I see you've managed to pry a few words out of Michael," he said.

"Yes. We're going to meet tomorrow so he can give me his pitch for organic farming. Is that surprising? I thought that was what GreenGrow did."

"Oh, I do believe he's just shy. Michael was always overshadowed by Jason. I haven't had the pleasure of speaking to him for a while—Jason managed to establish himself as the voice of the group and didn't encourage others to make themselves heard. Perhaps Michael will rise to his full potential now that the way is clear."

"Was he a disciple?"

"You mean, was he a blind follower of Jason's? I think not. But if you're meeting with him, you can get a better sense of his position." Christopher scanned the crowd, which had not grown. "Well, I suppose I should make my speech and be done with it. You don't need to stay, unless you wish to."

Meg shrugged. "You go ahead. I may slip out before you're done. But thank you for inviting me. You go give Jason a fitting farewell."

She watched as Christopher made his way to a podium in the corner.

"Friends," he began, "may I have your attention for a few moments? As you know well, the impetus for this gathering was the unfortunate death of one of our students, Jason Miller. While some of us may have had our differences of opinion with him, he was nonetheless a member of our small community, and we owe it to him to recognize his passing. As his thesis advisor, I must say I admired the sharpness of his mind and his dedication to the pursuit of his beliefs. He was not one to shrink from challenges, and . . ."

Meg tuned out and watched the faces of the others in the room. She thought she saw traces of skepticism on several, as Christopher's artfully crafted comments blurred the harsh edges of the truth about Jason. She moved quietly toward the open door, stepped into the hall, and was startled to find Detective Marcus standing just outside. Obviously he had been eavesdropping. He nodded to acknowledge her and then walked a few feet away. She followed.

"Detective," Meg said quietly. "What are you doing here?"

"Ms. Corey," he responded. "Just doing my duty, following up on a suspicious death. I'm a bit surprised to see you here, under the circumstances."

Meg lifted her chin. "I'm paying my respects to the man who was found dead on my property." *And I wanted to see who his friends were.* "What did *you* hope to find?"

He didn't answer immediately, looking beyond her as people began to drift out of the room. "Miller wasn't a very popular person, although he was well known in certain circles."

"With local law enforcement, you mean?"

"No, not really. He was too smart for that kind of trouble. But he did like to push people's buttons. Can I see you to your car?"

Was he telling her it was time for her to leave? Meg felt a spurt of annoyance, but she had no reason to stay longer. She had accomplished what she came for: to see what Jason's colleagues looked like. And she had an appointment with one of them the next day. Which she didn't see any reason to enlighten Detective Marcus about. She smiled up at him. "Why, certainly, Detective. How kind of you."

The detective waited until they had reached the sidewalk in front of the building before revealing his motive. "Ms. Corey, you didn't happen to mention that your employee knew the dead man."

It took Meg a few seconds to work out what he meant. "You mean Bree? I didn't know they were acquainted when I talked to you. She told me yesterday. Is there a problem with that?"

He ignored her question. "You didn't mention the pesticide in your barn, either."

So Seth had told him. "I didn't know about that, either, until yesterday."

"There seems to be a lot that you conveniently didn't know until yesterday."

Meg fought her impulse to give him a sarcastic answer. "Detective, I've been working on the house, and I haven't had a chance to explore the barn—I was waiting for warmer weather to do that. I have no idea what else might be in there. Since you know about the pesticide, you must also know that it was Seth Chapin who found it, identified it, and disposed of it properly, all before I knew anything about it."

"So you say, Ms. Corey. Still, it's a mighty handy co-incidence, don't you think?"

"Do you think Jason Miller came all the way out to my place and went snooping in the barn to find a means to kill himself? Or do you seriously think I used a pesticide from my barn to kill a man I had never met?"

"We have only your word for that. And it's early days yet. Nice to see you again, Ms. Corey. I'll be in touch."

"Wait! Did you ever find Jason's car?" Meg asked.

Marcus gave her a long look that could hardly be considered friendly. "Parked in Amherst." He didn't volunteer any details, but strode off toward his car, leaving Meg standing on the sidewalk, fuming.

How dare he? She had nothing to do with Jason's death, and it had nothing to do with her. As far as she knew, at least. But the way the coincidences were piling up didn't make her feel any better, and truthfully, she could see why the detective might have doubts. She sighed. Just what she needed: something else that had to be done immediately. Renovate house, learn how to run an orchard, solve a crime. If it was a crime. So, find out if Jason was murdered, *then* solve the crime. Sure, no problem.

Meg was in a foul mood by the time she let herself in the kitchen door. Then she recalled the battered file boxes Gail had given her, waiting for her in the dining room. Gail had once told her that prior to the untimely death of the hapless victim found in Meg's septic tank not so long ago—and now, possibly, Jason Miller—the last murder in Granford had occurred in the nineteenth century, so there should be nothing in a heap of old paper to remind her of her current problems.

She noticed that Gail had scrawled a large "#1" on one box, so Meg opened that first. On top she found a note from Gail, some sample entry sheets, and some pairs of white cotton gloves. She opened the note first and read it:

Thank you, thank you, thank you. I've included a CD with the cataloging software program and some instructions for you, and a few samples, but for now it's a pretty simple spreadsheet system and I'm sure you can handle it. To do this right, try to handle the documents with the cotton gloves— maybe we can make them last a little longer. I owe you!—Gail

Meg smiled: Gail had been pretty sure of Meg's help.

Meg looked around her dining room: the central table was bare, and the light fixture over it would provide adequate illumination, although maybe she should put brighter bulbs in. The cord of her laptop would reach the nearest plug. What more did she need? She sat down and put on the gloves, then pulled the first box toward her and fished out a three-inch stack of mismatched documents. An odor of mildew followed. She leafed through them, trying to make some sense of them. Deeds, newspaper clippings, broadsides, letters, maps—there was a little bit of everything here, in no particular order. She looked at one of the sheets Gail had sent and found she was supposed to record the item type, material, date (if known), and a brief summary of the contents. *Might as well start at the beginning, Meg,* she thought, and picked up the first item on her stack.

An hour later she had reduced the pile by less than an inch, although she was getting better at crafting brief descriptions. Meg rolled her stiff neck around and stretched. She was about ready to call it quits for the night, but the next piece of paper on the pile intrigued her. It appeared to be a hand-drawn map, brown ink on what she assumed was rag paper, clearly old and more than a bit fragile. It measured no more than a square foot. She could make out a date scribbled in one corner: 1797. It was in fact a map of the area, at a time when there weren't many roads in Granford. She studied it, and suddenly it seemed familiar. On a hunch, she opened a search engine on her computer and called up a map program, zeroing in on Granford. Yes! Looking back and forth between the two maps—the one hand drawn, over two hundred years old, the other pixels on a screen—she could see the bare outlines of the old town embedded in the new. There was the town green, which meant . . . Meg traced the roads she knew southward from town, then east. Yes: County Line Road, running along the bottom of the map. And, yes, a row of circles, apparently indicating homes, and next to one, in tiny letters, "Warren."

And next to that, tiny hand-drawn trees. The orchard, two hundred years ago. Meg reached out a careful gloved finger and laid it on the spot, as if touching it somehow connected past and present. Absurdly, tears pricked her eyes. The longer she looked, the more details she noticed—she could make out the names of the neighbors, and of the roads, although most of the latter were prosaic descriptions like "Road to Muddy Brook." There, just to the north of the Warrens, lay the Chapin property.

Meg sat back in her chair. Gail had known what she was doing, handing this task to Meg. Here under her hands was history made tangible. Meg knew she was hooked. Too bad she had other things to do, like manage the orchard. And that, as she could see, was an obligation passed down through two centuries—so she had better do it right.

11

As Meg drove to Amherst for her lunch with Michael, she wondered what she hoped to learn from him. She did want to hear his story about the glories of organic farming, not only to get a sense of GreenGrow's public position but also to satisfy her own genuine curiosity. All she knew was that organic produce seemed to cost more than the other stuff at the local supermarket. She had no particular preconceptions about it, and she felt obliged to at least consider it among her options. Ultimately, though, what she really wanted was to hear what Michael had to say about Jason, although she wasn't sure how to steer the conversation that way.

She was also beginning to worry that she hadn't heard from Bree. Meg didn't trust Detective Marcus, and he'd been known to be both wrong and pigheaded in the past. She hoped that her new orchard manager would at least let her know if she'd been arrested.

She had seated herself at a wobbly table in the restaurant and was looking over the sticky menu when Michael walked in and dropped into the chair opposite her. "I know who you are," he said abruptly.

Meg debated for a split second whether she should play dumb and decided there was no point. "I'm the one who found Jason's body," she said.

Michael slumped further and shrugged off his coat. "Yeah. You didn't mention that yesterday."

"I'm sorry, but I wasn't sure you'd talk to me if you knew. So I gather you did some checking?"

"Daphne told me. Look, I don't want to talk about Jason."

How did Daphne know? "Michael, I really am interested in organic farming. I'm new to the orchard business, and you know about local conditions and concerns. So let's just talk about that," Meg said. *And maybe I can work my way around to Jason later.*

"What do you want to know?" Michael picked up the menu and scanned it.

"Look, to be completely honest, all I know about the organic approach is what I read in the papers. It makes you sound like a bunch of crunchy hippies digging your bare toes into the good earth, with a sprinkling of self-righteous yuppies thrown in. Surely there's more to it?"

Michael snorted in spite of himself. "I hope so. Okay, if you're serious, I'll start at the beginning."

They were interrupted by the appearance of the student waitress, and Michael ordered a sandwich and fries. Meg settled for a sandwich and waited patiently for Michael to begin.

"Okay. GreenGrow sees organic farming as a sustainable alternative to current agricultural practices that put profits ahead of human welfare. At the moment, organic goods tend to be more expensive than nonorganic goods. So it's kind of a Catch-22: the prices for organic goods won't go down until organic processes spread on a wider scale, but people won't buy the higher-price goods that will make it possible for the market to grow." He looked at Meg to see if she was following.

She was; what he said made sense, in a broad way. "Sounds reasonable. So, I guess I have two questions: one, what does your group propose to do about it? And, two, how does that apply to what I'm doing as an individual grower?"

Michael was warming to his subject. "Well, we believe that organic farming is an environmentally friendly alternative. Do you have any idea of the impact of increasing levels of nitrogen compounds from fertilizer? They're contributing to global warming! They're in our watersheds, and that means they contaminate water tables and mess up biological zones at the mouths of our rivers. And they're not necessary! There are good alternatives—alfalfa or chicken manure, for example."

Meg struggled to suppress the image of herself trying to raise chickens to produce enough manure to fertilize her orchard. That was definitely something she hadn't signed up for.

Michael was still talking. "And look at weeds. There's no need to dump herbicides on them. You can use cover crops, you can mulch, you can burn them off. Lots of options. Keeping the organic matter in your soil is a big plus, and you don't have to add harmful chemicals."

"All right," Meg said cautiously. "But what about apples specifically? I've been told that buyers want big, flawless apples, and that means you have to control insects."

Disgust flashed across Michael's face. "Then we need to reeducate them. Organic fruits taste better, even if they have some blemishes. Sweeter, more flavorful. And there are economic tradeoffs, right? You may receive a little less money for your crop, but you aren't shelling out for all those chemicals, which don't come cheap. Or, heck, sell your apples for cider—then it doesn't matter what they look like."

"You make some good points. So why don't more people go this route?"

"They're lazy. Sometimes it does take more work to use natural methods. Or they've been brainwashed by the chemical establishment."

"And how does GreenGrow hope to change things?"

"GreenGrow is a nonprofit organization dedicated to providing information and support for organic farming practices here in the Pioneer Valley. We've been pretty successful, especially with some of the farmers' markets in the area. And with smaller farmers and growers. It's harder to convince the big corporate farms, but we're working on it."

"You rely on contributions for your funding?"

"Yeah. We've got a base list of local supporters, and the cooperatives chip in a bit. Why, you want to make a contribution?" Michael grinned, looking for once like an eager and attractive young man.

"Maybe. But what do you spend your money on?"

"Publications. Flyers, newsletters. The website. Memberships in national organizations."

Much to her surprise, Meg was impressed. Michael sounded as though he knew what he was doing, and he hadn't said anything she could disagree with. If it weren't for the issue of Jason's death hanging over them, she might actually have enjoyed this conversation. Maybe it was time to throw that out on the table and see how Michael reacted.

"You want some dessert?" she asked. At his nod, she waved the waitress over and they both ordered. At least that would keep him from getting up and walking out. When the waitress had left, Meg went on. "You know, Michael, you make a good case. You've given me something to think about, and I'll talk it over with my manager."

Michael looked away. "Bree? She's not that into it."

So Michael also knew Bree? And more—he knew she

was working for Meg? That was interesting. "Why do you say that?"

"Jason tried to persuade her, couple of years ago, but she blew him off."

Well, at least he had been the one to introduce Jason's name into the conversation. Meg tried to frame her next question as neutrally as possible. "Was that because she disagreed with GreenGrow's philosophy, or was it more personal?"

"You mean, like, her and Jason, were they together? None of my business. All I know is, he brought her into the group, and then she wasn't around anymore."

The waitress arrived with their gooey chocolate desserts and coffee, and Meg hoped that the interruption hadn't put an end to that thread of the conversation. "I understand that Jason was the founder of GreenGrow."

Michael grimaced around his mouthful of chocolate cake. "That's what he wanted people to believe, but we pretty much shared it, at least in the beginning. I guess he thought he was a better public speaker, which was probably true—I don't much like that kind of thing. But that meant I got to do all the scut work. You know, paying the bills, keeping the website current."

"So what did he do?" Meg forked up a piece of her own cake, keeping her gaze on the plate.

"Made speeches. Went around looking for places he could get attention. For himself, mostly."

Meg risked looking at Michael directly. "You know, you don't sound too happy about that."

Michael sat back in his chair, stretched, and grinned at Meg. "Lady, you're good. You've been plying me with cheap carbs just so you could pump me for information, right?"

Meg smiled back. "Something like that. Look, I never knew Jason, and then, boom, there he was, dead in my orchard. So I think I have a right to be curious. Don't you?"

"I guess."

"So tell me about him. What was he like? Do you think he killed himself?"

Michael snorted. "Jason? No way."

"So he wasn't upset about not finishing his degree, or about how things were going at GreenGrow?"

"Not really. I think he actually liked to believe that the university had it in for him because of his involvement with GreenGrow—made him feel like a martyr. And GreenGrow is doing okay."

"Say somebody killed him. Who would have wanted him dead?"

"That's a tough one. Lots of people might have thought about it. He could be really annoying. Pushy, self-important, and he had a one-track mind. Sometimes that worked; the guy really could give a good speech. Thing is, he never knew when to climb off the soapbox. He didn't have a clue about how to make nice to donors or the press. He thought he had all the answers, and if you didn't agree with him, you were obviously an idiot."

"Hey, don't hold back!" Meg laughed.

Michael swirled the dregs in his coffee mug. "Don't get me wrong. I liked the guy, or at least, the guy he used to be. We had a lot of fun when we were getting this thing started. But lately, I don't know. He was getting kind of extreme, you know? I think the university was pushing him to finish or get out, and he really didn't know what he was going to do."

"Had he finished the work for the degree?"

"Course work and stuff, I guess. He was having problems finishing his thesis, something about the research. Or maybe he just got distracted. He didn't share with me, that's for sure."

"Why would he even bother with a degree?"

"Credibility, I guess—it would certainly look better on the flyers if he could put 'PhD' after his name. And I think Mom and Dad were sending him a check now and then, as long as he stayed in school. GreenGrow doesn't pay much."

"Was there anyone else he was close to?"

Michael shrugged by way of an answer. Meg wondered if he was keeping something back or if he really didn't know.

Meg filed that fact away. "Okay, one last question. Any idea why he would've been at my place?"

"Hey, that one I can answer. He'd heard about you taking over the Warren place and figured he'd see if he could woo you away from the IPM people."

"He said that?" Meg said, surprised.

"Sure. Didn't he get in touch with you? He kept his eye on the local places, and of course he knew about your orchard, because Christopher's been taking students out there for years. He'd probably been there a few times already."

Meg felt a throb of anxiety in the pit of her stomach. So, not only had Jason had a reason to be on her property, but he'd also told other people. Except he hadn't told her; he'd just shown up—dead. It didn't put her in a very good light. "Did the state police talk to you, or anyone in your group?"

"Not me. I can't speak for the rest."

Meg wasn't sure whether that was good news or bad. On the plus side, Marcus presumably didn't know that Jason had been interested in her orchard; on the minus side, Marcus didn't seem to be trying very hard to find out about Jason's life. She'd have to mull that over. Meg took a quick look at her watch and realized it was after two. "Michael, I appreciate your talking to me. And I meant what I said about the whole organic thing. I do need to know more about it before I jump into anything, so if you've got some literature or can point me in the right direction, I promise I'll follow up."

"That's all I want. I'll see what I can pull together. And for what it's worth, I don't believe you had anything to do with Jason's death. It's just one of those things."

One of those things that just seems to keep happening to me. "Thanks, Michael. I'm glad we had this talk."

She looked at the check, then tucked a few bills under her plate and stood up. Michael clambered to his feet. He followed her to the door, then hesitated.

"Uh, listen," he began. "About Professor Ramsdell . . ."

"Yes?" Meg prompted.

"He talks a good line about IPM, and he's been willing to work with us, but I don't think he's quite as pure as he wants you to think."

"I don't understand."

"I don't have all the details, but I think he's in bed with the pesticide crowd."

"What do you mean?"

Michael shrugged. "Just that he's been taking funding from one of the big companies for research." He framed the last word with air quotes. "You might want to ask him about it. Jason knew about it, and he was really steamed. That's all I know. Thanks for the lunch." He turned and headed off down the street.

Meg stood for a moment, looking around the bustling Amherst intersection. It seemed so bizarre to have been sitting at lunch with a pleasant young man, talking about death. But then, a lot of her life had seemed bizarre to her recently. Jason had had a reason to seek her out, which was distressing, even if he hadn't actually made contact with her. And what was Michael implying about Christopher? With a vigorous shake of her head, she turned back toward her car, and her orchard.

12

When Meg pulled into her driveway, Seth was there, poking around the dead leaves and spindly bushes that clustered near the foundation of the house and in odd corners. He waited while she parked and clambered out of the car.

"I'm sorry, were you waiting for me?" Meg asked.

"Sort of—it's a nice day, so I thought we could do a walk-through of the barn. You want to change clothes? It's kind of dirty in there."

Meg looked down at her "lunch in Amherst" clothes. "I guess so. Give me five." Thanks to a couple of months' worth of renovations, she had an ample supply of grubby clothes, and upstairs in her bedroom she pulled on some paint-stained jeans and a similarly decorated sweatshirt.

Back outside, she picked her way across the damp grass to where Seth waited for her. "Ready to go. What are we going to be looking at?"

"A couple of things, I guess. You haven't been inside the barn much, have you?"

"Frankly the thing scares me—I'm afraid it's going to fall down on my head. When I wanted to keep the car out of the snow, I just pulled into the shed thing there." She pointed to the open shed that connected with the back of the house.

"Okay, let's start from this end." Seth gestured at the buildings. "Take a look—you've got the open shed, the old carpenter's shop, and the barn. They were all connected, so you could walk from the house to the barn without actually going outside. Those cold New England winters, you know."

"Okay," Meg said cautiously. "And?"

"There's some really neat old equipment in the carpentry part. As I told you, I've been thinking that I could use that for my shop—it's plenty big enough for an office, over there on the right, and there's room for the van inside, and storage above—although I might have to shore up the joists up there."

"You sure the barn wouldn't be better?" Meg asked.

"Actually, that's more space than I need for the business side, and it would be harder to retrofit. I might keep some of the heavier stuff—you know, those old cast-iron tubs and such—in there, but you're going to need the space yourself."

"For apple storage?" Meg looked skeptically at the structure, which seemed huge to her. It also appeared to be leaning a bit toward the north.

"Exactly," Seth replied promptly. "As Bree mentioned the other night, you're going to need a place to let your apples ripen."

"I meant to follow up with her on that point. I thought they were ripe when they were picked."

Seth shook his head. "Actually I understand a certain amount of ripening takes place after you pick your apples. And, like Bree said, that means you have to control the temperature and modify the oxygen–carbon dioxide mix. And you've got to cool them fast, which is why it's good to have your storage facility on site to process the apples as soon as they're picked, rather than shipping them to remote storage somewhere. What you need is what's called controlled-atmosphere storage."

"Sounds like you've done your research. And it sounds expensive." Meg wasn't surprised, since everything she had touched on this property had turned out to be expensive.

Seth grinned at her. "Hey, lady, I'm a plumber, remember? I think we can handle it."

Meg had to smile at his enthusiasm. "If you say so. How big does this storage system have to be?"

"I'm not sure, but I'll talk to Bree and some guys I know, and we can lay out what you need." Seth busied himself with unlocking the padlock that held the sliding barn door in place—sort of. "After you." He stood back to let Meg enter first.

Meg walked in and stopped after a few feet to let her eyes adjust. Her first impression was that it looked like a medieval church: long central nave, open to the rafters; side aisles split halfway up to form haylofts, but still open to the center. The central part had a plank floor, but Meg couldn't tell how far that extended, because all the aisles were clogged with . . . stuff. A forest of things she couldn't even begin to identify. She could see light through a multitude of chinks in the walls, and a steady breeze wafted through.

"Looks like it needs to be cleared out, doesn't it? What the heck is all this stuff?" She waved around the interior.

"My guess is nobody here ever threw anything out, so you've probably got at least a century's worth of defunct equipment. The building itself is probably at least a hundred years old, but there are later patches and modifications, and there's a lot of reused timber that is much older."

"What was it used for back then?"

Seth shrugged. "Just basic family farm stuff, if that's what you're asking. The family probably kept a couple of cows for their own use, a horse for farm work and transport—that lasted well into the twentieth century—and some kind of carriage or buggy. Mowing equipment. Maybe a pig."

Meg advanced cautiously into the center of the building, looking at the old beams. A rickety timeworn ladder leaned against one. Ropes hung from various hooks and nails, and massive cobwebs festooned the corners and swayed in the moving air. "This makes me feel incredibly ignorant."

"You and most other people nowadays. Nobody uses most of this stuff anymore. I recognize most of it only because I've lived around here all my life, and I've poked in a lot of basements and outbuildings. And I guess I'm just naturally curious. Want to take some wild guesses about what these bits and pieces did?"

"As long as you promise not to laugh." Meg scanned the dark corners, then pointed. "Okay, that's a grindstone, and that's an anvil, right?"

"Two for two. Go on."

She took another couple of steps forward, peering into the bays. "Now that one mystifies me."

Seth came closer and looked at the dusty cylindrical object on the floor. "That, ma'am, is a chicken fountain."

Meg's mouth twitched. "A what?"

"It's to provide water for your chickens. You fill the top part with water, and it trickles out the holes around the bottom, see? And your chicks can't fall in and drown in it, because it's not deep enough."

"What's this thing?" Meg picked up a long pole with a rusty tangle of wires on one end.

"For shame, woman. It's an apple picker."

"Oh." Once Seth had said it, it made sense. How long was it going to take her to get the hang of this? "If you say so." She crossed over toward the other side of the main area, and a flash of white caught her eye. "What on earth . . . bones?"

Seth came up beside her. "Yes. Animal—that's a cow's skull there. It's a fact of farm life, you know. And they might have kept them to use as fertilizer—bone meal."

"Good heavens!" At least they were animal and not human. "Can we get rid of them? I think they're creepy."

"Not a problem. Now, let me show you what I think we can do in here."

As they ambled toward the front of the building, Meg asked, "How much space is this controlled-whatever chamber going to take up?"

"Depends on the size of your crop—we'd better ask Christopher about that. I'm guessing we could build out the one or two bays closest to the doors, use the framing that's already there, add appropriate insulation . . ."

Meg listened with one ear to what Seth was saying. She could barely follow, but she was warmed by his enthusiasm. When he pursued something, he did it wholeheartedly. His attitude was so unlike that of the bankers she had known in Boston, who made a point of playing it cool about almost everything. Seth's openness was appealing, and Meg was pretty sure that his eagerness to help with this project went beyond the chance to get some nice work space for his own business.

"Thanks, Seth. I appreciate all that you're doing here." She drifted toward the door. "Oh, and can you show me where that pesticide was when you found it?" *In case Marcus comes asking.*

His cheerful expression faded. "Right. It was in the corner, here." He led her over to a dim corner and pointed at the floor near the front wall. "I wish I'd been paying more attention. I swiped off the dust on the front, found out what it was, and figured I'd better take it into town. I didn't notice whether it had been opened any time lately. I'm pretty sure it wasn't full, but that's all I know."

"The dust wasn't disturbed? There weren't any dribbles on the floor?"

"I wasn't looking. You can see how dark it is in here, even during the day. I know I made sure it hadn't leaked. I had no idea at the time that it would be important."

"You didn't have any reason to think so." Meg considered for a moment. "Have you ever noticed any tampering with the locks? Or, heck, how many doors are there to this building?"

Seth smiled ruefully. "Too many. The padlock up front here is mostly for show. The other doors are a joke, and there's a broken pane on one of them. And before you ask, no, I don't know how long it's been broken. Could have been a week, could have been years."

"We make lousy detectives, don't we?"

"Hey, Meg, don't beat yourself up about this. Nobody would expect you to have done a complete inventory of your outbuildings in the middle of winter, when you weren't even using them."

"I suppose." Still unconvinced, Meg was turning to leave when she heard something metallic fall, somewhere at the other end of the barn. "Did you hear that?"

Seth nodded. "Could be a bird."

"Or rats?" Meg's stomach clenched at the idea.

"Nothing for them to eat here—the place hasn't been used in ages. Ah, here's the culprit." Seth pointed to a cat, wandering down the central aisle in their direction, tail waving.

Meg recognized her. "She—or he?—stopped by to say hello the other day."

The cat was now rubbing against Seth's legs, and he squatted down to scratch its head. "I'd say she, and only a couple years old."

"She's not a stray, is she?"

"I don't think so. I think I've seen her around before—

there was a family over the hill, moved out a couple of weeks ago. Maybe they didn't want to take her along."

"That's awful, to just leave her like that. Especially if she's an indoor cat."

"I agree, but it does happen. Have you been feeding her?"

"Not yet. Should I?"

Seth straightened up. "Depends on whether you want a cat. Do you?"

Meg looked at the tabby sitting in front of her, completely at ease. The tabby looked back. "You know, I think I do." As if on cue, the cat stood up and walked over to Meg and began stropping her head against Meg's legs, purring. "She's a smart one, isn't she? Knows just who to suck up to."

"Obviously you're an easy mark. Listen, if you do decide to keep her, I know a good vet—you should check on her shots, spaying, that kind of thing."

"Good idea. Seth, is there anybody you don't know around here?"

He grinned. "Hey, I'd better be going. And looks like you're going to need to buy some cat food."

"Thanks for coming by, Seth. What's the next step?"

"I'll talk to Christopher, get a better idea about the size of your storage area. And, if you don't mind, I thought I'd get the office and shop space built out first. You won't need the storage until late summer anyway, right?"

"That's what I understand."

They left the barn, followed by the cat. After Seth pulled away, Meg shivered. The sun was sinking fast. She looked down at the cat waiting patiently by her feet. "Okay, lady, I guess it's time to go inside. Can you handle tuna? Because I'm pretty sure I've got a can of that. I'll deal with cat food tomorrow, all right?"

The cat stared up at her with green eyes "Do you have a name?" The cat didn't answer but strolled ahead of Meg, climbed the granite stoop, then turned back to look expectantly at her. *Meg, you really are losing it. You're talking to a cat . . . Well, in for a penny, in for a pound.* "All right, I'm coming." When Meg opened the door, the cat darted inside.

13

Meg's sleep was troubled by a vague sense of unease: there were too many loose ends, too many hints, too many unexplained coincidences surrounding Jason's death. The pesticide in the barn that nobody had known about—or had they? Poison in the barn, poison in Jason: were they the same? Bree and Jason: she said it had ended, but should Meg trust her word? How much did she really know about Bree? And what had Michael been hinting about Christopher at lunch? Christopher was supposed to be one of the good guys. Why would he have had any reason to eliminate Jason? Wouldn't denying him his degree be enough to get rid of him?

Reluctantly Meg got out of bed and dragged on some clothes. It wasn't until she reached the kitchen downstairs that she remembered the cat, who was sitting in the middle of the kitchen floor and waiting with admirable patience for . . . blast, for food, of course. Which Meg didn't have yet.

"Hi, cat. Did you have a good night?" Meg had fixed up an impromptu litter box using shredded newspaper and hoped fervently that the cat had put it to good use. Although based on what she'd found while removing crumbling shag carpet from several rooms in the house, Meg knew that various pets had left their calling cards in the past. "I'll go to the store today and stock up. In the meantime . . ." Meg opened the refrigerator and rummaged through her sparse leftovers. "Aha! How about some chicken breast?"

The cat's green stare was now fixed on the plate in Meg's hand, and her nose twitched.

"I'll take that as a yes." As Meg shredded meat from the bones, she sorted through her tasks for the day. Market, obviously, for cat food, and after that, the local home store. She needed more paint stripper and probably some gardening tools: now that spring was coming on strong, she should clear out her flower beds and figure out what might be growing. At the very least there was plenty of pruning to be done. Maybe somewhere in the barn there were tools, but she didn't feel like venturing back into the place alone to hunt for them, and most likely they were rusted into inert relics by now. She had some reading to do for her next class, but that could wait until after dark. As long as the weather held, she should work on those chores that required daylight. She set the plate of chicken on the floor, and the cat dove in as if she hadn't eaten in days, even though Meg knew full well that she had scarfed down a can of tuna the night before. If she had been an indoor cat before, no doubt she'd had a hard time of it foraging on her own.

Meg was startled to hear a rapping at the kitchen door and looked up to see Bree. She hurried to let her in. "Hi! I was wondering what had happened to you. Is everything all right?"

Bree stalked in, managing to look both defiant and

sheepish. "Yeah, sure. Sorry. I was trying to work some stuff out. Who's this?"

Meg followed her glance to the cat, who was still eating eagerly, untroubled—or undistracted—by the arrival of a stranger. "That's, uh, a cat."

Bree snorted. "Yeah, I figured that part out—I took animal physiology. Is she yours?"

"I don't know. I found her in the barn yesterday. Seth said she might have belonged to some people who moved away. Do you have any problem with cats? Allergies or something? And you think she's a she?"

Bree hunkered down and waited politely for the cat to finish eating. The cat then sauntered over to Bree and sniffed her outstretched hand before rubbing her head on it.

"I like cats. And yes, she's female. She have a name?"

Meg shrugged. "Not that I know of. I'm working on it. Can I get you some breakfast or something?"

"Coffee, if you've got it."

"Coming up. I fed the cat first, so I haven't had breakfast." Meg stole a glance at the girl. She figured that she might as well put breakfast together and let Bree talk when she was ready.

Five minutes later Meg set plates with scrambled eggs and toast on the table, added the coffeepot, and sat down. "Dig in."

"Thanks." Bree stalled for a few more minutes by eating her eggs, but finally she sighed and put down her fork. "I talked with that Marcus guy."

"About Jason?"

Bree nodded. "I told him we'd been together for a while, but it had been over for a long time."

"What did he say?"

"Not much. I couldn't tell if he already knew about it."

"Yeah, he doesn't like to share much."

Bree gave Meg a sharp glance. "You know him?"

"Better than I'd like but not very well. There was a murder here at the beginning of the year. Maybe you heard about it? Anyway, Detective Marcus would have been happy to blame me. To be fair, there were some good reasons to, but I didn't have anything to do with it."

"You don't like him," Bree said bluntly.

"It doesn't matter. He's the chief investigator. He has to investigate. But you know, I get the feeling nobody liked Jason much. And that includes his so-called friends."

Bree took a large bite of toast and swallowed before answering. "The GreenGrow bunch, you mean?"

Meg decided not to mention Christopher's guarded comments. Technically Bree was still a student, and it might not be appropriate to know what her faculty advisor was thinking. "Yes, and maybe some of his colleagues at the university as well. I didn't see you at the wake on Friday."

"You went? I thought it would be hypocritical for me to show up. I wasn't about to mourn for the guy."

"Fair enough. Look, Bree, you knew Jason, and you know about the organic groups around here. Would any of them have reason to want him dead? Was he really important enough to kill? Or was he just plain obnoxious? Not that that's enough of a reason to kill anyone, but sometimes it's tempting."

That comment brought a lopsided smile from Bree. She helped herself to more coffee, clearly more relaxed. "Nobody's said it's murder yet. But, yeah, I can think of some people . . ." Her smile faded, and she leaned forward, both elbows on the table, cradling her coffee mug. "Okay, here's the thing. A few years ago, Jason was kind of the wonder boy of the department, right? Smart, charming, funny. Kind of superfocused, but not in your face, if you know what I mean. But then he started to change. I guess that's about the time I met him. He got more and more extreme. He'd started up GreenGrow with a buddy of his—"

"Michael Fisher. I had lunch with him."

Bree looked startled, but she continued on with what she had been saying. "Well, for a while it went really well, but then Jason started trying to push a harder line, and that turned some people off and they dropped out. But he wasn't willing to compromise. I remember one argument—" Bree stopped abruptly.

"Bree, if you're worried about implicating someone, you don't have to tell me," Meg said.

"It's not that, exactly. Maybe I got it wrong. But once, when we were at the GreenGrow offices, Jason and Michael really got into it. Michael's a good guy, and he's better at handling publicity stuff than Jason ever was, only Jason wouldn't admit it. They disagreed about a lot of things."

"But this was two years ago, right?" Meg asked. "And both Jason and Michael stayed with GreenGrow?"

"They worked it out. Sometimes Jason listened to Michael. And Michael didn't really like being the public face, so he was happy to let Jason do that kind of stuff. At least until lately."

"What changed?"

"I haven't been involved with GreenGrow for a while, you know? But I heard things from other people. Jason just seemed to be getting more and more out there. Like he was on a crusade."

Meg nodded. "I think I see what you're saying." She thought for a moment before adding, "You think he was unstable?"

Bree considered. "I hadn't thought of that. You mean, like he was flipping out?" She finished her second piece of toast before going on. "You think the detective ought to know that? Maybe Jason went to health services or something, and there's a file on him. Although I'm pretty sure he wouldn't admit he had that kind of problem. He was always right and the rest of the world was wrong, you know?"

Briefly Meg weighed the option of presenting Marcus with this piece of insight—and rejected it. "Jason might have been overzealous, but that's not necessarily a sign of mental illness. Which leaves us with Jason being annoying, and that's not usually enough reason to kill someone."

"You didn't know Jason," Bree muttered darkly.

"No, I didn't. One more thing: do you think he was suicidal?"

Bree snorted. "Jason? No way. He had all the answers, and everyone who disagreed with him was just plain stupid. To kill himself would be to admit that he was wrong and they were right, and he wasn't about to do that."

Meg wasn't sure whether to be relieved or disturbed: if it wasn't suicide, then Jason must have been murdered. "Listen, Bree . . ." Meg hesitated, unsure of how to phrase her next question. "Are we all right? I mean, you and me, and the job and all?"

Bree looked startled. "What? You having second thoughts?"

"No! I just wondered if you were. I mean, finding a body here, someone you knew . . . That could make some people uncomfortable."

"I can handle it. I mean, sure, I'm sorry he's dead, I guess, and I wish it had been someone else, someone I didn't know, or he'd been found somewhere else, or . . . You know what I mean. But I still want to work for you. If you want me."

"I do," Meg replied firmly.

"Thanks. I can finish moving in soon—it's just as easy to commute to classes from here, and the dorms are so noisy, it's hard to get much done."

"That's fine with me. By the way, Seth was here yesterday, and he said he'd talked to you about building the apple storage chamber in the barn."

"Yeah, we talked about it. Nice having a plumber to work with—he knows what I'm saying."

"He'll probably be doing a lot of the construction work himself, or at least supervising it. You haven't seen the inside of the barn, have you?"

"Nope, not yet. We need to do a walk-through."

The cat had stationed herself halfway between Meg and Bree, clearly hoping for some fallout from breakfast but not exactly begging.

"Any idea for a name?"

"What? Oh, you mean the cat?" Bree studied the cat for a moment. "Lavinia."

"Why?"

"Emily Dickinson's sister. Lived at home, never married. Liked cats, a lot."

Meg laughed. "How do you know that?"

"I've lived in Amherst for four years, and I took an English class. She was called Vinnie for short."

Meg regarded the cat. "Vinnie?" The cat stood up, stretched, and left the room. Meg turned back to Bree. "Was that a yes or a no?"

"You've never had a cat, have you?"

"No. My mother had allergies."

"I'm guessing no. Vinnie sounds like a guy's name anyway. What else you got?"

"Lavvie? No, that's not even a name. How about Lolly?"

"Give it a try."

"Lolly?" Meg called out tentatively. No sign of the cat.

"Yo, Lolly!" Bree said loudly, and the cat reappeared in the doorway. "Guess that works." She stood up and then knelt to give the cat a head rub. "Hi, Lolly-cat." Then she turned back to Meg. "Hey, why don't we take a look at that barn again? I want to know what kind of space I'm working with."

Meg followed her outside and led the way to the barn. She opened the padlock, then hauled back the door. Seth had moved it easily; Meg hadn't realized how heavy it

was. She let Bree enter first, watching her: was she deliberately avoiding looking at the corner where the pesticide
had been? *Meg, you're getting paranoid.*

They spent a pleasant half hour examining the barn
and discussing what kind of chamber Meg would need.
Bree was well informed about concepts and technical
details, but less so about costs.

"So, Bree, tell me, what size crop should I expect?"

Bree puffed her cheeks and blew out a breath. "That's
not an easy one. You should ask Christopher."

"I will, but I just wanted a ballpark number. I've got
fifteen acres, right? So what kind of yield per acre am I
looking at?"

"Depends on a lot of things, like weather and pests.
And then some apples vary a lot from year to year—like
Baldwins. They tend to bear in alternate years."

"Bree! Just give me some idea, will you?"

"Okay, okay. In an average year, with decent weather
and no disasters, maybe five-fifty to six hundred bushels
an acre."

"Wow!" Meg did some quick math. "So that means
maybe nine thousand bushels for the season?"

"More or less. And you're going to need more than one
unit."

"What?" Seth hadn't said anything about that.

"Yup. Different varieties of apple like different conditions. We can juggle a little, but I still think we're gonna
need two."

"Great," Meg said glumly. More materials, more costs.
Meg had a business degree and a few years of hands-on
experience in municipal finance, and all her training told
her that she should take the easiest route and just ship the
apples off to somebody and not worry about optimizing
her profits by holding them. So far she was seeing a
whole lot of investment and not much return—not good
business.

Bree must have sensed her dismay. "Hey, it's not that big a deal."

"Easy for you to say—you're not writing the checks." Maybe she could get a home equity loan. But first she'd have to convince someone that there would be an income.

"What're you doing about a truck?" Bree's voice interrupted her dip into self-pity. Unfortunately the question didn't improve her mood.

"Shoot, I hadn't even thought about that. And what about boxes or crates or whatever I'm supposed to be putting the apples in?" Meg was embarrassed by the hint of hysteria in her tone.

"Hey, Meg, chill. Let me work up a list of what you're going to need and where we can get the stuff. Too bad your relatives here didn't hang on to some of that. Sure looks like they hung onto everything else, doesn't it?"

A half hour later she watched Bree pull out of the driveway. As far as she could tell, Bree and Seth were on the same page about this storage thing she needed, and it sounded as though it would be relatively simple to assemble, although the equipment would no doubt be expensive. Just like everything else on the property.

14

Monday morning Meg found a mailed flyer in her mailbox announcing a public meeting of GreenGrow, to be held at a senior citizens center on the fringes of Amherst. It must have been sent before her lunch with Michael, yet it had her name on it, rather than "Occupant." She felt vaguely troubled, although there was nothing menacing about the folded sheet itself. And she hadn't exactly been invisible in the Granford area over the past couple of months, so her presence was common knowledge. Still, Jason had known about her orchard; had he sent this to her before he died?

She looked again at the flyer, apparently run off quickly at a local copy shop on cheap paper, with labels slapped on askew—clearly an amateur production. But if she wanted information about GreenGrow's position, what they offered, what they fought against, the best way to find out would be to attend the meeting. Maybe even ask questions, if she could figure out what she needed to know. She checked the date: tomorrow night at seven.

Meg was still standing at the mailbox, her mail in her hand, when a regrettably familiar car pulled in, one with the Massachusetts State Police seal emblazoned on the door. It came to a stop, and Detective Marcus climbed out of the driver's seat, while another officer emerged from the passenger side. Marcus's face offered no warmth, but Meg didn't expect any from him.

"Detective, what can I do for you today?" *Might as well be polite.*

"Ms. Corey, I'm going to have to search your outbuildings."

"Do you have a warrant?"

"I do. This isn't a request. Are the buildings locked?"

"Yes, I keep them locked. The keys are in the house. I'll get them for you."

Meg turned and went back into the house by the kitchen door. So Marcus was taking Seth's information seriously, although that horse was already out of the barn, so to speak. She deposited the mail on the kitchen table, then snagged the cluster of keys from its hook on the way and went back outside. "Let me unlock them for you."

The detective held out his hand. "I'll do that."

Meg wondered briefly if she should protest, and if she should tag along after him in case he wanted to ask her anything. She decided against both. She wasn't hiding anything, and she knew so little about the barn that she would have trouble answering any questions, which would make her look either stupid or evasive, neither of which would help. "I'll wait inside until you're done."

"Fine," he replied, then turned away and led the officer toward the barn door. Meg watched as they unlocked the padlock and slid the door back, then disappeared into the dark interior. Meg went back to her kitchen and busied herself with tidying up the few dishes she had left. Lolly strolled in, cleaned off the last few crumbs of food on her plate, then leapt up onto a counter and began washing her face. Meg watched, wondering if she was supposed to object. Did she want a cat on her counter? But the house was perennially filthy, with plaster dust and who knew what dirt of the ages kicked up by the wheezing furnace, so the presence of a cat could hardly add much. She'd have to see if Lolly was smart enough to stay away from the stove.

It was close to an hour later when the detective completed his tour of the barn. He knocked at the back door, and Meg let him in. "You're finished?"

"I have a few questions for you."

"Sit down, please. What do you want to know?"

Detective Marcus sat heavily in a kitchen chair. "You keep the barn locked at all times?"

"Yes. Well, at least the big door in the front. I know there are some smaller doors on the other sides, and I'm not even sure I have keys for those. Nobody's used the barn for quite a while." *Meg, stop babbling.*

"What do you keep in the barn?"

Meg suppressed a stab of annoyance. "*I* don't keep anything in the barn. If you recall, I've been here only a couple of months, and it's been too cold to do much poking around, so I really don't know what's there. Anything in there predates my arrival."

"Have you been inside the barn?"

"Yes, a few times. Most recently this past weekend, on Saturday with Seth Chapin, and my orchard manager, Briona Stewart, yesterday."

"What were you doing in there?"

"We were looking at what improvements I need to make in order to store my apple crop in the fall."

"Hmm." The detective made a note in a small notebook, then pulled out a handkerchief and blew his nose. "The university's been overseeing the orchard for quite a while now?"

"About twenty years, I understand. I've agreed to let them continue their research here."

Marcus flipped through the notebook and peered at

his notes. "Christopher Ramsdell heads up that project at the university, right?"

"Yes."

"Do you know if he uses pesticides here?"

"You'll have to ask Professor Ramsdell about that."

"I intend to." The detective blew his nose again.

Meg turned over several questions in her mind, then decided it was time to stop tiptoeing around. "Detective Marcus, was Jason poisoned?"

"We haven't ruled it out."

Finally the man had given her a piece of information. "Do you know which poison?"

Detective Marcus shook his head. "Lab work takes time. We'll know in a couple of days."

"Do you think the pesticide that was in my barn is what killed Jason?"

"Could be."

Frustrated, Meg pressed on. "Can you tell me if he died here? Or somewhere else?"

"Vomit we found suggests he died here. It was definitely his."

This was not the news Meg had hoped to hear. The detective was looking around the kitchen. "You have a cat?" His eyes lit on Lolly, still sitting on the counter.

"I just found her. She's a stray, I think. Are you allergic?"

The detective nodded briefly, then stood up abruptly. "I think I have all I need for now."

Meg let him out the back door, and Marcus strode quickly back to his squad car. The other officer had been leaning against the car with arms crossed, waiting, but now he scrambled to climb in as the detective slammed his door. After the car pulled out of the driveway, Meg locked the door, then turned and leaned on it.

"Thank you for driving him away, Lolly. But what was that all about?" Lolly jumped off the counter and sauntered off toward the dining room. Meg wondered just

how many other toxic substances were lurking in the
dark corners of the house, especially the basement, which
she had also avoided. This might be a good time to find
out. Still, she really wasn't sure what might be poisonous
and what was safe; what might have been poisonous
once but had now lost its potency, and what might have
been harmless years ago but had by this time festered
and mutated into something deadly. *Seth would know*,
she thought.

As if conjured up by her thoughts, Seth's van turned
into the driveway. Meg went out and waited on the stoop
until he had climbed out of the vehicle. "Marcus was just
here, poking around the barn."

Seth shrugged. "I'm not surprised. That was pretty
fast."

"That man sets my teeth on edge. He always seems to
be looking for something to pin on me. Now he's made
me feel stupid for not knowing what's in my barn."

"Personal feelings aside, he's a decent officer. And his
reputation is on the line here. His boss—the DA—needs
some high-profile wins, or failing that, a good roster of
closed cases. It doesn't look good to have a lot of 'suspicious deaths' on the books. So he's going to put his best
efforts into it."

"I guess that's good news. As long as he doesn't think
I did it."

"Let's hope not."

"I guess every time Marcus shows up, I get upset, but
there's not a lot I can do about that. You want to come
in?"

"Only if you promise not to bite my head off."

Meg summoned up a smile. "I think I can manage
that."

Back inside, Meg discovered that Lolly had returned
to the kitchen. Seth squatted and rubbed her head. "You
decided to keep her?"

"Apparently. Or she decided to keep me. And there's

one piece of good news: Detective Marcus is allergic to cats. Maybe Lolly will keep him out of here."

"Lolly?"

"Bree suggested it. Well, we kind of named her Lavinia, Emily Dickinson's cat-loving sister, but she didn't like Vinnie, so she's Lolly."

Seth laughed. "That makes sense. Bree was here?"

"Yes, thank goodness. You want some coffee?"

"Sure. Why thank goodness?" Seth hung his coat over the back of a chair and sat down. Lolly jumped into his lap and settled herself.

"I guess I was worried that she wouldn't come back, what with Jason's death." As she put the kettle on to boil, Meg realized that Detective Marcus hadn't mentioned Bree at all. Had he already discounted her as a suspect? Or did he still not know about her relationship with Jason? Meg decided to change the subject. "Oh, did Bree tell you we'd need two holding chambers, not just one? Apparently different apples have different needs."

"I'll sit down with her again and get the details, when we get a little closer to building it in a couple of months. For what it's worth, from what little I've seen of her, I think that she's a good kid."

"I hope so. Tell me, what's the story about the Jamaican community around here?"

"You mean the pickers?"

"I guess. Is that what they are, mainly?"

"There's a long tradition around here, and in New York and Vermont, too. It's not exactly an itinerant group—most of these people have been coming back here for years. They're skilled, and they're proud of it. Some of them go home for the winter, others go for other crops, like sugar cane in Florida. The money goes a lot further in Jamaica—most of them own land, have families down there."

"And it's all legal?"

"Sure. The State Department and INS offer a handful

of options: green card, if they want to stay permanently; seasonal employment card; temporary work card. The government is really very supportive of them—they find them housing, even provide rides. There are some who think the Jamaicans are taking work away from local people, but mostly the locals don't want that kind of work. The Jamaicans work hard and don't get into trouble, so it's pretty much win-win."

Another whole area of her supposed business that she knew nothing about. "Seth . . . am I going to be able to do this? The whole orchard thing, I mean?"

Seth searched her face. "Are you having second thoughts?"

"I don't know. It's not that I expect it to be easy. I'm not afraid of hard work. But there's so much I don't know, and I don't have the luxury of time to learn it, so I have to rely on other people. And I've never been good at making snap decisions. I'm much more the research-it-to-death school. This is all way outside my comfort zone."

Seth nodded. "I can see that. To be honest, I do think it *could* work, but there are no guarantees. There never are when it comes to agriculture. But I hope you stay—I think you're an asset to the community."

And personally? "Just to the community?" she asked, trying to keep her tone light.

Seth didn't answer immediately, studying her face. "Meg, are you asking how *I* feel?"

Yes. No. Why had she even started this? She shook her head. "No, never mind. This isn't the time to get into this."

"Meg," he said gently, "there's never a perfect time."

He waited, and Meg looked down at her hands on the table, suddenly panicked at the thought of a relationship with her next-door neighbor slash business partner slash go-to guy for just about everything. She finally managed to meet his gaze. "Hold that thought, will you?"

He smiled. "No problem."

She smiled back. "Well, I don't intend to bail out on the orchard just yet. I've got to give it a year or two before I make any decisions, right? Oh, by the way, I found an old map of Granford in a batch of stuff Gail Selden gave me to catalog for the historical society. It shows this place, and yours, and there's even a sketch of the orchard. Isn't that amazing?"

"You'll have to show me sometime," he said. He stopped, clearly thinking. "You know, there's somebody you should talk to, if you're interesting in the history of this farm. Let me see if I can set something up. In the meantime, I'm going to go take some more measurements in the barn, and then I've got to head out for a job. Are we good?"

"Sure. You go ahead and measure."

Meg watched Seth stride across the muddy driveway toward the barn, whistling as he went. Apparently Jason's death wasn't getting him down. But Meg found she was restless. She didn't want to think about whatever Marcus was or was not telling her. She definitely did not want to think about dead Jason up the hill. She didn't want to think at all: she wanted something mindless to do, to distract herself. And then her gaze landed on the kitchen floor.

What had Rachel said? That there was likely to be ancient and tenacious glue lurking under the ugly vinyl? There was one way to find out, and before she had time to talk herself out of it, Meg armed herself with a putty knife and attacked a corner of the kitchen where the floor was already buckling. The first layer—twentieth-century vinyl—came up relatively easily, revealing older linoleum tiles. Meg pried up the corner of one and found . . . another layer of linoleum, this time in sheet form with a faded yellow pattern imitating tile. But the glue or mastic or whatever was brittle, and the layers parted easily. She dug in again and finally arrived at the bottom layer, then sat back on her haunches. Wooden flooring, and it looked nice. From her vantage point, Meg surveyed the kitchen. Wood would suit this room. And if this corner was any indication, getting rid of the ugly layers lying over the original floor would not be hard. Definitely something she could do. It was a plan.

Three hours later, as the daylight faded outside the windows, Meg finished scraping the last of three layers of crap off her kitchen floor and stood back to inspect the results. At the moment it was a patchy mess reeking of ancient food spills. The floor coverings had absorbed generations of cooking grease, and her best guess was that every half century or so someone had decided that something should be done about it and had slapped another layer on top, using rather nasty mastic. The mastic had outlived the linoleum, and it had taken a lot of determined scraping to get rid of it. Meg was convinced that it would live on under her fingernails for years to come.

But the end product appeared to be worth it. As she had hoped, the floor was wide board pine, as old as the house. The individual boards were probably two inches thick and still solid. A few more days of scrubbing and sanding, and she could think about refinishing. It was funny that she had removed so many layers of "improvements" merely to return to the way things had been in the beginning. But she could see it as it had been—and as it could be.

Lolly wandered in, picking her way reluctantly across the now-unfamiliar floor.

"That's right, lady, it's food time, isn't it? I'll feed you, and then I'll take a shower and feed me. That sound good?"

Lolly sat by her food dish, waiting.

Meg opened a can of cat food and dumped it into the dish. "Yo, you impatient creature—here's your dinner." She wished it was as easy to produce her own. Between the unpredictability of her appliances, the exercise all this renovation was providing, and her lack of enthusiasm for cooking for one, she was actually losing weight—chalk up one small benefit to this monumental rehab project. And it would get worse before it got better. But it felt good to make progress, to see the changes happening. Or, in this case, to feel them under her feet.

15

 By the next morning's cold light Meg felt far less pleased with herself. While the kitchen floor's boards lay revealed, they were still marred by generations of gunk that had to be removed somehow. Meg was leaning against a counter eating an English muffin when her phone rang.

"Meg? It's Rachel. You busy for lunch today?"

"I've got a class this morning, and I wanted to go to a meeting in Amherst this evening, but the middle's clear. What did you have in mind?"

Rachel giggled. "I've got a surprise for you. But you have to come here to get it. Can you meet me at the house at noon?"

"Sure. I hope I can get the black gunk out from under my fingernails."

"Gunk?"

"I decided to tackle my kitchen floor."

"Meg, you're nuts. See you later."

Meg smiled as she hung up the phone. Rachel sounded

gleeful, and she wondered what kind of surprise she might have cooked up. With the Chapin family, she never knew what to expect. She could only hope that it didn't take a truck to transport. Although, come to think of it, maybe she should trade her trusty two-door for a pickup truck. No doubt Seth could get her a deal on one. But she should think it through before she so much as mentioned the idea, or he'd show up with a truck the next day, pleased as punch.

After her class Meg arrived at Rachel's B&B promptly at noon, to find her friend waiting for her on the swing on her ornate porch, despite the chill in the air. Rachel stood up at the sight of her. "Good, you're on time. Let's go."

"What? Are we going out for lunch?"

"Sort of. You'll see. I'll drive."

Meg settled herself in the passenger seat of Rachel's car after dislodging a stack of kids' toys and CD cases. "Where are we going?"

"It's a surprise. Not far."

Rachel looked so pleased with herself that Meg stopped prying and settled back to watch the scenery. The deciduous trees were just beginning to show hints of spring color, more red than green, almost like fall in reverse. They passed farms, fields, convenience stores before Rachel finally turned into a long and winding drive. At the top of a hill they pulled up in front of a handsome one-story building that sprawled across the crest of the hill. Meg noticed a discreet sign next to the door under an imposing portico and looked at Rachel, who just smiled and climbed out of the car. Meg followed her into the building, where Rachel stopped in front of an oak reception desk.

"Can you tell Ruth Ferry I'm here?" Rachel asked the young woman behind the desk.

"Sure, Rachel. Bet she's been dressed for an hour now." The woman picked up a phone and punched a couple of buttons, then said, "Miss Ferry? Your friend is here."

Meg studied her surroundings. It was a retirement home of some sort, and a fairly luxurious one at that. Why had Rachel brought her here? And who was Ruth Ferry? She looked at Rachel to find her smiling at her.

"All will be revealed. Have patience."

Whether or not the mysterious Ruth had been dressed and ready, it was still a few minutes before she appeared. She was a tall, slender woman with gleaming white hair, freshly permed. She wore a well-fitted shirtwaist dress in a discreet pattern and had a cardigan sweater draped across her shoulders. She walked carefully with a single cane, and as she approached, Meg's estimate of her age inched upward. Eighty, at least. But still upright, and a commanding presence.

"Rachel, my dear, it's so kind of you to suggest an excursion. The food here is palatable but bland, and I do love to go to lunch. And this is Meg?"

Meg stepped forward. "Yes. I'm Meg Corey."

Ruth cocked her head at Meg, her eyes bright. "You have the look of the Warrens. But let's not get into that until we get to the restaurant. Rachel?"

"Yes, ma'am." Rachel threw a grin at Meg as she looped her arm through Ruth's and escorted her out to the car. "You sure you'll be warm enough with just the sweater?"

"My dear, let me enjoy the spring air without being bundled up in a cocoon. I've lasted eighty-seven years, and a little fresh air won't do me in."

Rachel settled her gently in the passenger seat, and Meg climbed in behind, still mystified.

Meg was surprised when Rachel pulled up in front of a small restaurant on the main street in downtown Amherst. "Would you help Ruth out of the car, Meg? And then I'll park."

Meg got out of the car, but Ruth already had the door open and had planted her feet firmly on the sidewalk. "If you'll just give me your hand, Meg."

Meg extended a hand and was surprised by the strength of Ruth's grip as she pulled herself upright. Rachel handed her the cane and shut the passenger door, then sped down the street to a newly vacated parking space, leaving Meg standing on the curb with a hand on Ruth's elbow. "We may as well go in. Have you eaten here before, Meg?"

They turned toward the building and began a careful progress toward the door. "No, I haven't. I haven't lived around here very long yet, and there are a lot of places I haven't discovered."

"The food is excellent—traditional French. I eat here as often as I can."

Ruth's statement was borne out when the maitre d' approached and welcomed her warmly. "Ah, madame, a pleasure, as always. Will you be comfortable in the corner table?"

"You know I will, Albert, since I always ask for it. I've brought a new friend along. This is Meg Corey. You do eat French food, don't you? I hope you're not one of those silly salad girls."

Meg laughed. "No, I love French food. I'm happy to meet you, Albert. And this place smells wonderful."

They had just settled into their chairs when Rachel rushed in and threw herself into the third chair. "There! Have you ordered?"

"I'll have the special, whatever that is—it's always excellent. Meg?"

"That sounds fine."

"Make it three." Rachel beamed at the young waiter, who scurried away, stopping to speak with Albert before heading to the kitchen. Albert approached the table. "Might I suggest the *potage aux moules* as a starter? And perhaps a glass of wine?"

"Of course," Ruth said. "Meg, you'll join me." It was an order, not a question, and Meg nodded assent.

"Nothing for me, thanks," Rachel said. "I'm driving."

Albert bowed slightly and vanished to the back of the small restaurant, leaving the three women alone.

Ruth sat back in her chair and looked at Rachel. "I gather you've said nothing to Meg?"

Rachel grinned. "Nope. Seth and I wanted to surprise her. I hope you don't mind, but that way you can tell your own stories."

Ruth turned to Meg. "Rachel thought we should meet because I used to know the Warrens, when I was much younger," she said. "I grew up on one of the adjacent farms."

"The Chapin place?"

Ruth sat up straighter. "The Chapins bought the land from the Ferrys, some years ago."

"I see. So you knew Lula and Nettie Warren?"

"I did. They were a bit older than I, but we attended school together, and they allowed me to tag along after them on occasion. Rachel tells me your mother inherited the place?"

"Yes. I gather Lula and Nettie remembered that my mother was descended from—let me see if I've got this right—Lula and Nettie's grandfather's brother? Apparently there was no one else left. My mother and I own it jointly now."

Ruth nodded. "It should remain in the family. It pains me to think of that lovely land chopped up into tiny lots with ticky-tacky houses. Although the meadow wouldn't permit such construction—too boggy. Yet Rachel tells me part of the Chapin land will be taken for commercial development?"

"If all goes according to plan. Does that bother you?"

Ruth sighed. "I have no say in the matter, and I recognize that life does move on. When I lived in Granford, we had little need of stores. We raised much of our own food, and we bartered for some things, or exchanged labor. There were a few crops that provided cash for those things we couldn't make ourselves. You're planning to manage the orchard?"

"I hope to. I thought I'd give it a try and see if I could make a profit. You remember the orchard?"

"Of course I do. Lovely thing, this time of year. Of course, when I was young everyone had at least a few fruit trees, if not an orchard. Warren's Grove . . ." Her eyes went vague.

She couldn't possibly remember that far back, Meg thought. "It hasn't been called that for years, has it?"

"What? Oh, not officially, but I remember my grand-parents talking about it. 'Warren's Grove's bearing well this year,' or, 'Warren's Grove's got blight problems.' Like it had a life of its own, apart from the people who tended it. Some great old varieties there, too, not like what you find in the markets these days. *Pfaugh!*"

Meg suppressed a smile—Ruth sounded just like Christopher, who was at least a full generation younger. "I haven't had a chance to explore all of it," she said.

"Do you know, the Warrens used to say that Johnny Appleseed himself planted some of those trees."

"Really? Was he from around here?"

"No, he was born well east of here. Didn't stay in Mas-sachusetts long. But he spread seeds and saplings very widely. Who's to say it's not true?"

Meg had a lot of questions she wanted to ask, but she did not want to be rude. Rachel sensed her reluctance, because she broke in, "Ruth, Meg's probably too polite to ask, but I'm sure she'd like to know about your life on the farm. Especially, I bet, how you managed the farm as a single woman."

Meg smiled her thanks at Rachel, while waiting ea-gerly for Ruth's answer. "You married, young lady?" Ruth began.

"No." Meg stopped, unsure if she should add some-thing innocuous like "not yet." But she didn't want to imply that she disliked being unmarried, especially not in front of someone who had never been married herself.

"You will be. You're the type. I never married and never missed it. Men are more work than they're worth, as far as I can see, but I know there are others who feel differently. I worked my farm all my life, with some hired help. Sometimes it was a hard life, and sometimes lonely. I laid to rest my parents, my brothers and sisters, even some of their children, and I just kept going."

"But in the end, you sold the farm?" Meg prodded gently.

"Had to. I couldn't manage the work anymore, on my own, and there was no one left to hire. All my nieces and nephews went off to college, to the cities. Didn't want to have anything to do with farming. In the end, I sold the land for a fair price to the Chapins, and I'd inherited enough money from the rest of the family—outlived most of them, you see—so I could afford to move into that fancy place on the hill. It's just as well. And there are a few younger folk, like Rachel here, and her brother Seth, who stop by and keep me company. Seth's a good boy— Chapins were always hardworking. Except that no-good younger brother of yours. Sorry, Rachel, but I have to say what I think."

"No offense taken, Ruth. I'm well aware of Stephen's shortcomings."

"No substitute for hard work." Ruth turned her shrewd eyes to Meg again. "How do you plan to manage? You're a city girl, aren't you?"

"I am. But I'm working with someone from the university who's helped a lot, and I've hired an orchard manager—also a woman, by the way."

"Good for you! Hope she's a smart one. You can hire muscle, but it's a lot harder to find brains. I wish you well, Meg Corey. Maybe I can talk Rachel here into bringing me over to see the place again, when the trees bloom."

"I'd like that, Ruth."

They'd talked their way through the main course, and Albert arrived bearing dessert and coffee. "Something for your sweet tooth, Miss Ruth."

"Albert, you spoil me. But I like it, so don't stop. Meg, try the tarte Tatin—it's extraordinary."

Meg complied—and agreed. The caramelized apples were soft and sweet, the crust flaky—and neatly concealed under the mound of apples. Meg wondered if she could duplicate the dessert, since she had no knack for making pie crust.

It was nearly three o'clock when they emerged from the restaurant. Ruth had insisted on paying for lunch, and Rachel had signaled Meg to go along. As Rachel went to retrieve the car, Meg stood holding Ruth's arm—for all her outward enthusiasm, the older woman seemed tired by the outing.

Ruth's voice cut into her thoughts. "Don't worry, my dear. I know how to pace myself. At my age it is a treat to meet new people, and our families share a long history. I daresay we're cousins of some sort, if you follow that kind of thing. But I asked Rachel to bring you because I wanted to talk to you."

"Me? Why?"

"I am not unaware of local events, and I know you've had a rather hard time since you moved to Granford."

No use pretending she didn't know what Ruth was saying. "You mean, the deaths?"

"I do, not that you are accountable in any way for those unfortunate events. But someone of weaker fiber would have turned and run. You haven't. There's Warren blood in you yet, and they were good people. You'll do fine with your orchard."

Meg felt an unexpected prick of tears. "Thank you, Ruth. I appreciate your saying that. And you're right, it hasn't been easy, but I think it's worth fighting for, and

I'm going to try. And in a few weeks, Rachel can bring you over to the house and I can show you what I've done."

Ruth laid a hand on her arm. "I shall look forward to that."

Rachel pulled up to the curb, and Meg helped Ruth into the front seat before settling herself in the back. She wasn't sure, but she suspected that Ruth dozed a bit on the silent ride back to the retirement home. Ruth refused Rachel's offer to escort her back to her room, and stood on the sidewalk outside to wave them away.

Back on the road, Meg turned to Rachel. "Thank you for introducing me to Ruth. What an amazing woman!"

"Isn't she? That's why Seth thought you two should get together. For a while, when we were kids, we thought of her as that crazy lady in the old house. But I got to know her—better than the boys did—and I really came to admire her. She lived her own life, never judged, never complained. She used to talk to me about the 'old days,' but I was a kid so I didn't pay much attention. Now I love to hear about it. When Noah and I got married, she sent a lovely old silver spoon, said it had been the dowry of one of those ancestors we shared. Remind me to show it to you sometime."

"I don't know how she did it. But I guess if she could manage as a single woman all those years ago, I certainly should be able to now, with so many more resources to call on."

Rachel sneaked a glance at her. "She seems to think so. And she's pretty smart about people. She never liked Stephen much, but she and Seth get along like a house afire."

"Now you're even talking like her. But I'm glad she approves of me, and I'd be happy to have you two over for tea or something. Assuming, of course, I finish my floor this century."

"You will, don't worry. And better now than later,

when the orchard stuff picks up. You give me a call when the orchard blooms, and I'll bring Ruth over, okay?"

"Sounds good to me. And thank you again for bringing us together." *With just a little nudge from Seth.*

"My privilege."

16

After she had retrieved her car from Rachel's house, Meg checked her watch: no point in going home and coming back again for the Green-Grow meeting, so she might as well stay in Amherst and find something useful to do. Lolly couldn't complain; Meg had left her plenty of food and water. She made another mental note to ask Gail if she could tell her more about the former Ferry farm, and what, if any, family connections the Warrens had shared with the Ferrys. Funny how everyone around here seemed to be related to everyone else, even if the link sometimes went back a century or two.

Meg stopped at the university library and spent a few hours tracking down some of the recommended reading for her course, then headed over to the GreenGrow meeting. She followed a trickle of people into a single-story cinder-block building behind the main street and found a seat among the rows of folding chairs. The group appeared to be a mix of academics and ordinary citizens, although most of the latter wore clothes made of natural fibers. She was early, so she pulled her class notebook out of her bag and started to review the notes she had taken at the class earlier in the day.

At ten minutes past the designated start time, Michael stood up behind the podium at the front of the room and tapped the microphone to assure that it was live. He scanned the audience, clearly disappointed: by Meg's count there were no more than twenty-five people in the room, including the cluster of people standing behind Michael. Had he hoped for more? Meg recognized a couple of faces, including the young woman—Daphne something—who had accompanied Michael to Jason's wake at the university.

Michael had to bend down to speak into the microphone, and he took a couple of seconds to adjust its height before he began. "Welcome, everyone, to this meeting of GreenGrow. Before we begin, we'd like to make a public statement about the unfortunate death of our colleague Jason Miller and to let you know of our plans going forward. Jason was a founder of this organization, and his efforts . . ." Meg tuned out Michael's actual words while studying his performance. He was good: earnest and sincere. He ended his quasi eulogy quickly yet gracefully, asking for a moment of silence for Jason. The room fell silent, and Meg looked at her hands. Although she hadn't known Jason personally, she was coming to know him through his associates—and she felt bad that she didn't like what she had learned about him. So far he had emerged as overbearing and fanatical. He had been emotionally invested in GreenGrow, but at the expense of his academic career, and it sounded as though he had been in the process of alienating many of his colleagues even here. He had had a vision, no doubt, but apparently hadn't been interested in tolerating anyone else's views.

Michael began speaking again, and Meg brought her focus back to him. "We at GreenGrow want to continue

Jason's work in eliminating toxic chemicals in our food, and to that end we have been working on developing a number of new programs to spread our ideas to the public." He went on to detail the updated newsletter they planned to distribute, the expansion of their website, the collaboration in the summer with the Pioneer Valley association that sponsored various farmers markets throughout the region. All good ideas, Meg thought, and she sat up straighter and paid closer attention. Occasionally she shifted her glance to the other members of the Green-Grow group. They appeared generally enthusiastic, though Daphne still looked sullen, as she had at the wake.

After another ten or fifteen minutes, Michael wrapped up his presentation. "We'd be delighted if you would all stay a bit longer and join us in some refreshments." He smiled. "We like to say they're our best advertising. All made from locally grown, pesticide-free ingredients. And please ask us questions about anything you like." He ducked his head shyly, still smiling, and a few people clapped in a haphazard way before standing up and stretching. The majority moved toward the front of the room, where Meg saw a table that until now had been concealed by the GreenGrow members. The surge of people suggested that either they were very hungry or the products, natural or otherwise, were very good. Meg decided to investigate more closely.

She was filling a small plate with an interesting if eclectic sampling of cookies, cakes, and cheeses when Michael came up beside her. "I'm glad you could come, Meg. What did you think?"

"I thought you handled that very well. And I'm impressed with what you've put together. I'll take a look at the website. Has it gone live yet?"

"In a couple of days. Jason didn't think that kind of thing was important, so it's something I've been working on in my spare time."

"It seems to me a website is an excellent way to draw attention to your efforts, and to reach a wider audience." She bit into a cracker she had slathered with what she hoped was goat cheese. "Wow, this is good. It's local?"

Michael nodded. "Yes. The cheese comes from a farm about five miles from here. We're not ready to compete with the artisanal cheese makers in Vermont, but we're getting there."

"What else do you promote here?"

"Honey, of course. Lots of fruits and vegetables, later in the season. Various milk products from cattle that haven't been dosed with antibiotics or chemical-laced feeds—all grass-fed. Eggs from free-range chickens. I can give you some more literature, if you're really interested."

"I'd like to know more about *all* of this," Meg answered, surprised to find that she really meant it.

Michael looked away from her and raised a hand to someone across the room. "Excuse me, but I need to talk to him—he's from the local paper. Why don't you talk to some of our other members?"

"I will." Meg refilled her plate, then wandered over to Daphne, who hovered near the edge of a group of people without really being part of it. "Daphne, right? I met you at the university."

Reluctantly Daphne peeled herself away from the group. "Yeah. And you're the woman who owns the place where Jason was found."

"Yes. Meg Corey. Did you know him well?"

Daphne drew herself up. "I was his girlfriend."

"I'm sorry for your loss." The words sounded lame even to Meg, but she had nothing better to say. Better to fall back on platitudes, since Daphne looked as though she would take offense at almost anything that Meg offered. "He sounds like he was a very committed man."

"He was. He really cared about natural foods and keeping our crops pure. Not like some of these people here." Daphne uttered the last sentence in a low voice, and Meg wondered if she was supposed to hear. So there was dissent in the ranks?

Daphne was on a roll. "The chemical establishment wants to make money off of the farmers, get them hooked on spraying or whatever, and keep them hooked. And when the pests become resistant to one form of chemical, guess what? There's the chemical company with something newer and better. And probably more expensive. Do you have any idea how much chemical treatments add to the cost of the food you eat? Do you?"

"No, I don't. I never gave it much thought until I ended up with my orchard," Meg admitted.

Michael, having finished his conversation with the local reporter, came up beside Daphne and laid a hand on her arm. "Daphne, you don't have to be too hard on her. I said I'd give her our materials, and she's willing to look at them."

Daphne gave him a sidelong glance laden with venom. "Yeah, right. She's working with Ramsdell at the university, isn't she?"

"He's been managing the orchard for years," Meg said. "I haven't heard any complaints. Do you have a problem with him?"

Michael answered, cutting off Daphne before she could protest. "Actually he's one of the more responsible scientists in this area. At least he doesn't dismiss Green-Grow out of hand. And he tried to help Jason."

"Help?" Daphne sputtered. "He told Jason his thesis research was sloppy and he'd have to redo all his analyses. And then he turns around and tells him that he's out of time. You call that help?"

"Daphne, I don't think he put it quite that strongly. He said he thought some of the analyses were a little superficial and Jason should look them over more critically. And he was only following university guidelines, as far as timing. Jason just wasn't very focused on the academic side of things."

Poor Michael looked uncomfortable airing Jason's dirty academic laundry in front of Meg, but he couldn't stem Daphne's tide of hostility. "And why should he have been, with an advisor like Ramsdell? Holds himself up as Mr. High and Mighty, let's all find a middle path and use chemicals responsibly, blah, blah, blah. All the time he's been sucking up to the chemical industry."

"Daphne!" Michael's voice had taken on an edge. "I think you're making far too much of that."

Daphne turned to face Michael. "What? I saw him with that guy Kurtz, the big man at DeBroCo. And they looked pretty friendly to me."

"That doesn't necessarily mean anything. Chemical companies come around all the time, looking for new opportunities. DeBroCo's been funding scholarships and research at the university for years. Ramsdell is probably on his regular call list."

"Michael, you are so naïve! Just wait—there's going to be a big announcement any day now, and then you'll see how he's pulled the wool over your eyes. You and a lot of other people!"

"Daphne, that's enough! This is not the time or the place to discuss this." He held Daphne's gaze for a moment, and finally she turned away from him to address Meg. "You—ask Ramsdell about the money DeBroCo is throwing at the university. He's going to come out of this smelling like a rose, and GreenGrow's going to get screwed. Again." She turned on her heel and stalked away.

Michael shook his head. "Sorry about that. She's upset about Jason's death. And I think his attitude was kind of contagious, and now she's seeing conspiracies everywhere."

Meg felt sorry for Michael, having to deal with such histrionics. "I can understand that. But what was she talking about?"

Michael shrugged. "We don't have all the details, but the rumors are that the university has been negotiating something big with DeBroCo Pharmaceuticals, and it's likely to be announced any time now."

"And Christopher has something to do with this?"

"Looks like it. I don't know much, only what I hear. Why don't you ask him?"

And then report back to you? Not likely. "I'll be interested to hear what he has to say," Meg replied non-committally. But she did wonder if there was any truth to the rumors, or if GreenGrow was just seeing evil pesticide promoters under every rock. What was the saying? Even paranoid people were right sometimes? Not that there was any reason for Christopher to have told her about university plans, public or private, confirmed or anticipated. But she knew that he was worried about his own future—he had told her as much when it had looked as though her orchard was destined to be paved over for parking for a planned minimall in her backyard. Even though that threat had been quashed, she knew that funding was always an issue within a university, and that popularity of disciplines and departments waxed and waned. But would Christopher sell out to corporate interests? It seemed out of character for him.

Michael seemed eager to talk to the rest of the dwindling crowd. Meg waved him off. "Michael, thanks for inviting me to the meeting, and for the information. You've given me a lot to think about. You make a good case for the organic viewpoint."

"Thanks." He hesitated. "Jason was a good guy and he really cared, but he was pretty pushy, and I think it put some people off. I try to present a more balanced and practical approach. But he did a lot for GreenGrow." The last statement sounded perfunctory to Meg's ears.

"I'm sure he did. And I hope that the police figure out what happened to him."

"So do I, Meg. Thanks for coming."

Meg watched him work the rest of the small crowd. He did seem at ease, and he was clearly knowledgeable. He might make a good leader, out from Jason's shadow.

As Meg drove home in the dark, she wondered, *Why is it that everything I look into turns out to make everything else more complicated?* Did she now have to add Christopher to the list of those who might have wanted Jason dead?

17

Wednesday morning after breakfast, Meg climbed up the hill to the orchard, hoping to find Christopher there. She was in luck: he *was* there, and even better, he wasn't accompanied by his students. He waved when he saw her, and she approached him with an uncomfortable mix of anxiety and hope. Surely the rumors she'd heard at the GreenGrow meeting were only that.

"Good morning, my dear!" Christopher said warmly. "It looks as though the buds are forming well. It shouldn't be long now until we start to see some color."

"Green tip, right?" Meg said. "Listen, can I talk to you about something?"

"Of course. Is this about Bree?"

"No, we're fine. This is about you, and your department."

"Oh dear, that sounds serious. Perhaps we should go inside?"

"No, I'd rather walk, if that's all right with you."

"If you prefer." As Meg set off down the cleared space between two rows of apple trees, Christopher fell into step alongside her. "Is something troubling you?"

Meg fumbled to begin, then decided to work her way around to her real concern. "Christopher, you told me you use some pesticides in managing this orchard?"

"Yes, I do, judiciously."

"How do you get them? Can any ordinary citizen go online and buy whatever they want?"

Christopher paused to seize a low-hanging branch, examining the buds on it. "Of course a person such as yourself may go to any garden center and buy and store small amounts of any number of pesticides and herbicides, for home use. For agricultural use, on a larger scale, there is a paper trail. Moreover, handlers—anyone who mixes, loads, or applies pesticides—are given formal safety training. Pesticides must be clearly labeled and identified as toxic. When they are applied in the field, clear warnings must be posted."

"So the short answer is, there are lots of regulations in place for large-scale use?"

"I think it would be accurate to say that. Not that they are always followed precisely, but I have always maintained strict standards, personally and to protect my students." Christopher stopped walking, forcing Meg to stop as well. "Meg, I'm happy to answer your questions, but I have a feeling you're leading up to something. Why are you asking? Is this about Jason's death?"

Meg met his gaze. "Yes, it is. Look, I told you about the pesticide that was found in the barn, right?"

"You did. Methidathion. I checked my records, and we haven't used it on this site for several years. Particularly after we started having troubles with bees dying off."

"Could the container in the barn have been left over from then?"

"Meg, I would say with some degree of assurance that any chemicals found in your barn did not belong to the university. Is that what you wanted to know?"

"In part. Do you still have any methidathion at the university?"

Christopher shook his head. "I can't say definitively. It has other applications than in orchards, and other faculty members may be using it. And the amount required to kill a single person would probably not be significant. Let me ask *you* a question: have the authorities determined that methidathion was the cause of death?"

"If they have, they haven't told me, but that's no surprise. All I know for sure is that the authorities believe Jason was poisoned, but I don't know if they've narrowed down which poison or how he took it. I'm just trying to understand how someone would go about getting hold of a poison." Meg decided to try another tack. "Can you think of any reason why Jason would have been here? I mean, I'd never met him, never had any contact with him. Why here, why now?"

"I'm afraid I can't answer that, my dear. The department's involvement with this orchard is well known and has been going on for years. Perhaps he hoped he could persuade you to adopt his philosophy rather than mine. I'm sorry if I have in any way dragged you into something unpleasant, but I confess I have no idea how that could have come about."

"I know. Listen, Christopher . . ." Meg wondered whether bringing up what she had heard from Michael and Daphne was worth it, but she might as well get it all out into the open now. "I went to a GreenGrow meeting in Amherst last night," she began.

"Ah. Has Michael taken the reins in hand?"

"Yes, and he seems to be doing well. But we got to talking afterwards, and he mentioned something that bothered me."

"What would that be?"

"Apparently some people believe that you are working with a major pesticide company. He and others saw you with one of their executives."

Meg hoped that Christopher would deny it. When he sighed and took his time answering, she felt a chill that had nothing to do with the March breeze sweeping over the hillside.

At last he spoke. "Meg, I don't wish to mislead you. Michael is no doubt referring to DeBroCo, which has sponsored various programs in the Life Sciences Department for years. If I recall, Bree has benefitted from their scholarship funding. Recently I have met with a representative of DeBroCo about something new, and no doubt some well-meaning member of GreenGrow saw us and misconstrued the situation. But I can't say more at this time."

Meg wavered. She had known Christopher only a short time, but she would have said they were friends, and his evasiveness troubled her. Did he have something to hide?

He was still talking. "Please don't take this amiss, Meg. I can understand how this might look to you, and if it were only I who was involved, I would share the details in a moment. But there are others who have an interest, and I am not at liberty to speak for them. Let me assure you that this matter will be resolved shortly, and then I will be able to give you a full account."

She remained unconvinced, but what could she do? She had no reason to distrust Christopher, save for the gossip of a few people from GreenGrow, and she wasn't sure whether she had any grounds to believe them.

She summoned a smile. "Christopher, I'm sure you have good reasons for not telling me, and I look forward to a full account whenever you can speak freely."

"Thank you, my dear. I will not abuse your trust." He glanced at his watch. "Heavens, I've overstayed. I have office hours in half an hour. You'll excuse me if I run?"

"Of course."

He lingered a moment longer. "Please don't trouble yourself, Meg. This will all be cleared up soon. In the meantime, we should schedule some time to review your plans for the storage units. Bree mentioned them to me."

"Fine, Christopher. I'll be here." By then she was speaking to his retreating back, as he hurried toward his van.

She had no more answers now than she had had earlier. Christopher had disavowed any knowledge of the pesticide from the barn, and she couldn't prove or disprove anything. He had admitted that he was involved somehow with a pesticide purveyor, a fact that had set off alarm bells with the GreenGrow people. There might be a perfectly innocent explanation, but Christopher was not willing to share it with her. Things were getting murkier by the day.

18

Meg was in the middle of trying to put together something for lunch when Seth appeared in her driveway. She opened the kitchen door as he approached. "Hi, Seth. Come on in."

"Wow!" Seth had made it three feet inside the door and was now staring at the denuded floor. "When did you do this?"

"Um, Monday? I wanted something to take my mind off . . . everything, and this is what happened. You approve?"

"You've still got some work to do, but it looks great. You are planning to leave it bare?" he added anxiously.

"I think so. Seems a shame to cover it up again, now that I've put so much work into cleaning it off, and the wood looks nice. Anyway, to what do I owe the pleasure of your visit? Did you drop by to chat or was there another reason?"

"Actually, I stopped by to ask if you've done anything about a tractor."

"What?" That was the last thing she expected to hear.

"Bree said you were going to need something to haul your apples around."

"Oh, right. We didn't find one buried in all that junk in the barn, did we?"

"No. The sisters probably sold off whatever they could, since they weren't using it."

"And left the rest to rust in the fields, apparently." She had seen several rusted tangles of machinery scattered around the place.

"That they did." Seth was all but bouncing with repressed excitement. "But the good news is, my friend Eric's got a line on a great used tractor, and he can get you a good price for it."

Meg recalled that Eric Putnam was a long-time friend of Seth's; his day job was teaching at UMass, but he spent most of his free time prowling for antique salvage. Eric had sold Meg the antique clock that graced the space over her mantel. And Seth gladly took all of the antique plumbing fixtures Eric could find, for his growing plumbing and renovation business.

"You know I don't know squat about tractors. Or how to use one." Meg still wasn't sure what she would do with a tractor, of any age or condition.

"You're smart—you can learn. You interested?"

"What, I have to decide right now?"

"If you don't want it, Eric will find someone else. But the seller's in a hurry to get rid of it."

Seth looked so excited that Meg hated to disappoint him. "I guess. Where is this thing? Does it even run?"

Seth waved a dismissive hand. "Don't worry about that. I can get it running and figure out what attachments you'll need."

"Attachments? Wait a minute—I don't even know how it works, and now you're adding stuff to it?"

"Just a way to move your apples from one place to

another, and maybe something to mow between the trees. No big deal."

"Easy for you to say."

"Don't worry, it'll be fine. When I was a kid, I used to pick up some spare change after school during harvest season, picking apples. I have a good idea what you'll need. And I like machines. You want to go?"

"Okay, okay. Where are we going?"

"Williamsburg—it's a small town north of here. Let me give Eric a call, let him know we're coming."

Seth finished up his call in less than a minute. "He's good to go. He thinks it hasn't run for a while, but it's in pretty good shape."

"Lead on. I just love having my nose rubbed in all the things I don't know about farming."

"You're learning fast."

"I'd better."

Seth was driving his car today rather than the plumbing van, and Meg settled herself in and buckled her seat belt. "Listen, I don't want to get stampeded into a decision about a piece of major machinery without time to think about it."

"Hey, relax. We'll let you know if it looks like a good machine for you, and if you want it, your handshake is good enough to hold it."

"That's not the point. Everything I touch is expensive these days, and I want to be sure I'm spending my money wisely."

"What, you don't trust my opinion, or Eric's?"

"I do, but I still want to pretend to be in charge of this. You big strong men will let me get a word in now and then, right?"

"Of course we will."

They bantered easily during the drive, past Northampton and north, paralleling the Connecticut River until they arrived in Williamsburg. They drove past a cluster of shops and a restaurant, then climbed up a steep road to where a house and barn, in dire need of paint, clung to the hillside. Meg recognized Eric leaning against a battered pickup truck parked in front of the barn. He was talking to a fortyish woman in faded jeans and a more-faded sweatshirt.

Meg climbed out of the car, watched by a pair of curious goats behind a rickety fence.

"Hey, Seth, Meg. This is Florence Lucas."

The woman stepped forward and Meg shook her hand. Her grip was strong, her palm rough. "I'm taking my own name back—Florence Lusardi. Eric here says you need a tractor?"

"That's what people keep telling me. I just took over an orchard in Granford, and I'm kind of starting from scratch." Meg was conscious of Florence's cool stare, and she wondered if she looked as clueless as she felt.

"You're not from around here, are you?"

"No, I'm from Boston."

"Think farming is a cute hobby?"

Meg immediately felt defensive. "No, I don't. I realize it takes hard work, and I'm not just dabbling. I want to make this orchard economically viable, and to do that I need equipment. Eric said you had a tractor to sell?" Meg realized that the two men hadn't said anything, and wondered if Seth was trying to suppress a smile.

Florence finally softened and produced a smile. "Sorry, didn't mean to give you a hard time. But I hate these city types who come out here and buy a place, and then get fed up and leave again. Like my ex. He used to have a decent job in Springfield, and then a few years ago he ups and decides he wants to be a farmer. I told him he was crazy, but he didn't listen to me. He went out and bought all this equipment, and he used it for a few months, and then, surprise, he lost interest. So, yes, I've got this tractor to unload. Want to see it?"

"Sure. Does it run?"

"Don't know, really. I let my idiot husband worry about that. Come on." Florence led the way into the dim recesses of the barn; the goats followed along the fence, bleating plaintively. Eric and Seth trailed behind, talking to each other.

"You don't need a tractor?" To Meg's eyes, the barn was substantially newer than hers but possibly in worse condition. The wood planks had been slapped on carelessly and as they'd dried, gaps had opened between them, letting in both light and wind. Wisps of straw scurried across the cracked concrete floor.

"*I* never needed it. My ex—Alvin—he saw this thing on eBay and thought it looked cool, and next thing I knew, it showed up here. Not much use on a place like this—pretty much all hill. He never did figure out how to hook up the snowplow. Which was the only part we really needed."

They reached a bay that held a lump shrouded by a blue plastic tarp. Florence grabbed one edge of the tarp and hauled it off, revealing a large green tractor. "There it is."

Eric and Seth surged forward, their eyes alight. They began walking around it, pointing and poking. Meg turned back to Florence. "Is it yours to sell now?"

"Sure is. Alvin moved in with the receptionist at his dentist's office in Hadley—he said he was having a root canal. Ha! If he wants anything, he can take me to court. Me, I've had it. I'm going to move to Springfield, where my daughter lives. Just as soon as I unload all this crap." She waved vaguely around.

Before Meg had to reply, Eric and Seth joined them. "Flo, it looks good. Can we start her up?"

"Go for it. I can't tell you how much gas there is."

Eric and Seth, like Tweedledum and Tweedledee, went back to the dusty machine and started looking at more dials and gauges.

"You planning to run this orchard place all by yourself?" Florence's question startled Meg.

"That's the idea."

"How big's your place?"

"Fifteen acres of established trees, another ten of wetlands, and an old house and barn," Meg replied promptly.

Florence eyed her critically. "You've got your work cut out for you. I've got plenty of relatives around here trying to keep their heads above water financially. And farming can be lonely and frustrating. A lot of people have just given up the past few years. Not enough money in it, and one bad turn can wipe out your profits."

Meg sighed. "That's what people keep telling me. But I hate to give up before I've even started. Will you sell me the tractor?"

"You want it, it's yours. Who knows—maybe you'll make this whole thing work."

"I hope so." Meg heard the roar of an engine, and the tractor jerked to life. She and Florence stepped back to let the tractor sputter past, and watched as it moved into the unpaved driveway. "They look like they're having fun, don't they?" Meg asked.

"Sure do. Boys and their toys, huh?"

"My thought exactly."

It was hard to make herself heard over the noise of the machine, so Meg contented herself with watching Eric take it through its paces, all the while with a huge grin on his face. Seth egged him on from the sidelines. After a few minutes, Eric shut off the motor and stepped down.

"Seems good," he said. "What're you asking for it?"

"Alvin paid five grand," Florence said, "but I thought he got ripped off." She shot a glance at Meg. "I'll take two, and throw in the attachments."

"That's a great price, Meg," Eric said.

Meg looked at Seth, who nodded. She sighed. "Okay, guys, if you say so. Florence, looks like I'll take it. If you guys can figure out how to get it to Granford. And if you can teach me how to use the thing."

Seth grinned. "No problem. I know a guy with a flatbed. And I can show you how to work it. Bree may already know."

"We've got a deal," Florence said.

"Thanks, Florence," Meg said. "You guys ready to go?"

"Happy to be rid of it. Good luck, Meg—you're gonna need it."

"I'm going to stick around and check out some of Florence's other stuff," Eric said. "Seth, swing by the barn sometime this weekend—I've got another load for you. Bye, Meg. Enjoy the tractor."

Once back in Seth's car, Meg muttered, "Yeah, right, enjoy the tractor. What am I getting into?"

"Meg, you need a tractor," Seth said patiently, "and you're getting a really good deal on this one. Hey, it's a new skill—it'll look good on your resume."

Meg laughed. "Yeah, right. 'Municipal bond analyst, can operate heavy farm equipment.' Damn, I just hate feeling ignorant all the time."

"The older tractors were well made and simple to operate—that's how they've lasted this long. You can drive a car, so I'm sure you'll catch on fast. You know, you really sound down. Is anything wrong?"

"I talked to Christopher this morning, and it's still bothering me."

"Why?"

Meg proceeded to lay out the events of the Green-Grow meeting, the oblique comments from Michael and Daphne, and her talk with Christopher. "What I don't understand is, if it's all so innocent, why can't he just tell me?" Meg turned in her seat to face him. "I'm so dependent on him to keep this orchard thing going, at least for a while, and that makes me uncomfortable, you know? But I guess what is really gnawing at me is the possibility that Christopher could be selling out to the pesticide interests, and that Jason somehow got in the way."

"Meg, are you saying that you think Christopher is a killer?"

"No! I mean, I hope not. I like him. I trust him. But I've been wrong about people before."

"Look, he said he could tell you about this mysterious thing soon. Give it a few days and see what happens. And, remember, we still don't know if *anyone* killed Jason."

"I haven't found anybody who believes that Jason was the type to kill himself."

"Still, it's not ruled out, either. And there's nothing you can do about it right now, is there?"

"I guess not. Besides, I have to learn to drive a tractor. That should distract me, right?"

"Piece of cake."

Meg sat back, obscurely reassured. Maybe she was just feeling overwhelmed. She wanted to trust her instincts about Christopher. She was pleased that Seth had implied faith in her decisions—and in her ability to learn to drive a tractor. She could practice in the middle of a nice, flat, open field—how much trouble could she get into?

19

Meg's Thursday class at the university seemed to drag on and on. She knew the notes she was taking covered a lot of things that she would need eventually, but right now it was hard to put the information into any context. A book could give you facts, but the smelly, messy, unpredictable reality was something you had to deal with personally. If she had known she was going to end up running an orchard in rural Massachusetts, she might have planned her undergraduate courses a bit differently. But how could she have known?

When she emerged from the lecture hall, she spotted Daphne sitting on a bench in the hallway. When Daphne saw her, she jumped up quickly and approached Meg.

"Hi, Meg," she began with uncharacteristic enthusiasm. "Can I talk to you? Can we go somewhere and maybe get a coffee? Unless you've got somewhere you have to be?"

Meg didn't, but neither did she really want to spend any time with this girl, who up until now had been nothing but rude to her. Still, somehow Daphne's abrupt about-face intrigued her, as did the fact that apparently this chat was important enough for Daphne to have tracked her down. "Okay. Somewhere on campus?"

"Could we go into town? I know this coffee shop."

"That's fine. I have my car here—do you want a ride?"

"Sure. I don't have a car."

Meg led the way to the parking lot, still puzzling over what Daphne might have to say to her. Daphne made no effort at small talk, plodding along in her heavy shoes and shapeless coat. The poor girl definitely lacked social graces. Or maybe, Meg thought, trying to give her the benefit of the doubt, she was mourning Jason.

Daphne directed Meg to a restaurant near the middle of town—which turned out to be the same one where she had met Christopher for lunch. Amherst really was a small community. Meg ordered a large coffee, while Daphne asked for herbal tea, then quizzed the waitress about the ingredients of the pastries listed on the menu. After dithering for a few minutes, she finally settled on apple crisp, having been assured by the waitress that it was homemade and contained no artificial ingredients. Meg suspected the waitress would have said almost anything at that point just to escape Daphne's whining.

As they waited for their orders, Meg prompted Daphne. "You said you wanted to talk to me?"

Daphne took a moment to struggle out of her bulky coat, then blew her nose on a paper napkin. "Yeah. Look, I think we kind of got off on the wrong foot. I mean, you were the one who found Jason." She paused to sniff and swallow. "So I kind of held that against you. But Michael told me that I wasn't being fair and that you really are interested in what GreenGrow is all about, so I thought I'd try to patch things up. If that's okay."

Meg didn't believe a word of it, but Daphne had piqued her curiosity. At least she could use this opportunity to find out more about Jason. "I can understand that. How long were you close to Jason?"

Daphne sniffed again. "He was my boyfriend, for, like, two years. He brought me into GreenGrow. He was amazing!"

"Tell me about him." Meg sat back and prepared to listen to Daphne heap praise upon the dead. She was not disappointed. Daphne didn't even stop when her food appeared, apart from requesting a new napkin. According to his adoring girlfriend, Jason had been a paragon of all possible virtues: smart, funny, idealistic, honest, hard-working, a true friend—the list went on and on. When Daphne finally started to repeat herself, Meg decided it was time to step in.

"Daphne, he sounds like he was a wonderful man. I can see why you must be devastated by his death."

For a moment Daphne looked honestly bereft, and Meg felt a stab of pity. Sad, dumpy Daphne had apparently lost the only person who cared about her.

"Yeah," Daphne said, blotting her eyes on the clean napkin, then blowing her nose again. "I really loved him. It's not the same without him."

"You're a student here, too?"

"Sort of. I mean, I was, full-time, you know. But lately I've been taking only a couple of courses a semester. There was so much to be done at GreenGrow, and I really wanted to help Jason."

"Were you a science major?"

"No, literature. But I've done a lot of temping, summers and stuff, so I knew how to run office equipment, get mailings out, that kind of thing."

"You must be very useful to GreenGrow." Nothing like a willing slave to do all the unappealing work. "Are you a paid staff member?"

"Oh, no. Michael and Jason were the only people who got paid, and they didn't make much. Almost all the money they raised went back into business expenses, promotional materials—heck, even keeping the lights on at the office. The rest of us are volunteers. We're involved because we care about organic farming."

"That's really admirable." Meg could say at least that much with sincerity. "So are you still working there?"

"I guess. Michael's a good guy, but it's not going to be the same without Jason. He was really the spirit of the organization, if you know what I mean. I guess I'll stick around and see how things play out. It's too late in the term to add any classes now, so I might as well."

Time now to turn the tables. "Have you talked to the detective investigating this case? Since you were Jason's girlfriend?"

"That jerk? Yeah."

"What did he ask you?"

"When did I last see Jason. Who were his other friends. What was his mood like. That kind of thing."

"When *did* you last see Jason, before . . . ?"

"Before you found him? Two days earlier—Saturday night. I know it was then because GreenGrow has these staff meetings once a month, and because everybody's so busy, working and all, we usually just get together for dinner and talk about stuff. We were all there—Jason, Michael, me, a bunch of the other regular volunteers. And that Bree person." Daphne sniffed again, but this time she was angry.

Bree had been there? She had never mentioned that. If anything, she had said—or was it only implied?—that she had avoided Jason and GreenGrow since they broke up two years ago. Why would Bree have gone to the dinner meeting? "What did you talk about?"

"The usual. Money, and how to get more. How to get the word out better. Michael wanted to upgrade the website, but Jason thought that was a waste of time. He was more into direct action."

"Was there any conflict between them about these different approaches?"

"No more than usual. You know, we're all really into what we're trying to do with GreenGrow, so sometimes we argue. But mostly we agree, in the end."

"When the dinner was over, did you and Jason leave together?" And where had Bree gone?

Daphne shredded her napkin. "Yeah. He had a car, so we went back to his place for a while, and . . . you know. Then he told me he wanted to work on something, and I should go home."

"He didn't drive you home?"

"Nah. I usually walked—I don't live in campus housing anymore, and it was only a couple of blocks. But I never saw him again . . ." Daphne appeared to be struggling to hold back tears, and pressed the ragged remnants of her napkin to her mouth.

Meg's estimation of Jason slipped down another notch. He had used Daphne, in more ways than one, then sent her on her way. "Did he say anything about going out again that night?"

Daphne shook her head vehemently. "No! But . . ." She hesitated, chewing on her lower lip.

"Yes?" Meg prompted gently.

"When I thought about it, after . . . Look, I know he'd been kind of down lately. One of our main supporters at GreenGrow said he wasn't going to renew his funding. And Jason was getting pressured by the university to finish up or he'd be out. There was just a lot of bad shit coming down, you know? And he was kinda sweet to me that night. So I wondered . . . Maybe it all got to be too much, and he killed himself?"

"Do you think that's what happened?" Finally, someone who had been close to Jason and might actually be in a position to know. Maybe Jason, seeing his empire crumbling, had decided on one last political gesture, swallowing a lethal dose of pesticide and laying himself down in the middle of an orchard that offended his principles.

Meg could believe it, almost. But then she realized something. "Daphne, how did he get to my place? It's, what, ten miles from Amherst to Granford? He couldn't have walked, could he? And wasn't his car found in Amherst?"

Daphne slumped in her seat. "I don't know. Maybe he had help. Maybe he asked someone else . . ." She dissolved into a sobbing lump, and Meg felt as though she had kicked a puppy. An annoying puppy, perhaps, but one who didn't need any more pain.

"Were Jason and Michael close?" She had to say something to shut off Daphne's tears.

"Huh? Oh, yeah, once. Maybe not so much lately. But they were still tight."

Could Michael have helped Jason kill himself? For the good of GreenGrow? Meg had a feeling that Michael had come to regard Jason as more of a hindrance than an asset recently. But that was still a long way from helping Jason kill himself . . . or killing him.

At least Meg's interruption had had the desired effect. Daphne was mopping her nose with the sodden napkin, but she seemed to be under control again. "Hey, thanks for listening. I've been spending so much time with Jason that I guess I kinda lost touch with most of my women friends. And you seemed so nice, coming to the wake and all. I mean, you never even knew him."

And I truly wish we had never crossed paths, Meg said silently to herself. "I'm sorry I never had that opportunity. Clearly he will be missed."

"Yeah." Suddenly Daphne bounced out of her chair and started pulling on her coat. "Look, I've gotta go. I really appreciate you listening. See you."

Before Meg could protest, Daphne was out the door, leaving Meg bewildered. Also, leaving her with the check, although that didn't surprise her. Had Daphne been embarrassed by her frankness with Meg, whom she barely knew? She was apparently friendless and still heartbroken about Jason's death.

After settling the bill, Meg drove back to Granford in a pensive mood. She arrived at the house to find Seth leaning against the tractor, grinning. As well as two goats in the pen next to the driveway.

"Goats?" she protested, climbing out of the car. They looked kind of familiar.

Seth grinned like a mischievous boy. "When we went over to pick up the tractor, Florence said she was going to sell them to the Greek restaurant in Hatfield and they'd be on the menu next week. If you don't want to keep them, I'll find another place for them."

"Oh," Meg said. She stared at the two animals, who returned her gaze—with rather peculiar eyes. Horizontal pupils? They looked alien. "I guess they can stay there for now. Will that fence hold?"

"I'll check it out, but it looks okay. And there's the shed there. I think somebody back a ways used to keep sheep in this field."

"What am I supposed to feed them?"

"When there's grass they can forage, but it's still early. There's a feed store on the highway towards town. I can pick up some hay and some grain feed for you."

Wonderful, Meg thought. One more expense she really didn't need.

Seth was still talking. "Just give them a few days, see how they settle in. Kind of makes the place seem more like a real farm, doesn't it?"

She hated to disappoint Seth. He was so pleased with his surprise. "I guess. I don't have to clean up after them, do I?"

"No. And you don't need to milk them either, at the moment."

That hadn't even occurred to Meg. "You mean they're both female?"

"Yup. Male goats stink—I wouldn't do that to you. In case you want to know, the bigger one is a Nubian. I'm not sure what the other one is."

Chalk up another set of new facts. "Fine, whatever. Just make sure they can't get out, will you? I don't want to go chasing goats all over the neighborhood. You have any other bright ideas while you're at it? Chickens, maybe?"

"Maybe. Hey, you might like them. Plenty of eggs."

Meg sighed. "Can I just get through one apple harvest before I decide to become a theme park for agricultural America?"

"Sure. Look, let me go get the feed, and then I've got a job in Chicopee. You and the goats can get to know each other."

"Sure." After Seth left, Meg walked over to the wire fence—which looked none too sturdy—and contemplated the goats. Together the goats walked over to the fence and looked up at her expectantly. "Hi, goats. Do you have names?" The goats continued staring, but the younger one butted her head against the fence. "Am I supposed to pet you?" Did goats bite? Spit? Meg had heard that llamas spit. She felt a tug and realized that the smaller goat had managed to reach through the fence and grab a corner of her jacket.

"Excuse me, that's my jacket. Give it back." Meg pulled, and Smaller Goat released it. Meg could have sworn the goat was smiling at her.

Meg sighed again and realized she was doing that altogether too often. Now she had to go inside, boot up her computer, and research goats.

What had Seth been thinking?

Meg let herself into the house to be greeted by Lolly, who sniffed her suspiciously. Maybe female goats weren't as pungent as males, but cats had sensitive noses. Lolly turned tail and disappeared toward the living room at a trot. Meg made herself a cup of tea and then followed.

She had a couple of hours of peace, something to be

treasured. Bree was still living part-time on campus; Seth was off on a job. Meg knew that such solitary moments would become increasingly rare as the apple season progressed. Part of her wanted nothing more than to curl up with her tea and a book, but another part itched to dig into the stacks of historical documents in the boxes scattered around the room. That task would be both enjoyable and useful. Decision made, Meg sat down and booted up her computer.

Ruth Ferry had given her some insight into the relations between neighbors in the past century. It seemed to Meg that people had been more aware of each other in the past—although of course, there were fewer of them back then. Right now Meg couldn't even name her nearest neighbors, with the exception of Seth over the hill. But Ruth had also mentioned the memories and tales that had been passed down in her family; Ruth could remember what her grandparents had said about the Warrens, who had lived in this house more than a century ago. Meg had to admit she was curious now. Who were they? What had they been like, and how could she find out? Were there any hints in the boxes of musty papers at her feet?

One way to find out, she thought. She donned her cotton gloves and dove into the box she had already begun to sort through. Such a jumble of materials—she could understand why Gail was swamped. Meg was intelligent and computer literate, yet after three hours she had made little progress in cataloging the items in the boxes she had. She didn't want to guess how many hours it would take to go through just those four—and how many more boxes were there? And how many people willing to do it?

She was hungry and cranky. Lolly had stationed herself at Meg's feet, waiting for dinner. Meg wished someone would come along and hand *her* a plateful of dinner. But at least she could point proudly at the one box she had sorted and made basic data entries for. And she had turned up a couple of treasures along the way: old photos of her house, with indistinct figures she had to assume were Lula and Nettie, the sisters who had been the last Warrens on the property, in long black dresses, standing in front of the house along with an unidentified man in a hat and a reclining dog; and an indistinct photo of what was labeled "Warren's Saw Mill" in pencil, showing a tangle of unfamiliar equipment, with the house—or the one next door?—in the background. Men rendered ghostlike by the long exposure moved about the machinery, planing the boards that had probably gone into one or another renovation of the house, or other houses nearby. All in all, a good day's work.

"Dinner, Lolly?"

The cat's ears pricked up, and she stood up and headed toward the kitchen. Smart cat.

20

Meg awakened in the dark. She checked her clock: not even six, and the sky was barely light. Why was she awake?

The answer came quickly, as she heard the goats bleating in the pasture. Goats, indeed. What was she supposed to do with goats? She had no idea what kind of care they required. And didn't she have enough to keep her busy at the moment? Why were they making noise at this ungodly hour? They couldn't possibly be hungry again, could they? She had seen Seth spread hay and fill a large pan with the grain he had bought at the local feed store. Had Florence been neglecting them? Were they starved? How was she supposed to know? Or maybe there was an intruder. Was there such a thing as watch-goats? Reluctantly Meg hauled herself out of bed, disturbing Lolly, who had been curled into a snug ball near her feet. The cat gave her a baleful glare and went back to sleep.

Downstairs Meg put on water for coffee, then shrugged into her coat and rubber boots and went out to investigate

the commotion. The goats trotted eagerly toward the
fence when they saw her. She checked the pan that had
been full of grain the day before: only half-empty. So they
weren't hungry, even though they were still looking at her
expectantly. Lonely? But they had each other. Bored?
What was she supposed to do to keep goats entertained?
"Hey, guys, think you can keep it down until the sun
comes up?"

They didn't move, and she found their stares unnerving. Bad enough that she talked to her cat, but now she
was initiating a conversation with a pair of goats. Maybe
she really was crazy. At least there were no near neighbors to overhear her—or the goats. They could just learn
to entertain themselves. The tough-love school of goat
rearing.

She could hear the kettle in the kitchen whistling.
"I'm going back inside now," she told her audience. "Try
to amuse yourselves, huh?"

Meg detoured to retrieve the morning paper from the
head of the driveway. She was still learning her way
around the Springfield daily paper—she missed the *Boston Globe*, but that paper didn't provide much information about what was happening in her end of the state,
and she hadn't bothered to subscribe. She had the odd
feeling of floating between two worlds, her old urban one
and her new rural one. At the moment she didn't feel like
she belonged in either.

She had finished reading the paper and had cleaned up
the kitchen when Bree arrived at the back door.

"Come on in. No classes today? You want some coffee?"

Bree sidled in. "Nope, no classes, not today. I thought
I ought to check in here, since things are speeding up in
the orchard. We've got to put together a spraying schedule. And I brought over a few more boxes of my stuff.
What's with the goats?"

"Complicated story. I'm still trying them out, so to speak,

but they came with the tractor. Do you know anything about goats?"

"Not much. They're nosy, and they get into things. And they make a great jerk—you marinate the meat with hot peppers and stuff and then grill it. The tractor was my next question. Where'd that come from?"

"A friend of Seth's found it and got a good deal for me. Or so he says. Please tell me you know something about driving a tractor?"

"Only since I was seven."

"Thank goodness!" Meg handed her a cup of coffee. "Can you teach me?"

"No problem. Hi, Lolly." She greeted the cat and scratched behind her ears. "Hey, what'd you do to the floor?"

"Peeled off all the floor coverings. I have to strip it or sand it or something, but I wanted to find out what kind of shape it was in before I decided what to do."

Bree eyed it critically. "Looks pretty good to me, or it will when you clean it up. Nice wood. I can help if you want, not that I know much, either."

"I may take you up on that. You have any idea when you might be moving in to stay?" Meg asked.

Bree kept her eyes on the coffee. "Like I told you, I'll probably be going back and forth for a while. I know there's lots to do here, and I don't have that much more stuff to worry about for my last classes."

"No rush. You do whatever works best for you." Meg suppressed the thought that Bree was wavering. About the job? About living with her? She didn't want to press. She refilled her own cup and sat down. "Listen, I've had a couple of odd conversations over the last few days, and I wondered if you could give me your feedback."

"I guess. What's the problem?"

"Well, let's start with Christopher. Have you heard anything connecting him to a pesticide company?"

"What do you mean, 'connecting'?"

"Well, maybe I need to explain. I went to the Green-Grow meeting in Amherst the other night, and I talked to some of their people afterwards. And last Friday I had lunch with Michael Fisher, and he said something to the effect that Christopher might be in bed with the pesticide makers."

Bree twirled her mug around and around on the table. "I told you about the scholarship, and I know other people in the department who have gotten them, too. The pesticide makers like to make it look like they're real concerned, but they've paid my way, so I guess I can't complain. I don't think Professor Ramsdell would tell me about a bigger deal—I'm just an undergraduate. Come to think of it . . . there've been a couple of closed-door meetings in the department recently. You know, a bunch of the faculty holed up somewhere together, and you can't find them when you go looking. And then they don't explain why. I get the feeling something's going on, but I don't have a clue what. Of course, that doesn't mean it has anything to do with a pesticide company. Just a coincidence, maybe?"

"Could be. I have a hard time believing that he'd be involved in anything underhanded. Okay, next question: do you know where they keep the pesticides that the department uses? Are they kept under lock and key?"

"Students don't play with that kind of stuff too often—the university's scared of liability issues, you know? But there are very specific regulations for storage and use of poisonous materials. If you're using it, you're supposed to have official training. The university offers a course so you can get certified, and I've done it, in case you're wondering. Maybe you should think about doing it, too. I know the stuff itself is kept at the research field stations. There are all sorts of regulations about what kind of containers to use and what kind of safety provisions you need to have handy. And of course everything is kept locked, with big signs all over the place. Why do you want to know? Like, how could Jason or anyone else have gotten his hands on some?"

"I guess that's what I'm asking. Sounds possible, although he hadn't been spending a lot of time on campus recently. Anyway, if there's some sort of oversight, then that would have made it more difficult for him."

"And easier to figure out who could get at it," Bree pointed out. "I mean, a stranger can't just wander in and help himself. The students are taught from the beginning to treat this stuff with respect. That's part of the IPM philosophy. You don't just go out and dump buckets of poison on whatever bug shows up that week. You have a balanced, long-term strategy, and you reassess regularly throughout the growing season."

Meg sighed. "Bree, there's something I have to tell you." She laid out the details about the methidathion Seth had found in the barn. "The problem is, we have no idea who brought it here, or even when. Christopher says it wasn't his, and Seth said it was way past its expiration date. No one around here seems to have ever thrown anything out, so it could have been there for decades, and who knows how many people saw it there."

"Yeah, that's a good point." Bree swallowed some more coffee. "You said you had more than one weird conversation?"

"Yes, and the other one is kind of related. Yesterday Daphne waylaid me after class and wanted to have coffee with me. You know her, right?"

Bree made a face. "Yeah. I don't like that woman."

"Why not?" Considering how reserved Bree usually was, Meg was surprised by the vehemence of her response.

"For starters, she doesn't much like me. She knew Jason and I had dated, and I guess she thought I was still a threat to her."

"But that was over, what, two years ago? Wasn't that before they got involved?"

"Yeah, but she's incredibly insecure. She probably thought I might come back for more. Poach on her territory. Or what she thought was her territory."

"She said she was Jason's girlfriend."

"Ha!" Bree snorted. "In her dreams. She hung around him as much as she could, and . . . You know the term 'friends with privileges'?"

Meg nodded.

"Well, he was happy to sleep with her, but were they together, like a couple? I don't think so."

"She says she was, uh, with Jason Saturday night— which is probably when he died—but then he sent her home. He said he had work to do."

"You mean they had sex? And then he made a crappy excuse and told her to go home? Sounds about right. Jason took what was offered."

Meg struggled to find a tactful way to ask her next question. "Bree . . . why do you know so much about what was going on with Jason and Daphne? I thought you and Jason had gone your separate ways a long time ago, and you stayed away from GreenGrow."

Bree looked away. "It's not that big a department. It was hard not to run into Jason now and then, and wherever he was, Daphne usually wasn't far away. She'd always glare daggers at me when she saw me. Of course, I think she hates a lot of people. But she had a real thing for Jason. That was obvious."

"From what she told me, it sounds as though she does most of the unglamorous work at GreenGrow."

"Yeah, but she volunteered. Nobody was forcing her, but she wanted to stay close to Jason. I'd feel sorry for her if she wasn't so obnoxious."

Meg had to admit she agreed with Bree's assessment. She tried to put a kind spin on her own reaction to Daphne, but she had to admit to herself that she really didn't like the woman any more than Bree did. But there was one more thing she had to bring up, much as she didn't want to. "Bree, Daphne said you were also at the Green-Grow meeting Saturday night. Why?"

"Michael asked me to come."

"Michael? Why?"

Bree shrugged, then looked away. "I think he was try-ing to take a bigger part in GreenGrow, maybe balance out Jason's side a bit. They need more members."

"Did Michael know about you and Jason?"

"Yeah, of course. And I went because I figured they couldn't cut off my scholarship money this late, so why not?" She jumped up from her chair and took her empty mug to the sink. "So, you want to go play with your trac-tor?"

Meg stood up more slowly. Bree's answer made sense, at least on the surface, but why had she chosen that particular night to return to GreenGrow? One more coin-cidence to add to the list. "I guess. I don't even know where to start. I don't think this thing came with an in-struction manual. It's not exactly new."

"Not a problem—there's plenty of documentation on-line. Look, this is way simpler than a car. You drive a stick?" When Meg nodded, Bree went on. "So you've got the basic idea of a clutch and shifting. The biggest thing you're going to have to worry about is getting a feel for the steering, and for balance. Why don't you just try it out for today, and we can worry about all the attachments later?"

"Shoot, I hadn't even thought about those. What else am I supposed to need?"

"I think I saw a mower attachment—that's good for cleaning up between the rows of trees. You don't want to let the weeds and stuff get too far out of control—great place for pests to hide, and it makes it harder to get around the orchard anyway. The most important thing is to be able to move the apples from the orchard to your storage area."

"And how do I do that?"

"That's one of the problems with apples, and why you need experienced pickers. It's all done by hand. You can't just go by and shake the tree or wait to pick up what falls, unless you're planning to make cider, and fast. If you're selling them for eating, the pickers have to take them off the tree and put them in these bags or baskets they strap on. And when you transfer them to bigger containers, again, you can't just dump. Bruises the apples. You have to be careful with them, because bruised apples sell for a much lower price than ones that aren't. So the pickers have got to be good, and they've got to care about what they're doing."

Meg groaned, and Bree grinned. "This is a relatively small operation. It just means you and I and the pickers have a lot of lifting to do. It'll build up your muscles fast enough."

"I bet. You ready to go tackle the tractor now?"

"I am. Let's go see what you've got."

Bree led the way eagerly. She stalked around the tractor in the driveway, looking at tires and parts Meg couldn't even begin to identify. Then she climbed into the seat and inspected various knobs and dials. From what Meg had seen, there weren't many, and most were clearly labeled. Maybe there was a plus side to having an older machine.

"You know anything about what shape it's in?" Bree called out.

"I think Eric checked it over before he delivered it. Does it have gas?"

Bree looked back at a dial and nodded. "Full tank. You ready?"

"I guess." Meg approached the tractor, and Bree climbed down again.

"Okay, first of all, safety check. Your tires look good. You've got gas. But we need to make sure there's oil and the radiator isn't dry. Who'd you say this belonged to?"

"Some guy who didn't use it, I gather. He bought it over

the Internet. He and his wife split, and she was clearing
out his stuff. Seth says I got a good deal on it."

"Figures. It's old, but it's in pretty fair shape." Bree
poked around some more. "Oil and radiator, good." She
took a critical look at Meg. "And you're dressed all right—
nothing that could get snagged. You want me to start it
up, get a feel for it?"

"Please!" Meg stepped back out of the way and watched
as Bree climbed into the seat. She adjusted it slightly, then
turned the key in the ignition. The machine roared to life,
belching smoke, then settled down to chugging steadily.
Bree gave a thumbs-up, released the parking brake, and
slowly let out what Meg assumed was the clutch, while
giving it some gas. After an initial lurch, the tractor moved
forward smoothly. Bree, her slight form dwarfed by the
machine but with a huge smile on her face, drove in a few
tight circles in the driveway, then reversed before pulling
up in front of Meg. She set the brake, turned off the engine, and jumped down.

"Sweet! She runs really well. Think you can do it?
Just try her out on the driveway for a bit, and if you think
you can handle it, we'll take her out on the grass. One
thing to remember, though: watch for slopes or steep
banks. It can tip over if you're not careful. But as long as
you stick to flat ground, you'll be fine."

Bree's warning did little to boost Meg's confidence.
"Uh, the orchard is up a hill, you know."

"Don't worry. You've got plenty of time to practice
before you have to worry about that."

"If you say so." Meg climbed into the high seat and
before doing anything else, looked around her at the house,
with all its tacked-on bits and pieces, and the barn, and
then the view down toward the Great Meadow. This was
a whole new perspective; it felt odd to be elevated, and on
such a rickety piece of machinery. The big modern tractors she had seen online had enclosed cabins, and even air-
conditioning and sound systems. Hers was the no-frills

model. Still, this was supposed to be a practical piece of equipment, not a pleasure ride. She located and attached the seat belt. "Now what?"

"Put your clutch in and start 'er up. Keep the brake on until you're ready to move."

"Right." Meg imitated what she had seen Bree do and was rewarded by the roar of the engine. The whole machine vibrated, and Meg couldn't imagine what it would be like to travel over a rough field or unpaved lane. She looked uncertainly at Bree, who yelled, "Go on!"

Taking a deep breath, Meg disengaged the brake, let out the clutch—and prayed.

The machine lurched, and she released the clutch too fast, stalling it. She started it up again and shifted more cautiously this time, managing to make some forward progress—at about two miles an hour. But at least it was moving, and she was in the driver's seat.

A half hour later, Meg wondered what she had been worried about. On level ground the machine putted along happily. She hadn't pushed its limits, but she definitely felt that it had more power in store, which no doubt she would need when she started hauling around trailers laden with apple boxes. And her posterior was already sore from the bouncing. She looked over at Bree, who had shifted her attention to the eager goats, and yelled, "Can I stop now?"

Bree gave the larger goat a final pat and walked back to the edge of the driveway. "Sure. You want to put her in the barn?" she yelled over the engine noise.

"Let's not worry about that now," Meg yelled back. "I still need to clear enough space for it. I'll just leave her where I found her, okay?"

"Let her idle for a minute or two to cool down, okay? And don't forget the brake!"

Meg stopped the tractor in front of the barn doors, then pulled on the hand brake and pushed in the clutch pedal. She looked around again but with an entirely different perspective this time. She had mastered the tractor; she had laid claim to her land. Did this make her a farmer? Maybe not yet, but one big step closer. She felt ridiculously proud of herself. "Long enough?" she yelled at Bree.

Bree nodded, and Meg, with a little pang, turned off the engine. The sudden silence startled her.

Bree came alongside. "Hey, you did great. I told you it was easy."

It wasn't until she had climbed down and brushed off the seat of her pants that Meg realized she'd doubled her audience: Art Preston was leaning against his squad car, grinning.

"Looking good!" he called out. "Your first time?"

Meg matched his grin. "Hi, Art. Yes, it is. Seth found this for me, and Bree's teaching me how it works."

Art nodded a greeting to Bree, then turned to Meg. "You got a minute?"

Meg felt a small chill, and her smile wilted. "Sure. You have some news?"

"I just thought I should bring you up-to-date. I take it our friend Marcus hasn't been in touch?"

"No, not that I expected to hear from him. And I wasn't about to call him."

Bree was shifting from side to side, looking uncomfortable. "Meg, I should go. I'll come back tomorrow and we can take out the tractor again, okay?"

"Sure, Bree. And thanks for the help."

Without any further formality, Bree headed for her car and pulled out.

Art watched her departure. "She working out?"

"I think so. She seems to know what she's talking about, and thank heavens she knows how to drive a tractor. You have time to come in?"

"Sure." Art followed her into the kitchen. As Meg

puttered around, fixing another pot of coffee, he sprawled in one of Meg's kitchen chairs and shrugged off his coat. "Getting almost too warm for the coat these days."

Meg didn't feel up to chitchat: Art had to be here for a reason. "Marcus was here, looking at the barn, after Seth told him about the pesticide. I don't think he found anything useful."

"So he's taking all the right steps, if a little late. I guess he's got to go through the motions."

Meg poured two mugs of coffee and set them on the table before sitting down. "Okay. Tell me." *Might as well get it over with.*

"Got the word from the ME. The formal report won't be ready for a while, but thanks to our heads-up, he looked for methidathion and found it."

Meg couldn't say she was surprised, though she had hoped it wouldn't be true. "From here?" she asked.

Art shook his head. "There's no way to know where that particular batch came from, at least not without a lot of fancy and expensive testing. So we can't eliminate that stuff from your barn as the source. And the same stuff was in the vomit, too, so we know he was still alive when he got here."

Not good news. Jason had died here, and Meg still didn't know why. "Art, is there any chance it was suicide?"

"Physically? Well, there's no sign of struggle, no injections. Nothing conclusive. But, Meg?"

"What?" she said dully. She had a feeling she didn't want to hear what he was going to say next.

"There's a lot to suggest that it wasn't suicide. The ME puts the time of death sometime early Sunday morning, maybe between midnight and six. Jason had dinner with a bunch of folks on Saturday night."

"The GreenGrow meeting," Meg interjected.

"Yes. Plenty of witnesses say he was in fine form there, nothing out of the ordinary. He left with this Daphne

Lydon woman, and she says she spent an hour or two with him, and he was fine when she went home."

"She told me."

That surprised Art. "You've talked to her?"

"More like, she talked to me. She found me and told me all about how close she and Jason were. And that they were together that night and then she went home."

"That's what she told the detectives. She lives in one of those places that rents out rooms to students, but it sounds like she's kind of a loner and nobody pays much attention to her. Okay, so, the ME says the dose Jason got would have killed him within six hours, or at the very least incapacitated him. Marcus says his car was still in Amherst. So how'd he get from Amherst at midnight to your place?"

Meg met his eyes. "I asked Daphne the same question. She didn't know. But clearly he would have needed help," she said slowly. "No way he could have walked. So somebody else knew. Somebody brought him here and left him to die." She sat silently for a few moments, then said slowly, "You know, it bothered me that if he had killed himself, he didn't leave a note. I would expect Jason, from what I've heard, to have left a detailed manifesto or something. The police didn't find anything like that at his place, did they?"

"No. And they didn't find any pesticide, either."

"Why here, Art? What did I have to do with this? I didn't know the man or his friends. Although I've certainly met a few people who might have wanted Jason out of the way."

"Meg, I can't answer that. Even if it was political, or even if he was depressed, somebody had to help him die."

Meg debated with herself before saying, "Art, Bree was at that dinner. She had a relationship with Jason, though she says it ended two years ago. Still, I don't know her well enough to be sure there wasn't more to it than what she's told me."

"Huh. Why'd she go to the meeting? Did she say?"

"She said Michael Fisher—he's one of the founders of GreenGrow—asked her to come. She said she thought Michael was trying to balance out Jason's radical bent by bringing in more middle-of-the-road members. Anyway, I assume Marcus knows this. What's he doing now?"

"Investigating. Say what you will about the man, he's a competent investigator. I'm sorry it doesn't clear you completely, Meg, but it's going to be hard to prove you had anything to do with this."

"But even if I'm clear, there are people I know who are still under suspicion, aren't there? Christopher, Bree, even Seth?"

Art shrugged. "Maybe. Don't borrow trouble, Meg. Marcus is stubborn, and he'll get to the bottom of this. Look, I've got to go. I just wanted to let you know where things stand." He stood up.

Meg stood as well. "Thank you, Art. And I hope Marcus is very good at his job."

At the door, Art turned and smiled at her. "You just hang in there, okay? Hey, you looked pretty good on that tractor."

Meg recognized that he was trying to change the subject and was warmed by his effort. "Thanks. It was kind of fun, and easier than I expected. Look, Art, I do appreciate your coming by and filling me in."

"Hey, I don't want you to sit here and stew. If I hear anything new, I'll let you know." He opened the door. "I'd better be getting back. Thanks for the coffee."

She smiled. "Thanks for the update."

After Art left, Meg sat down again with her cold coffee, staring into space. She tried to reconstruct that Saturday night. Nothing had awakened her; nothing had seemed out of the ordinary on Sunday. The road that ran past her property was a quiet one, little traveled. And there were few houses from which people could have seen anyone dragging around a dying man. Even the presence of her fence wouldn't have stopped anyone who was really determined.

It seemed so peaceful here. Funny—she would have said she was happy living in Boston, with all its lights and noise. Somehow in the short time she'd lived in Granford, she had come to appreciate the silence. But now the isolation bothered her. It shouldn't be so easy to just wander around the countryside disposing of dead bodies.

Why her orchard?

21

The next morning Meg was surprised to see Christopher and Bree arrive together in the university's van. Even from a distance Meg could see that Christopher looked extraordinarily pleased with himself: there was an extra spring in his step, and he never stopped smiling.

She opened the back door before they reached it. "Good morning. You're here bright and early. Are you coming in or heading straight for the orchard?"

"Good morning, Meg. What a grand day! We'll go up the hill later, but first I need to talk with you. Both of you, in fact."

Despite his smile, Meg felt a tingle of fear. Recently nobody's surprise announcements had been happy ones. "Come on in, then. Coffee?"

"You wouldn't happen to have any tea, would you?"

"Coming up."

"I'll do it," Bree interrupted. She had followed Christopher into the kitchen, looking wary. Meg tried to read her expression. What had Christopher said to her on the way over?

"Thank you, Bree. Come, Meg, sit. We have much to discuss." For the first time he noticed her piebald floor. "Good heavens, my dear! What have you done?"

"It's my latest home improvement—and I use the term cautiously. I plan to refinish it soon."

"Ah. Well, the wood appears to be in excellent condition. I shall look forward to seeing the finished product. Shall we sit now?"

With a sinking feeling in her stomach, Meg sat.

Christopher laughed. "Meg, you look as though I'm a dentist and I've just told you you need a tooth pulled. I have excellent news."

"All right," Meg said cautiously. "What?"

"I admit I was perhaps less than forthcoming the last time we spoke, but only because I had a superstitious fear that things would not work out. But they have, in fact, and I thought you should know. No doubt there will be press coverage, in any event."

"Christopher, what's going on?"

"DeBroCo has agreed to fund a new integrated pest management research institute at the university, and the department has asked me to assume control of it."

"DeBroCo? The chemical company? Don't they make pesticides?"

"They do, but they recognize the importance of using them responsibly, in coordination with other strategies. I don't know if you are aware of it, but insects can develop a resistance to pesticides, which renders the pesticides useless. If you wish to be cynical, you can say that the company is just protecting its future profits, but this way everyone benefits. And they're not attaching any strings to the institute. They're willing to support all aspects of research, including natural viruses and natural enemies. They agree that a coordinated program is the most practical approach for the future."

The knot in Meg's stomach unraveled. "Well, then, I guess congratulations are in order. What will this involve? Are they going to build something?"

"Indeed they are—a new building on campus, which will of course bear the corporate name. But I have carte blanche to lay out the laboratory requirements."

"Does that mean you'll have to give up your own research efforts? With the orchard, for example?" Something new to worry about?

Christopher was quick to understand her concern. "Meg, there will be many demands on my time, but I wouldn't abandon you now. Your orchard has been the centerpiece of the university's pomology research for a generation, and of course I plan to maintain our studies here. Rest assured that I will continue to provide oversight, and Bree can call on me whenever she needs me, although I have every confidence in her ability to carry on. And you as well, once you have acquired some experience. You might not see as much of me on site, but I will remain a part of this project."

Christopher looked so happy that Meg was reluctant to complain. She knew he had been concerned about whether the orchard would survive at all in the face of the threatened public development in Granford, and at least Meg and Seth and the town had staved that off. But Christopher wasn't far from retirement age, and this new institute would no doubt be the crowning achievement of his professional career. From a business perspective, she was less sure that DeBroCo's generous gift would come with no strings attached, but she had to trust the university to look out for its own interests, and Christopher to keep them on track. "Well, then, I'd say a toast was called for, if it weren't so early in the morning. Congratulations, Christopher. It sounds wonderful, and I'm happy for you. When will all this start?"

"There will be a press conference on Monday, and we

should break ground soon. The building should be completed within the year."

"That fast?"

"The plans have been under way quietly for some time, and as I'm sure you're aware, there's been a construction slump in the region of late, so we should have no problem finding willing workers. In any event, I wanted to come here today with Bree so we could go over your spring needs together. I want you to be fully prepared, insofar as possible. I know you've been auditing the orchard management class, but nothing matches hands-on experience."

"All right, I'm game. What do I need to know?"

As Christopher extracted papers from a file folder, Meg glanced at Bree. She didn't look happy. Did she have issues with the involvement of a major chemical company in her department? But since the company had been funding her education, it wasn't as if Bree wasn't already aware of DeBroCo and its activities. She'd have to ask Bree later, when Christopher wasn't around. For now, Meg needed to focus on what Christopher was telling her.

"Forgive me if this sounds like a lecture, my dear. Our goal in your orchard is not to eradicate all insects but rather to maintain a low level so as to encourage the population of natural enemies and to discourage the development of pesticide resistance. It isn't easy to achieve this balance, but that is our intention."

Meg held up a hand. "You're saying you actually *want* to keep some of the bugs? How do you even know what I've got out there?"

"We do regular inspections, which are a bit labor-intensive, but yours is a small plot, so it is feasible. We also do leaf sampling, once the trees are leafed out, and we use some insect traps."

Meg had a brief image of trying to snag a fruit fly with a bear trap and suppressed a giggle. "Traps?"

"Pheromone traps, which lure insects with a synthetic sex hormone. Then there are bait-lure traps, which we use to monitor for apple maggots. And also light traps, which may attract other types of insects. But they're harder to maintain."

Meg's head was spinning. "Am I supposed to do something with all these, or do your students and staff take care of that?"

"Most assuredly the latter. This is an ongoing research project, and the data collection must be scrupulously maintained. No reflection on your skills, Meg."

"I'm more than happy to let you handle it. Okay, once you've identified the pests, what do you do?"

"That is when we begin to lay out our pesticide program. You have your organophosphates, your carbamates, and your pyrethroids. And there are a few other approaches—for example, *Bacillus thuringiensis*, a microbial insecticide that works well on caterpillars, and various lepidopterous apple pests. Endosulfan, a chlorinated hydrocarbon for apple leafhopper. Oh, and insecticidal soaps, which work well on soft-bodied arthropods."

Meg didn't know whether to laugh or cry. Christopher could have been speaking a foreign language for all she understood.

"Could you just give me a bottom line? How much of this do I need to know? I don't mean to sound stupid or lazy, but it's a lot to take in all at once. Can't I just delegate it all to you and Bree?"

Christopher looked contrite. "Of course. I'm so sorry—I've been absorbed in the subject for so long that I forget how new you are to all this. And there's no reason why you should know the details at this point. I would hope you would involve yourself in the process as we move forward, but you're quite right—you have skilled people at your disposal."

"Thank you! And I will do my best to learn, but right

now I need the broad outlines. Say you figure out what pests you're fighting, what's next?"

"We spray—carefully, I assure you! Given the size of your orchard, and the density of your plantings, we have been using alternate middle spraying with good success. This works particularly well for codling moth and apple aphid. What's more, the process reduces the amount of spray material you need to use and is less harmful to beneficial species. We've kept your trees pruned low, both to facilitate spraying without heavy-duty equipment and to make harvesting easier—no ladders."

Christopher's words reassured her. "Christopher, I know you've done a good job keeping the orchard going this long, and I certainly don't know enough to interfere. Please keep on doing whatever you've been doing. And I really appreciate your taking the time to explain it to me. Maybe at some point I'll feel confident enough to have an opinion, but right now I trust you to do the right thing. And to help Bree take over the reins. Right, Bree?"

"Sure, Meg, Professor. I can handle it."

"I'm certain you can." Christopher stood up quickly. "Well, shall we head up the hill and see what's going on?"

The more Meg learned, the more interested in the reality of the orchard she became. Christopher pointed out scars from prior-year infestations and nodded to a few tattered traps still hanging on branches, soon to be replaced. When he and Bree put their heads together to confer on some technical point, Meg wandered from tree to tree, studying each, trying to discern similarities and differences. She was becoming impatient to see them in bloom, and with fruit hanging from them. Soon, soon . . .

After a couple of hours, they made their way back down the hill. "Are you leaving now, Bree?" Christopher asked.

"Yeah, I've got stuff to do." Bree turned to Meg. "Why don't I come back tomorrow? I can show you how to hook up the tractor attachments. And, Professor, we need to go over the pickers' contracts, right?"

"Indeed we do. You are on top of things, my dear. Meg, thank you, as always, for your attention. You're a good student. Don't forget to check the paper in the morning!"

Warmed by his compliment, Meg waved them off and returned to the house. *It will all work out.* It had to. She had a lot riding on the success of the orchard, and she knew how little she knew. And she could apply good business practices: choose competent people, and don't second-guess them.

She felt reassured that she now had an explanation for why Michael and Daphne had seen Christopher with a representative of the evil poison merchants. The Green-Grow people were more than a little paranoid, Meg thought, seeing conspiracies under every rock—or was it leaf? Perhaps it was Jason's influence filtering down to his followers. Classic cult mentality: personal charisma could overcome intelligence and common sense in a small group, particularly one outside the mainstream to begin with.

What now? Meg didn't feel like starting a new project this late in the day. Maybe she should do a little online checking into this pesticide company and see what she could learn about the agreement. She was sure that the university would have done its homework before accepting the deal, but Meg still worried about Christopher. It was possible he might get pushed in a direction he didn't want to go, if the company somehow had the upper hand. And at the same time, his new responsibilities might keep him so busy that he wouldn't have time for her small orchard. Thank heavens for the Internet: she could learn about DeBroCo from the comfort of her house. And if she found any red flags she could get more details from her former banking colleagues in Boston.

An hour's worth of research left Meg vaguely troubled. She had long known the name of DeBroCo as a major diversified producer of chemical products, but she had been less aware of their recent financial difficulties. Even more disturbing was a spate of pending lawsuits filed against the company, alleging falsification of safety records, notably in their agricultural products division. One would not have been significant, but there were several that had reached the public eye in the past year or two, and taken together they suggested a pattern. Even if the suits were baseless, Meg knew that negative publicity could have a real impact on the company's sales, not to mention its reputation. In that context, launching this joint endeavor with the university made good public relations sense. It would send the message that the company had taken heed of the complaints (without admitting anything) and was working to change its approach. No doubt the outlay involved in setting up this new program and its new building was small change compared to national profits from the division. Overall it was a smart move, and Meg would have expected no less from a long-established company such as DeBroCo.

But Jason Miller would almost certainly have seen it as a cover-up, or at the very least an empty gesture to placate the naysayers. Still, GreenGrow and Jason would have been no more than gnats buzzing in DeBroCo's ear. That must have been hard for Jason to take. What would he have done about it?

22

When Seth stopped by on Sunday morning, Meg wondered whether she would ever get used to people simply dropping in all the time. Why was it that back in Boston, getting together with people—whether for business or pleasure—had always involved multiple phone calls or e-mails and complicated scheduling, while here in Granford people just showed up assuming you'd be home? No calls, no e-mails, no negotiation: they just knocked on your door. Meg wasn't sure yet which she preferred.

"What brings you here so early?" she asked Seth as she let him into the kitchen.

"I've got a couple of days free this week, and I wanted to get started on building out the shop." He looked down. "When are you going to do something about the floor?"

Meg poured him a mug of coffee. "I don't know yet. You have any ideas?"

Carrying his coffee, Seth paced around the kitchen, studying the floor, bouncing on the balls of his feet now and then. "Nice pine, good thick boards—no give. Built to last. I'd leave it exposed, though you need to finish it—three coats of oil-based polyurethane would do it. Sooner rather than later—if you leave it bare like this, you'll start getting grease stains and dirt ground in."

Meg sighed. "Okay, so how do I do it?"

"You need to sand it down to get rid of the old glue and any leftover finish. No need to strip it—that old glue is pretty much as dry as it could be. So, sand the floor, get rid of the sawdust, and start with the polyurethane. But you need to let it dry at least overnight between coats, so you won't be able to use the kitchen for a couple of days."

"It figures. And there are *so* many wonderful restaurants in Granford."

Seth ignored her sarcasm. "I've got a disk sander and a detail sander back at the house. You busy today?"

"What? You want to do it right now? I thought you had something to do in the shop."

"Why not? If you've got the time. My stuff can wait for a day, and I can help get you started. You up for it?"

"I guess. I can get the polyurethane tomorrow, right?"

"Sure. Let me run back to my place and pick up the equipment, make sure I have the right grades of sandpaper. Back in ten."

As quickly as he had appeared, Seth disappeared, leaving Meg shaking her head. Not only did people show up unannounced, but they also planned your day for you. Still, Seth had a point. Now that the floor was exposed, she should protect it or else live forever with stains from whatever she dropped on it. Obviously she hadn't thought this whole thing through when she started in on the project. Trust Seth to have the necessary equipment at hand. He seemed to have one of everything, and if he didn't, he knew who to ask.

It was eleven minutes later that he wheeled a piece of equipment to her back door. Meg watched as he set it down, then went back to his van for a second, smaller item.

When he returned, she said, "Those are sanders, I assume?"

"Yup. The big one's for the major passes, and the small one's for all those corners you can't reach with the big one. What about your cabinets?"

"What about them?"

"I mean, are you planning to save them or replace them?"

"I really haven't thought about it. Why does it matter right now?"

"Because you might want to remove the lower ones— and the stove and refrigerator—so we can sand the whole floor at once. Then you can do whatever you want later."

It made sense, but Meg had not anticipated a major deconstruction effort when she woke up this morning. On the other hand, there was little in the cabinets, which would make things easy. On the third hand, some of them looked to be nineteenth-century in origin, with beaded board panels and simple moldings. Time for an executive decision. "Okay, let's take out the modern junk and leave the older ones. I like them. They feel right in the house."

"Good choice—they're probably late Victorian, but they're in decent shape. Let's start with moving the table and chairs out, and we can take it from there. Oh, and did you plan on replacing the stove? Because it might not weather the move."

Meg eyed the appliance dubiously. She really didn't want to lay out cash for a new stove right now, but the current one was probably older than she was, and it would make her life easier to have one she trusted to keep working. Damn, another decision to make. It was too early in the morning for all these decisions. "Let's just get it out of the way and decide later, okay?"

"Fine by me. Let's go."

It took a surprisingly short time to clear the kitchen of the most modern cabinets, mainly because they were cheap units probably added for or by renters. Meg hadn't brought much cooking equipment with her, so there was little of that to remove. She was standing on a chair reaching into the farthest corner of an upper cabinet when she pulled out a glass jar filled with dark brown sludge. "What the heck?"

Seth took it from her hand. "Look, it's labeled. It used to be apple butter, a few decades ago."

Meg took it back. "Check out the handwriting—make that a lot of decades ago. What do you bet that Lula and Nettie put this up, from the apples from the orchard? Hang on—I can show you their picture."

Meg went to the dining room and rummaged through the box of historical society papers she had processed. She pulled out the pictures of the house and the map, and returned to the kitchen, where she laid them on the counter in front of Seth. "See? Those are the sisters, although I have no idea which was which. But they look about five feet tall. Neither one could have seen a jar in the back of that cabinet." For a moment she wondered if the departed Warren sisters were trying to send her a message, but the antique apple butter was more likely a remnant from one of several generations of sloppy housekeepers. "And here's the map I told you about, with the orchard."

Seth leaned closer to get a better look, and Meg was suddenly aware of his nearness. He seemed oblivious, though, as he pointed to the map. "And here's the Chapin property—you can see where the creek formed the northern boundary. Stills does."

"I don't think I've gone that far yet. So this part over here would be the wetlands?" As she pointed, Meg moved to put a little space between them.

"Yup. Anyway, as far as the antique apple butter goes, I think you'd better get rid of it—maybe away from the house? Who knows what it's turned into by now. You might want to keep the jar, though. Nice artifact."

"I'll add it to my collection," Meg said drily, depositing it cautiously in the sink. "Can we get on with it? I'd like to finish this project before summer."

When Seth had unscrewed the newer cabinets from the wall and hauled them out of the kitchen, Meg was cheered by how open the room felt. She was less happy with the dirt of ages that emerged from under the cabinets and appliances. She didn't know whether to be pleased or depressed to find that she was not the only careless housekeeper to inhabit the house. Seth went back to the van and hauled out a Shop-Vac, which took care of the floor debris in short order. Before doing anything else, he squatted, studying the floor while raking over it lightly at a low angle with his hand. "Good news—no protruding nailheads. They can destroy a sandpaper disk in no time. We're all set."

He stood up again and wheeled in the big machine, parking it proudly in the middle of the kitchen. "This, ma'am, is a disk sander, which uses, as you might infer, disks of sandpaper."

"Um, yes, I can see that. So you swipe that over the floor and it removes . . . whatever?"

"Not quite that simple. This should take a couple of passes, with different grits of sandpaper. The coarse grits will remove most of the dirt and any old wax that might still be there. Then you switch to a finer grit to smooth things off and remove the obvious scratches."

"Aren't you worried about taking too much off?"

"Well, with a modern floor you should consider that, but you've got some serious boards here. I doubt they've ever been sanded. I'd worry more about rippling or gouging with the machine, although that's more of a problem with a belt sander. Anyway, the wood's been seasoned for a couple of hundred years and should be pretty hard. Best way to find out is for me to try a patch, get the feel of it."

"Hang on a sec, Seth. Do I get to do any of this, or do

I just watch you do all the work and hand you a cool drink and make admiring noises now and then?"

He grinned at her. "Am I taking over again? It's your kitchen, so of course you can do the honors. I was just trying to tell you what to watch out for."

"Duly noted. So what do I do?"

"Safety first. Ear protection and a dust mask. Otherwise you'll be coughing up sawdust for weeks." He handed her a pair of plastic ear protectors and a disposable mask, which she put on.

I must look like a Martian by now, Meg thought, but at least she knew she was well protected. "Now what?"

Seth ran an extension cord from an outlet and plugged in the machine. Then he came up and stood behind her and guided her hands to the sander's handles.

She was startled by the feel of his body against hers, although she tried not to show it; after all, it wasn't as though he hadn't ever touched her before. But he hadn't made any move toward repeating it, since that one night . . . And now he was just trying to demonstrate how the machine worked, right? He didn't mean anything by it. She tried to focus on what he was saying rather than on the way his hands closed over hers, guiding her motions.

Seth seemed unaware of her stiffness. "This thing here turns it on. This one lowers the disk. Once the disk is down, move slowly along the grain of the wood. It's no big deal if you go sideways, but try to stick to the grain as much as you can. If you have to stop moving, don't leave the disk down or you'll end up with dips or gouges. Think you can handle it?"

She nodded. She wasn't about to admit to him that she wasn't sure. This was her house, and she was going to do whatever came along, not just sit back and watch someone else do the work. It was a point of pride. "Let's go!"

She turned on the switch, then lowered the rotating

disk until it was on the floor. Immediately the whole machine tried to skitter sideways, but she wrestled it under control and aimed it down the length of the pine boards.

"Keep it moving!" Seth yelled. Seth kept his hands on the controls until she got the hang of it, then stepped back and watched.

Meg took a step forward, then another, struggled to keep the beast moving in a more-or-less straight line. She looked down at the area she had already passed over and almost stopped: the difference was startling. What had been grimy and yellow emerged as clean and golden. Sawdust floated through the air; the scent of wood filled the kitchen. Meg felt an unexpected surge of emotion. This wood had been cut over two hundred years earlier, probably by her own ancestors in her own backyard, and had stood the test of time. Now she was bringing it back to life.

She reached the end of the floor and realized she hadn't asked Seth how to turn around. Quickly she turned off the machine, which quivered to a stop. She turned to find Seth leaning against one of the remaining cabinets, with a big grin on his face. "Problem?" he asked.

"No, I love it. I just didn't know if there was a right way to turn and go back the other way. That looks amazing!" She pointed at the newly clean strip. "I had no idea it would look so good."

"Yeah, that's one of the rewards of sanding. It's like making it new. Well, since you're shut down, just swing the whole thing around and come back this way."

"Right, chief." With greater confidence she switched it on again, lowered the disk, and plowed forward, this time pivoting smoothly at the far end. At the end of ten passes the floor stood revealed, with only the edges to remind her of what it had looked like before. She turned off the machine again.

"Wow. I really like this. What do we do now?"

"Change the sandpaper to a finer grit and do it all again.

Oh, maybe we should clean up the edges so they match. Not as much fun, but necessary."

"With that smaller sander?"

"That's right. You want me to do it?"

"Sure, you do it. I want to save my strength for the real work."

Seth gave a snort but grabbed the smaller sander and, kneeling down, started sanding around the perimeter of the room with it. He moved with practiced skill, and as Meg watched, sawdust coated his arms like powdered sugar on a donut. Meg laughed at the image and realized she was actually giddy with a sense of accomplishment. All those years of apartment living, and she had barely changed a lightbulb; now she was sanding floors. How much her life had changed in only a few months—and Seth had been a big part of that change. If she hadn't needed a plumber in a hurry, she probably wouldn't have met him. And if she hadn't met him, she probably would have packed up her bags and left town as quickly as she had arrived, overwhelmed by both events and by the dauntingly unfamiliar task of renovating this house. At least now she could look around and see real, tangible progress. More than progress: improvement. What she had done actually looked good, and she was beginning to enjoy the process.

What would her Boston friends think? Yesterday she had learned to drive a tractor. Today, she was sanding the floor. And she had a pair of goats in the pasture. Those so-called friends would be shocked, amazed—and probably contemptuous. *Poor Meg, she's gone country. Thinks she's a rustic Martha Stewart now. Next she'll be baking bread and putting up jam. Or making goat cheese and spinning her own yarn.*

Meg realized she didn't care. When she'd been suspected of murder, only one of her Boston friends had even bothered to talk to her. The people of Granford had shown more concern and consideration for her than anyone from her past life. Particularly Seth and his sister Rachel. And here Seth was, sanding her floor—and looking as though he was happy to do it. She was startled by the silence when he shut off the smaller sander, and realized he had made the full circuit.

He stood up and dusted himself off. "Why don't you run the Shop-Vac over the floor so we can see what we're doing, and then you can make another pass with the big machine? I'll change the sandpaper."

"No problem. Seth, I can't tell you how much I appreciate this. I wouldn't have known where to start, and you've made it so easy."

"That's what friends are for, right?"

Friends? *Is that what we are?* Meg thought as she plugged in the vacuum. The term seemed kind of inadequate, considering what they'd been through together in the past couple of months. And once he moved into her barn, he was definitely going to be a part of her life on a daily basis. Was that good or bad?

She shoved the question away. *Not now, not yet.* And Seth was equally helpful and engaging with everyone he knew. Wasn't he?

The floor now clear of sawdust, Meg turned off the vacuum. "It looks terrific. It changes the whole room, doesn't it?"

"It does. This is a great room, with all the light— those windows on both sides. And maybe you can match the old cabinets with something similar, if you need more storage space."

"And appliances, don't forget. This looks so good, I can't see putting those old pieces of junk back in here. I guess I'd better take myself over to the home store and order something."

"Listen," Seth began, "I know a guy over in—"

"I'm sure you do," Meg broke in, laughing. "Fine, tell me his name. But first we've got to use the fine sandpaper on the floor, right?"

"Your sander awaits." Seth installed a fresh sandpaper disk and handed the sander over to her.

Another round of sanding, vacuuming, sanding, vacuuming. Finally Seth gave his approval to the smooth and dust-free floor. "You do good work, Meg."

"I'm learning. Now polyurethane?"

"Three coats. And you need to give the polyurethane time to dry in between. So even if you start tomorrow, you won't be able to use the room before Friday, most likely."

"That's not a problem—I can make do with the microwave for a few days."

"Why not call Rachel? She'd love to have you."

"Oh, no, Seth. I can't expect Rachel to bail me out. I'll be fine here. Besides, I have a cat to feed."

"It's up to you. Now, when you go to the home store, you're going to need—"

"Stop!" Meg held up a hand. "Leave me something to figure out on my own, okay? I can read a label, and there's always the Internet."

"I guess I take the big-brother role kind of seriously. I'm sure you can handle it." He stretched. "I should head out—Mom's expecting me for dinner. Good luck, and let me know if you run into any problems."

"I'll do that." Meg watched as he hauled the big sander out of the kitchen and loaded it into his van, then followed suit with the smaller one. From start to finish, the whole thing had taken her less than six hours, and the floor looked wonderful. Lolly wandered in from wherever she had been hiding to escape the noise and mess and stopped at the threshold, looking surprised. She took a tentative step onto the now-bare surface, then decided it was acceptable and crossed the floor to Meg.

"You want dinner, huh? Well, let me tell you, you're going to be eating in the dining room until I get some finish on this, you hear?"

She fed the cat, then rummaged for her own meal in the refrigerator—now standing monument-like in the dining room—and found herself at loose ends by eight o'clock. She could do nothing more with the floor at the moment, but she could at least do a little online research into the finer points of floor finishing, old-house variety. She opened her laptop and started searching. As she read through the various sites, she felt more and more smug that she (with a little help from Seth) had already accomplished the first, difficult sanding phase. She pulled out a pad and started jotting down the equipment she was going to need: a lambs-wool applicator; a respirator, perhaps; more sandpaper, definitely; a pole sander, which was basically a sanding pad on a long handle, but which would save her from trying to do the whole thing on her hands and knees; and tack cloths, whatever they were.

She wandered from one website to the next, learning such useful trivia as the fact that oil-based polyurethane finishes had been around for over seventy years and had first been developed for bowling alleys. In that case, it should be more than sufficient to protect her floor, which received far less wear and tear than a bowling alley.

Meg rolled her shoulders to loosen them and realized she was exhausted. It had been a busy day, and tomorrow promised to be as well. She had a class on Tuesday and hadn't yet managed to finish the reading. She should go to bed and get a fresh start in the morning. But as she sat staring at her computer screen, she found herself thinking about Jason's death. Perversely, she admitted to herself, she wanted to know how long it might have taken Jason to die. Daphne had said that he was fine at midnight when she'd last seen him. How long would he have been able to function after he was given—or took—the poison?

She typed in "methidathion" in her search engine and waited for results. She was rewarded with a wealth of information, and it wasn't pretty. Symptoms: headache, dizziness, blurred vision, anxiety, restlessness, weakness, nausea, cramps, sweating, salivation, runny nose, teary eyes, twitching, confused or bizarre behavior, convulsions, coma. Something for everyone on that list. But how long would it take to act? She scrolled through pages. Finally she found a brief mention buried in the midst of a long list of warnings and disclaimers: symptoms develop within twelve hours, and more likely within four. That fit what she knew, especially if it had been a large dose. She printed out the most succinct of the warning pages, because she wanted to study it more closely.

Still, she knew the printout would not hold the answer to her other pressing question: why here? Even if Jason had been out of his head, it seemed unlikely that he would have gotten into his car and driven here, then climbed the hill and sat down and waited to die. He would have needed help—but who?

With a sigh she logged off and shut down her computer, closing the lid with a click—no need to clog it up with sawdust. She would get up early tomorrow and buy the materials she needed, and she would start the long process of finishing her floor. And try to put the image of a writhing, vomiting Jason out of her head.

"Come on, Lolly—bedtime." The cat raced past her as Meg made her way slowly up the stairs.

23

 Meg had just entered the home improvement store yet again when the ringing of her cell phone stopped her.

It was Christopher. "Ah, my dear, I'm so glad I caught you. I know this is short notice, but there's to be a press announcement of sorts late this afternoon about the new building, followed by a small reception. I thought you might like to join us."

"That was fast!" Meg ticked off the items on her to-do list: buy floor-finishing products, finish floor, avoid walking on floor for the next twenty-four hours. She could do all that and still make it to the function at the university, and in fact she was curious to hear what the spin would be. All she had to do was manage to apply one coat of polyurethane to her naked floor before heading over to the university. That couldn't take too long, could it? "Sure, I'd be delighted. What time?"

"Four o'clock. I believe they hope for some local television coverage. And then cocktails to follow. As DeBroCo is footing the bill, I daresay the food will prove superior to the usual university offerings. I'll look forward to seeing you then." He rang off quickly.

Meg had loaded a shopping cart with tools and buckets of polyurethane, and was trying to maneuver the cart toward the checkout line when her cell phone rang yet again. She retrieved it from her pocket: Rachel.

"Hi, Rachel. What's up?"

"Seth tells me that you're refinishing your kitchen floor and need a place to stay."

Did Seth really think she was so helpless? "I think he's exaggerating a bit. Yes, I'm doing the floor, but I told him I was fine. After all, I have my trusty microwave, so I don't really need the kitchen."

"Oh." Rachel sounded disappointed. "Well, why not come anyway? Noah's away at a conference, and I don't have anyone booked for the B and B. We can have a girls' night, at least after I've put the kids to bed. Please?"

Meg recalled that she was going to be in Amherst anyway for the reception, and she had a class there the next morning. Why not? "Okay. But I've got this thing over on campus, and I'm not sure when that'll let out."

"You're going to the press conference?"

"Yes, Christopher asked me. How do you know about it?"

"I have my sources. Come on over whenever you break loose. I'll feed the kids early to free us up."

"Okay, sounds good." One more thing to add to her list: pack overnight stuff. Meg sighed.

Back at the house after her errands, she read the instructions on the polyurethane container dubiously. The manufacturers made it all sound easy, but she knew from experience that things were seldom as simple as they first appeared. Still, worst case: she could just strip off whatever she laid down and start all over again.

Lolly trotted down the stairs and wound around her ankles, and Meg reached down to scratch her head. "You can't be hungry again, can you?" But Meg realized that before she plunged into the project, she needed to remove some things from the kitchen—starting with the microwave and cat food. And something to drink out of and eat off of. And something to clean up after her inevitable spills. And if she didn't get started soon, there was no way she would be finished in time to clean herself up and make it to the reception in Amherst.

Two hours later she stood on the kitchen threshold admiring her efforts. The floor gleamed, in part because it was still wet, but also because the finish had brought out the rich golden tones of the old wood and the new gloss intensified them. Applying the polyurethane had in fact been as easy as its can claimed, once Meg had learned to be patient and take her time spreading it around, to avoid bubbles. Maybe for once something would work right the first time. She felt ridiculously proud of herself.

She was checking her watch when she noticed Lolly approaching cautiously, evidently put off by the strong odor but curious nonetheless. Meg stepped in front of her to block her and quickly closed the door behind her. "Sorry, cat—I don't want little paw prints all over my nice shiny floor." Leaving the cat sniffing the crack beneath the door in fascination, she hurried upstairs to pack, shower, and change clothes.

Standing in front of her cramped closet, contemplating her meager wardrobe, Meg wondered what she was supposed to wear to a press conference. Would there in fact be press there? That suggested something a cut above blue jeans. But why should she care? Christopher had invited her as a courtesy, and she was merely an interested observer. In the end she pulled out a pair of dark pants and a sweater—it was still cold, whatever the calendar said, and the IPM Department was not generous with heating their building. She threw a nightgown, toiletries, and some clothes for the next day into a bag, shrugged on a jacket, and went back downstairs to set out a full dish of food for Lolly.

She arrived at the university in time to find a parking space vacated by a departing day student, and made her way to the Life Sciences Building. A hastily scribbled sign tacked on the bulletin board near the entrance directed her to the largest lecture hall on the ground floor, where she found several camera crews already set up. Apparently DeBroCo Pharmaceuticals had a very effective public relations team to get the word out so quickly and to garner press attention. And maybe the abruptness of the event had forestalled the appearance of any Green-Grow protesters. At the moment the members of the press outnumbered spectators, but that wouldn't show on camera. Meg found a seat a few rows from the front and settled in to watch the action.

At precisely four o'clock, Christopher, his face beaming, approached the podium and tapped the microphone. "Friends and colleagues, I am delighted to see you here on this auspicious occasion. I have the great pleasure of announcing a new collaborative venture for the university and this department . . ." His enthusiasm was evident, and Meg was happy for him. From her online snooping she recognized Anson Kurtz, vice president for public relations for DeBroCo, immaculate in his well-tailored gray suit, standing behind Christopher. After a few more remarks, Christopher turned the microphone over to Kurtz.

Meg's mind wandered as Kurtz worked his way through the standard corporate boilerplate. Chemical giant, friend of the farmer. He certainly did not raise the specter of his products' demonstrated toxicity and the resultant lawsuits, but why would he? This was a feel-good moment that would polish DeBroCo's public image in exchange for a relatively small capital outlay. And that was how business was done. A year earlier Meg would have paid little attention, but now, with an orchard to run, it mattered to her. Was this an alliance with the devil?

When Christopher wrapped up the formal presentation and the news folk began packing up their equipment, she stood up and hesitated. Christopher noticed from where he stood, and nodded toward the side door. Meg guessed that he was directing her toward the reception, so she nodded in reply and made her way through the door and down the hall, following the sound of clinking glasses and the good smells emanating from a smaller lecture hall farther along the corridor.

She was happily surprised when she arrived at the room. DeBroCo had laid out a pretty penny for this spread. No shabby potluck, this. Why? Meg wondered idly as she filled a plate with smoked salmon and some tasty-looking puff-pastry hors d'oeuvres. Why would it be important to the company to woo the lowly assistant professors, lab techs, and graduate students? She wasn't going to pass up the treats, but something about the whole package made her uncomfortable. It was all too slick, and too calculated.

As she juggled canapés and a glass of white wine, she considered what had been said—and not said. The company stood to gain a high-profile, respectable partner in the university and could point to its efforts to be a good friend to the farmers. There was nothing wrong with that as a corporate strategy—it happened all the time. De-BroCo recognized that it needed to repair its public image, so this was a reasonable expense. Did that mean the cooperative effort with the university was a bad idea? Not necessarily, and the company would make sure that it was successful—at least for a while.

Meg smiled at Christopher on the other side of the room. He raised a hand without interrupting a spirited conversation with his colleagues, so she headed for the door. As she passed through the long and now-quiet corridor, one small question nagged at her: had GreenGrow known about this project, and publicly opposed it? If they had, would their opposition have had any noticeable impact? She shook herself. Time to go to Rachel's and have some cheerful conversation with a friendly human being—one with no hidden agendas.

24

Rachel's Victorian home—and bed and breakfast—beckoned through the gathering dusk. Meg parked at the side of the house, pausing to admire its frilly gingerbread and warmly glowing windows, and went around to the kitchen door, which was unlocked. Rachel wouldn't have heard anything as quiet as a knock, immersed as she was with marshaling her two children to clean up the kitchen table so that they could start their homework. She looked up when Meg walked in.

"Hi! That was fast."

Meg dropped her overnight bag by the door. "The bigwigs were still busy patting each other on the back, and I'd tried all the hors d'oeuvres, so I figured it was time to leave."

"You can tell me all about it as soon as I get these two sorted out. Chloe, please put that plate in the sink. Matthew, you get a sponge and wipe off the table. No, now! And say hello to Meg."

"Hi, Meg," the kids mumbled dutifully in unison.

"There's a humongous casserole in the oven, and there's bread and salad on the dining room table. You want something to drink? Wine?"

"Whatever you're having is fine."

While Rachel bustled around, putting some things away and removing other things from the refrigerator and cupboards, Meg studied the kitchen, wondering what elements she could use in her own. Not much, apparently—Rachel's house boasted high ceilings and large windows, which left little room for cupboards. But the adjacent walk-in pantry more than compensated. Rachel's floor was covered with a modern, neutrally patterned vinyl, designed to hide dirt. Meg thought briefly of her shining floor and felt absurdly pleased.

Rachel opened the oven door and pulled out the bubbling casserole, setting it on the stove top. "There. Let's see, is that everything? Meg, can you grab the, uh, plates, napkins, and wine bottle? Then we can clear out and let these two get down to work. You hear me?"

"Yeah, Mom."

Meg picked up the requested items and followed Rachel into the darker, quieter dining room. Rachel deposited the casserole dish on a trivet on the table and dropped into a chair with a sigh of relief. "There, done. Help yourself—we aren't formal around here. And then you can tell me all about the big press conference."

Meg took a plate and dished up casserole—a yummy-smelling concoction involving chicken and mushrooms—added salad, and sat down gratefully.

Rachel leaned forward and filled her own plate. "So, give me all the dirt. Shiny new building on campus, big boost to the agricultural programs. What's the real story?"

"Good PR, for a start. They had all the major local networks there. But I wouldn't expect less from a big company like DeBroCo. You want what they said, or what they didn't say?"

Rachel chewed vigorously. "The second, please. The rest I can read in the paper."

Meg sipped her wine before answering. "I did a little Internet digging about them when I first heard about the deal. They've been getting a lot of flack about some of their products—inadequate labeling, cutting corners in the testing, maybe even concealing test results. Probably typical of the stuff that kind of company faces all the time, but DeBroCo's gotten a lot of negative publicity. I think they see this as a good opportunity for them to mend some fences and to come out looking like the good guys."

"Are you saying they aren't?"

"Good guys? I don't know. I don't think they're any worse than any big company in the business."

"But?" Rachel stopped eating for a moment to look at Meg.

Meg shrugged, and picked up a forkful of salad. "There is no but, really. It just felt wrong, somehow—too calculating."

"Well, that's why you left the big, bad business world, right? All those jerks in suits."

"In part. But that doesn't mean the company is rotten or the deal is bad. And I trust that Christopher and the university know what they're doing. Certainly better than I do."

"And Christopher gets to keep working with your orchard, and the university gets a nice gift, and all's right with the world. Right?"

"I guess." Meg hesitated for a moment before adding, "The police have decided that Jason was poisoned with a pesticide."

Rachel sat back in her chair. "Damn! That's too bad. Do they have any suspects?"

"Not that I know of, but it's not like they would tell me anyway. I wondered if DeBroCo had tried to eliminate him, but that seems ridiculous."

Rachel speared a few more pieces of chicken from the

casserole. "I agree. Face it, Jason was small potatoes, strictly local. He was more bluster than bite, and most people around here knew it, including the members of the press. At worst he was an annoyance, but I can't see a big company going to the trouble of taking him out. You think they would hire a hit man? Where are they based, New Jersey?"

Meg smiled in spite of herself. "Delaware. And that's pretty much my conclusion—why would they bother? It's just so frustrating that the police aren't making any progress. Okay, Jason was irritating, but who wanted him dead? Do you know, so far I haven't found anyone around here who even liked him, unless you count his would-be girlfriend, and from what other people have told me, he barely noticed her. Even Michael, who was his friend and partner, was getting tired of him. Sad commentary, isn't it? To leave the world without anyone to mourn for you?"

"Let's hope his parents loved him, at least. Meg, are you getting depressed sitting in that house of yours, or are you sniffing too much solvent from your floor finishing? Because you are sounding a little odd."

"Gee, thanks. And, no, I read the instructions for the polyurethane very thoroughly and provided adequate ventilation. As for depressed—who has time? I have a cat, and now I have two goats to feed, thanks to your softhearted brother. And I can drive a tractor! There's one achievement I never expected."

"Okay, I'll believe you, for now."

"But Jason is still dead, and I just think that somebody should care. And I'd like to know who did it, so I don't have to worry about it anymore."

"Fair enough. I would, too, if I were in your shoes. But what are you going to do about it?"

"I don't know. The easiest thing to do would be to just stay out of it." Meg stopped abruptly.

Rachel snorted with laughter. "Don't be ridiculous. You found the body, in your own backyard, literally. Of course you want to know what happened. Just don't drive yourself nuts, okay? Excuse me while I go check on the kids and make sure they're getting something done."

Rachel stood up and went through the swinging door to the kitchen, where Meg heard her barking orders to the kids. She could pick out the word "bath" and heated protests from Chloe and Matthew, and then she heard the thunder of reluctant young feet stomping up the back stairs. Meg stood up and drifted around the room, admiring the ornate Victorian sideboard filled with mismatched china and the opulent dark wallpaper with clusters of anonymous fruits. Everything was handsome and fit together well, but truthfully Meg preferred the cleaner, simpler lines of her own house. She wondered what she was going to do about buying furniture. The orphaned junk the tenants had left behind was not even worth considering, and she didn't have much of her own to show for her years of apartment living. She was going to need something to sit on and something to put things in, but her budget was already strained and she still needed to buy new kitchen appliances. If it wasn't one thing, it was another. Maybe she could start growing her own vegetables to save a little money? Surely there would've once been a vegetable plot somewhere near the house—she'd have to go looking for it. And she could can and pickle and . . . whatever it was people had done in the old days.

Rachel returned. "Well, they're upstairs and they say they're going to take their baths, but if I don't hear running water soon, I'll have to go prod them. Okay: more wine or ice cream now?"

Meg considered. The only journey she had before her at the moment was up the stairs. "One more glass?"

"Done." Rachel tipped the wine bottle over Meg's glass, then refilled her own. "Do you know, I can't remember the last intelligent conversation I've had with a friend? I talk to the kids, I talk to Noah, sure. I talk to the guests, but they don't stick around for dinner, and I don't want to be pushy if they're here on vacation. But because I do have guests often, it's hard for me to join other organizations or just go out, beyond the essentials like PTA meetings. So this is a real treat for me, Meg."

"Thank you. I can't tell you how much it means to me to have a friend around here."

Rachel waved an airy hand. "You'll make friends. Just give it time. You're still the new kid. So you want to discuss world peace, or which movie star is sleeping with someone else's husband, or something closer to home?"

"Like where to get a deal on a new refrigerator?"

"Ask Seth. He'll know."

"He always does. He knows everybody. I can't imagine being that connected anywhere."

"Look, there's a downside to living in one place all your life. Everybody knows your business, and your parents' and your grandparents'. Sometimes you can get claustrophobic, if you know what I mean."

"Maybe. But I lived in Boston for years and I didn't even know the names of the other people in my apartment building. There were a lot of people around all the time, but it was easy to feel lonely. I suppose that was one reason why it was so easy to leave. So I'm still learning about how this place works."

Rachel swirled her wine in her glass, watching the whirlpool. "Listen, Meg, about Seth . . ."

Meg tensed. "Uh-huh," she said neutrally.

Rachel must have noticed her response, because she looked up and grinned at her. "No, it's nothing bad. I just didn't want you to get the wrong idea, and I mean that in a good way. Sure, Seth's Mr. Nice Guy, always helping everybody out. But he's gone an extra mile for you. Look, it's none of my business, but I know he likes you."

Meg suddenly felt nervous. "Wait—before you go any further, Seth is a good friend and neighbor, and a business partner of sorts. But I'm not at a point where I can deal with anything more than that right now."

Rachel was watching her. "I'm sorry, I didn't mean to make you uncomfortable. I'll stop. And Seth didn't ask me to play go-between. It's just that I'm happy with my life, with my husband and kids, and I want to see other people happy, too, and I love Seth, and I've been worried for him ever since his divorce, and . . ."

"I get the picture, Rachel. But give me a little time, will you? I've been here, what, a few months? And in that time I've had an awful lot to deal with, not even including trying to learn how to run an orchard when I usually have trouble keeping an African violet alive, and working hard to keep my house from falling down around my ears. I guess what I'm saying is, I really don't have the time or energy to even think about anything like a relationship at the moment. I can promise you that when I do, I'll put Seth on my short list, okay?"

"Good enough. I'll shut up. So, ready for ice cream now?"

Later, full of three flavors of ice cream and tucked into one of Rachel's delightfully frilly guest rooms, Meg thought back on Rachel's comments about Seth. Meg meant what she had said: after all of the recent upheavals in her life, she had no energy left to give to a relationship. No matter how nice it felt to have someone watching out for her, no matter how good it felt to have someone's arms around her. *No, Meg, stop right there.* Right now she needed friends, and she needed to get her life together. She still didn't know if she could manage to make a living from the orchard, and she was painfully aware of how little she knew about agriculture in general. She was forced to rely on others, like Christopher and Bree, and hope they knew what they were doing. The whole situation was unsettling. She couldn't deal with everything at once. So she just did what she could to keep moving forward.

Maybe having the house to work on was a good thing. There were specific, concrete tasks she could tackle, with real results. Like the kitchen floor. It had looked so good that afternoon, clean and fresh, gleaming with its first coat of finish. She couldn't wait to see it when she was done, and then she would get to enjoy the results each and every day.

She fell asleep thinking of the kitchen floor.

25

 When Meg woke up, the sun was shining, and all she really wanted to do was get back to the house and see how her kitchen floor looked in the morning light—and whether the finish was dry enough to sand. But she had a class to go to, so the floor would have to wait. Just as well—it hadn't had a full twenty-four hours to dry yet. She checked her watch: six thirty. Early still, but she could hear sounds coming from the kitchen, including childish voices. What time did school start these days?

She showered, pulled on a clean shirt and jeans, and made her way downstairs. Rachel was coordinating a scene of controlled chaos. "Eat your oatmeal, Matthew. I'm not driving you to school just because you don't like the stuff. It's good for you. Chloe, please put on a sweater. I don't care how trendy that top is—you've already got goose bumps and you haven't even left the house. Hi, Meg—grab yourself a cup of coffee."

Meg followed instructions and then stayed out of the

way while Rachel orchestrated the children's departure. When the door shut behind them, Rachel filled another mug for herself. "I can't understand why we go through the same arguments each and every morning. And they aren't even teenagers yet!" She dropped into a chair across from Meg. "You're up early."

"I woke up thinking about checking out the floor while there was natural light in the kitchen, but then I remembered I've got class this morning."

"I can't wait to see the results. I would've gone that route with this floor here, but it's crappy subflooring, and we get far too much traffic in here anyway. This stuff is tough and easy to keep clean. But I'm still jealous."

"Really? I've still got to find new appliances and cupboards and all that stuff. And I gather none of that is cheap. Last time I was at the home store, I was looking at refrigerators, and they were going for well over a thousand dollars."

Rachel waved a dismissive hand. "That's if you want all the bells and whistles, like in-door ice cube dispensers. You don't have to spend that much for a plain vanilla model. You'll find something you can afford."

They chatted amiably while Meg nibbled on Rachel's memorable muffins, and by eight she was ready to hit the road. She sat through her class, then drove home on autopilot, her mind reviewing lists: check if the floor was dry. Sandpaper? Did she have the right grit? Could she do it with a pole sander, or was she going to have to get down on her hands and knees and go over it by hand? How much sanding was enough? Too much? What was she supposed to mop with to get rid of the dust from the sanding?

She was surprised how quickly she arrived at her own driveway—and surprised to see two other cars parked there. One was Bree's, but she didn't recognize the other one. She let herself in the front door and was greeted by an annoyed Lolly. "Hello?" she called out as she knelt to rub Lolly's head. She hung up her coat on the stand in the hall, then walked through to the dining room. Lolly's dish was half-full of fresh food, so Bree must have fed her. Was Lolly complaining about still being banned from the kitchen, or was she annoyed about having someone else in the house? "Bree? You upstairs?" She scooped up Lolly, then cautiously opened the door to the kitchen, knelt down, and felt the floor. The surface felt completely dry, and the satin polyurethane looked even and smooth. *Well done, Meg!* Lolly was squirming in her arms, so she shut the door again and put the cat down. Time to change clothes and get back to working on the floor. Maybe she could even press Bree into service—two hands would make things go a lot faster.

She was near the foot of the stairs when she saw Bree coming down. And she wasn't alone: behind her trailed Michael, barefoot. When she spotted Meg, Bree raised her chin defiantly; Michael looked sheepish and uncertain. Meg stifled a laugh, although she felt a twinge of concern. She was unaccustomed to having a roommate, at least in recent years, and she and Bree had never discussed issues such as "gentleman callers." Not that she had any moral objections, though it might be a good idea to set a few guidelines. But Michael? That was a surprise.

"Hi, Bree, Michael. Have you guys eaten?" A lame question, but safe.

"No, we were about to go out and find something. I didn't want to mess with the kitchen. Floor looks good." Bree relaxed slightly, now that the first awkward moment had passed.

"Thanks. I've got to sand it down and put on a second coat this afternoon. Did you have plans for today in the orchard?"

"Professor Ramsdell said he was coming by later, and I need to talk with him. Why, do you want some help with the floor?"

"If you've got the time. Why don't you two go find

some food, and I'll get set up here. Nice to see you again, Michael."

Michael was sitting on the stairs pulling on his shoes, and he mumbled something, avoiding her eyes. Meg, feeling old, went back to the dining room to inventory her supplies. She heard the door slam as they left, heard two cars start up. She went up the stairs to change into work clothes, thinking hard. Bree and Michael: how long had that been going on? More specifically, had they been involved—if that was what they were—before Jason's death? Did it matter? Bree had made it clear that she'd had no interest in Jason, but how would Jason have felt about Bree and Michael together? Would he have been ticked off? And what might he have done about it?

Not that Bree's love life was any of her business, but Meg was going to have to ask her about it.

She shut Lolly in the front parlor, propped open the doors to the kitchen, opened the windows wide, put on her dust mask, and was down on her knees sanding when she heard Bree's car return. She stood up and dusted herself off, and went to intercept Bree in the front hall. "Hi."

"Listen, I didn't mean—" Bree began abruptly.

Meg stopped her. "Bree, don't worry about it. I'm not your mother, you're an adult, and you're free to do whatever you want. If you want to have guests, that's your business." Meg hesitated a moment. "I was just kind of surprised to see Michael."

To her surprise, Bree looked almost shy. "Yeah, well, it's kind of new. I mean, I haven't had much to do with the whole GreenGrow crowd again until recently, you know? Trying to stay away from Jason in particular. And I guess I assumed that Michael would be a lot like Jason, since they were friends. But he's not. He's really nice, and a lot less pushy. So we just sort of connected."

Meg interrupted. "Was it before . . . ?"

"Before Jason died? Yeah."

One more question. "Did Jason know?"

Bree shook her head. "I don't think so. Like I said, I stayed away from GreenGrow, so Michael and I went other places. Anyway, sorry if I should have asked you before bringing Michael here; I lived with my auntie growing up, and she was pretty strict, and then I've been living in a dorm, where nobody much cares what you do as long as you don't burn the place down. So I'm not sure what the rules are, you know?"

"I know. I'm new to this, too. But it doesn't have to be a problem. And Michael seems like a good guy." Meg squashed the thought that if Jason had known about Bree and Michael, Jason might have done something about it. But what? Started a fight with Michael? Killed himself in despair? "Look, I want to get the floor sanded down so I can put on another coat of finish before it gets dark. Can you help me with that? This round of sanding is just to smooth out the bubbles and whatever fuzz got stuck in the finish, not to mention cat hair. I'm sure there's plenty of that. And then we can talk to Christopher."

"Sounds good to me. You got sandpaper?"

They were about halfway through the sanding process, working in different corners of the room, when Bree spoke up. "Hey, listen, what's going on with you and Seth?"

"What?" Meg bristled, but then she realized that if she had a right to talk about Bree's visitors, Bree probably had a fair claim to ask about hers. Seth was around a lot. "Well, you know, he's using the shop for his new office. And he's been helping me with other stuff about the house."

"Yeah, but is that all?"

"We're friends."

"Okay. I just didn't want to say anything stupid. It's cool."

Gee, thanks, Meg thought. *Time to change the subject.* "I think we're just about done with the sanding. Let me run a tack cloth over the floor and then the buffer. Thanks for helping. I think applying the finish is a one-person job."

Bree stood up and brushed off her pants. "It's looking great. Listen, Meg, I'm glad you're okay about Michael. I don't know if it's going anywhere, but we'll see. And I didn't mean to be pushy about you and Seth."

"That's okay. If we're living under one roof, you have a right to know what's going on, too. Let me get this finished up, and by then Christopher should be here."

As Meg mopped, buffed, and spread finish, she turned over in her mind what she had heard—and not heard—at the press conference the day before. She hadn't had time to watch the news or to read the morning paper, but she could guess what the local press would say. The announcement of the new project following hard on the heels of Jason's death troubled her. She was going to have to lay some of these demons to rest, assuming the state police didn't manage to do it. What the heck were they doing, anyway?

With a second coat of finish applied, Meg carefully closed the door to the kitchen and went upstairs to change yet again. From the front bedroom she spotted the U-Mass van pass by, so she hurried into her clothes, found her coat and keys downstairs, and went out to meet Christopher in the orchard.

He greeted her happily. "Meg, I'm so glad to see you. You left quite quickly last evening, and we didn't have a chance to chat."

"I thought you and the corporate types would have more than enough to talk about."

"Ah, Meg, you sound a bit jaded. So you weren't impressed by the fuss and feathers?"

Meg shrugged, not sure how far she wanted to go. "Christopher, are you sure this is on the up-and-up? I mean, is this just a nice PR stunt for DeBroCo, and in a year or two there'll be some mysterious construction delays or the university will decide it wants to move in a different direction?"

Christopher looked at her with something like sadness

before he answered. "I can see how it might look to you, but in fact we have been negotiating this agreement for quite a while. Multimillion dollar agreements do not happen overnight, as I'm sure you know. They first approached us about two years ago. And I'd like to think that DeBroCo is a responsible and forward-looking partner. They have been aware of the shortcomings of various pesticide approaches for some time, and they have chosen to be proactive in their approach—hence this new collaboration. Does that ease your mind?"

She backpedaled quickly. "Christopher, I'm sorry. I don't mean to question your professional judgment or the university's motives. I'm sure it's a good deal all around. It's the timing that bothers me—that Jason died just as this new project is announced."

He searched her face, and gradually his expression softened. "Jason would have had no impact on the outcome—he simply wasn't important enough, although he might have believed otherwise. But regrettably, that unfortunate young man is creating as much trouble dead as he did in life."

Isn't that the truth? Meg thought.

26

Bree and Christopher headed back to campus, and Meg tried to decide what to tackle next. She was reluctant to take the tractor out by herself just yet; she wanted a few more practice runs under Bree's tutelage. The floor would take a day to dry, so there was nothing more to be done there, and she didn't want to risk other renovations stirring up dust that might mess up the floor. She had learned from experience that the doors and windows and, for all she knew, even the walls of the old house were not precisely airtight, and dust and odors migrated freely through the house.

She realized there was one thing she hadn't scheduled yet: a vet appointment for the cat. Who knew what nasty bugs or parasites Lolly might have picked up when she was fending for herself in the wild? Though she had never owned a pet before, Meg had a vague idea that there were shots that cats were supposed to have, and she really ought to find out whether Lolly had been spayed. And what would this cost? One more bill she hadn't anticipated.

Did the goats need any medical attention? Was she going to keep the goats? If she was, she needed to name them: Smaller Goat and Larger Goat were not going to work for long.

Seth had recommended a vet, and Meg recalled that it was a woman, but the name had slipped her mind. No way was she going to call him to ask such a simple question—she could figure this out on her own. A quick check of the phone book showed that there was only one who fit the bill within ten miles. Meg dialed and spoke with the harried receptionist.

"Hi, I'm Meg Corey over in Granford, and I recently inherited a cat and wanted to get her looked over. Can I—"

Before she could finish the sentence, the woman on the other end snapped, "We've got a cancellation. Can you be here in an hour?"

"Uh, sure, I guess."

"Great. You're Corey. Cat's name?"

"Lavinia."

"See you then." The woman hung up without saying good-bye.

Meg was left staring at the phone. She figured it would take half an hour to get there, which left her time to find a map on the computer, and to find some sort of carrying container for Lolly. Meg had an ominous feeling that the cat wouldn't like that part. Slowly she climbed the stairs in search of a box that Lolly wouldn't manage to claw her way through in the time it took to drive to the vet's.

Half an hour later she was on the road, and the cat's yowls from the box had subsided to the occasional low growl. She managed to find the vet's office with only one wrong turn, and she struggled to extricate the box containing Lolly from the front seat, without jostling the poor cat too much. "Sorry, sweetie, but I have to do this. It'll be over soon." Lolly did not bother to comment. Meg wondered how long it would take the cat to forgive her for such rude handling. Still, she would rather put up with short-term hostility than risk losing Lolly to rabies or distemper or whatever other ailment was making the feline rounds.

Inside, Meg was relieved to find the waiting room empty except for a woman about her age wearing a slightly soiled blue jacket, talking to the receptionist. "I wish you'd asked me first, that's all. This is the last appointment of the day, right?"

"You were busy, and I figured it didn't matter if I dropped someone into that empty slot." The receptionist, her plump face florid beneath a frizz of blondish hair, didn't look at all intimidated by the doctor's comment, and from the look on the doctor's face, this wasn't a new argument. They both saw Meg at the same time, alerted by Lolly's renewed complaints. The doctor smiled and walked toward her. "Hi. You must be, uh—we didn't get your first name, but you're the three o'clock? With Lavinia?"

"That's me. I'm Meg. I take it you're the vet?"

"Yup. I'm Andrea Bedortha. Come on back and we can exchange all the details. Vivian, can I have a patient record form, please?"

Vivian slammed a clipboard down on the counter, and Andrea smiled sweetly at her and took it. "Thank you, Vivian. Follow me, Meg."

Andrea led the way down a narrow corridor, with Meg following behind, carrying Lolly's box. "Interesting surname, Bedortha. Where's it from?" Meg asked over the cat's complaints. The neutral linoleum was threaded with claw marks, and a faint smell of urine lingered in the air.

"Right around here, in fact—mainly Springfield. Goes back to the seventeenth century." The doctor opened a door and gestured her in, closing the door behind them. "Meg, why don't you let the cat—Lavinia, is it?—out of the box so she can calm down a bit while we talk. That should make things easier for everyone."

"Okay," Meg said dubiously. "By the way, I call her

Lolly—Lavinia's the official name." She placed the box on the floor and opened the top flaps, and Lolly sprang out, gave her a baleful glare, stopped for a moment to wash a particularly critical spot on her flank, then started to prowl around the room, ignoring the people in it.

Andrea gestured toward a plastic-covered chair. "Sit. She'll be fine. Had her long?"

"No, only a week or so. She kind of showed up one day and adopted me. Seth said he thought he recognized her as one of the neighbors' cats and said they'd left town. I can't imagine just abandoning a pet like that, but here she is."

"Seth Chapin?"

"Yes. He's my next-door neighbor, and my plumber, and he's going to be moving his office into my annex shortly, and . . ."

Andrea laughed. "That's Seth, all right. So you're *that* Meg."

Meg wondered which stories Andrea had heard about her, and from whom. "How do you know Seth?"

"We met when he and the other selectmen organized a one-day public rabies clinic in Granford a couple of years ago. But he's been trying to convince me to set up shop in that new development you all are building."

"You work alone here?"

"No, it's a partnership, and I'm junior, so I get a lot of the boring or messy stuff, lousy hours, that kind of thing. But no way could I afford to start off solo until I pay off my vet school bills. Seth's idea is that we can establish a satellite office in Granford now, and after I've pulled in enough clients in a year or two, I can take it over on my own. I'm still thinking about it. You like living in Granford?"

"I've only been there a few months, but I like the people, and I'm trying to make a go of it with an orchard. I'll give it a couple of years, I guess. Seems like it would be a nice place to work, assuming there are enough pets to keep you busy."

"Oh, I handle my share of farm animals, too."

"Then remind me to ask you about my goats."

Andrea cocked her head. "You don't look like a goat type to me."

Meg smiled. "Another one of Seth's bright ideas. Someone was getting rid of them, and he thought they'd be a nice addition to my farm. I know next to nothing about goats."

"Don't worry, I can give you some literature. Why don't we take a look at your cat first?" Andrea leaned over in her chair and snapped her fingers near the floor. Lolly came running immediately and began rubbing against Andrea's chair leg.

"I guess she's calmed down," Meg said. "What now?"

Andrea picked Lolly up and cuddled her against her chest, carrying her to the steel-topped exam table, murmuring soothingly. She set the cat on the table, keeping one hand on Lolly's back, and Meg could almost see the cat shrug and accept the inevitable.

"So you have no history at all on her, I assume," Andrea asked as she ran her hands over the cat. "Hang on a sec and let me check something." She picked up the phone on the wall, punched a button, then said, "Vivian, can you pull a record for Pendergast in Granford? They had a cat, came in last year sometime. Yes, now, please." She hung up and turned to Meg. "That woman is going to drive me nuts. We'd replace her, but I don't think we'll find anybody else for what we pay. Okay, for the cat, if we were starting from scratch, you'd need FHV1, FCV, FPV, and rabies."

"Uh, if you say so. Could you translate that into English?"

"In simple terms, that's feline herpes, feline calicivirus, feline panleukopenia, and the rabies you should know—that's the core group. There are some others, like feline leukemia, feline immunodeficiency, but those are optional. The good news is, I can tell she's already been spayed. But she did pick up some fleas."

They were interrupted by a knock on the door. "Can you get that, Meg? I'll hang on to the cat."

Meg opened the door, and Vivian shoved a folder at her through the crack. "Here. You about done in there?"

"Just a few more minutes, Vivian," Andrea said. When the door closed, she sighed. "That woman . . . Here, I'll trade you. I'll take the file, and you can keep Lavinia— Lolly calm."

Meg approached Lolly cautiously, not sure of her welcome. The cat looked balefully at her, then decided not to protest when Meg stroked her back.

"Great, I thought so," Andrea said. "Seth was right: she's the Pendergasts' cat, and she was current on her vaccines as of six months ago. Wonder why they left her behind? Or maybe she really didn't want to go and jumped ship. Did you, lady?" Andrea scratched under Lolly's chin, and the cat closed her eyes in bliss. "So we don't have to do any more to you today, right, girl?" Andrea looked at Meg. "You want to know what the Pendergasts called her?"

"I suppose. I don't have to change her name back, do I?"

"Kitty. Original, right? You should be fine with Lolly. Or Lavinia—Emily's sister, right? The cat lover?"

Meg smiled. "You got it, except that Lavinia seems kind of formal, so mostly it's Lolly. So we're good?"

"We are. You can take her home. I'll give you a monthly treatment for the fleas—it's going to get worse when the weather warms up. You keeping her inside?"

"So far. Is that all right?"

"If you want to keep her around, I'd recommend it. It's a mean world out there if you're a house cat. She was lucky to find you. You want me to swing by sometime and take a look at the goats, maybe next week?"

"Sure, if it's not too far out of your way. I wouldn't have had a clue how to cart them over here."

"I'll walk you out. You owe me for a basic checkup, but no vaccines. And I'll give you a sample of the flea meds. You might want to get a cat carrier before the next visit."

"It's already on my list." Meg laughed.

Lolly was quiet on the trip home, to Meg's relief. Back at the house, Meg lugged the box to the front door and struggled with her keys. As soon as she opened the flaps, Lavinia jumped out and disappeared up the stairs. Having a pet was a whole new experience, and Meg didn't know what to expect. Still, she wasn't surprised when Lolly later reappeared at the sound of a cat-food tin popping open, and by evening, as Meg sat reading in her parlor, Lolly relented enough to sit on her lap, although she remained stingy with her purr.

27

Wednesday morning Meg finished applying the last coat of polyurethane to the kitchen floor and stepped back through the kitchen doorway to admire her work. She thought that for an amateur, she'd done a pretty good job. No sanding gouges, no bubbles or clots of sawdust. Maybe she'd finally gotten something right the first time around. Reluctantly she shut the door behind her. The floor needed time to dry, one last time. Maybe by tomorrow morning she could tiptoe across it in stockinged feet, but she couldn't move the table back in, or install appliances, until three days had passed, or so said the online experts she had consulted, and she didn't want to risk messing up what she had worked so hard to accomplish.

Thinking of appliances, Meg realized she needed to call Seth for advice. Her apartments had always come fully equipped, and she had given them little thought, except when they stopped working. Seth had promised to help out, and much as she wanted to do this on her own,

he was, after all, a plumber, and he had far more expertise than she did in choosing appliances—which wouldn't
be hard, since she had no experience at all. So even
though she knew how busy he was, and even though this
would put her even more deeply in debt to him, she didn't
see any way around it. She picked up the phone and dialed his number.

He picked up on the second ring. "Hi, Meg. What's
up?"

"You have a moment to talk? I need to ask you about
appliances."

"Oh, right—well, this afternoon's clear. Want to go
shopping?"

Meg laughed. "Seth, I never thought I'd hear that coming from a guy, but at least it involves machinery. Sure,
let's say one o'clock."

Seth arrived promptly at the front door at one. "Do I
get a preview of the floor?" he asked as he came in.

"Sure. Just look, don't touch."

"Yes, ma'am. I have done this a few times, you know."

"I know, but I haven't, and I'm playing by the rules."
Meg led the way to the kitchen and flung back the door.
"Voilà!"

Seth studied the floor for a moment. "Looks great.
Nice and even. You done good, lady. So, you ready for
appliances?"

"Stove and refrigerator, I guess. I think a dishwasher's
going to have to wait. And let's keep them simple. Or
maybe I mean cheap. This is another one of those 'extra'
items in my budget."

"Are you seriously short of money? Because—"

"Stop right there. I have to be careful with my money,
that's all. I can't go running around throwing money at
things I don't need."

"Don't worry—I can get you a good deal. And if it
makes you feel better about replacing it, that stove of
yours probably wasn't safe."

"Gee, thanks—just what I wanted to hear." Meg followed him out to his van and clambered into the high seat. She waited until they were on the road before asking, "Anything new about Jason's death?"

"Wish I could say yes. I talked to Art yesterday, but he hasn't got anything more than he told you. No big surprise there."

"You know, almost nobody seems to have liked Jason much, and everyone I've talked to seems relieved that he's out of the way. Isn't that a terrible way to go?"

" 'Any man's death diminishes me, because I am involved in mankind,' " Seth said, his eyes on the road.

"John Donne, isn't it?" When Seth nodded, Meg went on. "I guess that about describes it. Only this is smaller than all mankind—it's one closed community, in a way. The university, the farmers, the towns."

"I won't tell you that you shouldn't feel bad about his death. Jason may have been a jerk, but he didn't deserve to die."

Choking in his own vomit, alone in a field in the dark. Or maybe he hadn't been alone; maybe there had been a witness. Meg suppressed a shudder. "Amen to that. So let's talk about more cheerful things. What do I need to look for in a stove?"

"For a start, do you want gas or electric?"

"I don't know. What are the pros and cons?"

"Depends on how you like to cook. But if you go for gas, we'll have to run a line to the house. You've got an oil furnace. You do know that, right?"

"I guess. I figured it wasn't coal." When Seth cast a bemused glance her way, she said, "Joke. I know I've been paying someone or other for oil deliveries, although I can't say I've seen anyone come by." Meg thought a moment. "I assume it would cost me more money if I had to install a gas line?"

"I'm afraid so."

"Then let's go with electric."

Meg had expected Seth to lead her to a major store at a local mall, but instead he followed a two-lane country road for a few miles and pulled into the parking lot in front of what looked like a dilapidated warehouse. A peeling sign identified it as Anderson's Appliances. The parking lot was all but empty. "We are buying new, aren't we? This place looks like it hasn't done business in years."

"Trust me. Bob's a good guy, and I throw a lot of business his way. And he owns the building, so it keeps his overhead low. Come on."

Seth led Meg into a dim and somewhat dusty warehouse where appliances in varying shades of white, black, and stainless steel marched off into the distance. Bob said hello and then had the good sense to leave them alone, and an hour later they emerged from the drafty depths of the building with what Seth assured Meg was an excellent deal on a midprice stove and refrigerator. Meg's checkbook was seriously depleted, again, but she thought she was getting good value. Bob had guaranteed delivery on Saturday, and Seth had promised to come by on Sunday to move them into the kitchen—the extra day would give the finish on her floor a little more time to cure. Meg felt that at least she had made progress.

"Lolly's certainly been taking all this upheaval well," Meg said as she watched the fields roll by, the newly turned earth now showing hints of green. "How come you don't have a pet, Seth?"

"I did—a Golden Lab. Lost him a couple of years ago, and I just haven't met the right replacement yet."

"I thought you seemed like a dog person. Although I'm not sure I see myself as a cat person. You know, one of those crazy old ladies who lives alone and talks to her cat. Lolly and I are still getting used to each other, and all the noise and smells from this floor project haven't made that any easier."

"I thought she seemed remarkably well adjusted, all things considered. Cats are adaptable."

They drove on for a bit, and then Meg asked, "What's going into Granford Grange?"

"We haven't firmed up a lot yet. We're hoping for some sort of café, maybe a card shop. Or a gift shop. Or a bookstore. Or some combination of the above."

Meg laughed. "Yeah, sounds really organized. But you're not going after the major chains?"

"No. Too expensive, and the town's not really big enough for them. And that's fine with us. I'd like to see it keep a local feel. Maybe that's old-fashioned, but I like to know the people I'm dealing with."

"Hear, hear."

Seth pulled up to her house, and Meg hopped down from the van. Before she closed the door a thought struck her. "You think you'll have everything up and running Sunday morning?" she asked.

He smiled. "Since all that's involved is wrestling the appliances into place and plugging them in, I think so. And before you ask, yes, you do have the correct electric lines. I checked."

"Thank goodness you looked. I totally forgot. But what I was thinking was, maybe I could have a dinner party, sort of a christening for the new floor and appliances? There hasn't been a whole lot to celebrate lately."

"What, you can cook?"

"You've eaten my food and survived. And I'm told I make a mean spaghetti sauce."

"Sounds good to me. Sunday night?"

"Make it early. Say, sixish?"

"It's a deal. I'll bring some wine."

"Thanks. And thanks for the help." *Again.* She shut the van door and watched Seth pull away, all the while wondering if she would have gotten anything done in the last two months without his help. When she walked into the house, she found Lolly curled up in one of the old overstuffed chairs in the parlor; she opened one eye, then went back to sleep.

She had just volunteered to host a dinner party. How odd was that? Meg had almost never entertained when she was in Boston. It was so much easier to eat out in one of the many restaurants there. But that wasn't an option in Granford. She felt a momentary panic: what if the appliances didn't work? She didn't have enough plates or glasses or cutlery. Heck, she didn't have enough guests to call it a party. Who else should she ask? Christopher? Bree, certainly. Rachel? Gail? No, she seemed to recall that Gail had a husband and kids, which would just complicate things.

Half an hour later, she had left Christopher a message on his office phone, Rachel had told her she had two bookings for the B&B and couldn't get away, and Bree had agreed to come, then asked shyly if she could bring Michael, to which Meg had agreed promptly. It was coming together. She started jotting down a market list, then backed up and made a note to herself: inventory pots and pans.

She realized she was smiling. She could picture the dining room with its old woodwork gleaming in candlelight, the broad table set with china. Happy people, enjoying her food. Maybe she was her party-loving mother's daughter after all.

What *would* her mother make of all this? Certainly she hadn't foreseen Meg's decision to settle down in Granford, though Meg was still rather amazed that her mother hadn't already descended on her with a fistful of fabric swatches and paint samples in hand, once she'd heard Meg's plan to stay. But her mother didn't do country *or* winter—and maybe she realized that her daughter needed a little time to lick her wounds in private. But Meg had a suspicion that once the weather warmed up, Mom would put in an appearance.

In any event, the house deserved a housewarming, or maybe she meant a rewarming. It had survived neglect and abuse, and she wanted to welcome it into the twenty-first century with laughter and warmth.

28

Thursday passed in a blur. Meg dutifully attended her class in the morning. On her way she ran into Christopher, rushing in the opposite direction. He stopped when he saw her and said, "Thank you, my dear, for your kind invitation, but I fear I have a prior commitment. I hope I may look forward to a rain check?"

"Of course, Christopher. I'm sorry you'll miss my little party, but I certainly hope there will be more. I get the feeling that the house wants more people in it. It must have seen quite a history, when it was a more active farm."

"No doubt. And the kitchen would have been the heart of it, as at any farm. I'm glad you're working on that room now."

"It's turned out quite well, if I do say so myself. Although there's more work to be done, as always. I'd love to have you over sometime."

"That would be grand. Oh, and I needed to speak with

you anyway. I'm planning on spraying the orchard tomorrow morning, weather permitting. We had a small
problem with apple scab last season, and I'd like to ensure that it doesn't persist this year. We're using a fungi-
cidal spray, but if we act now we can minimize later
applications. I can explain in more detail in the morning,
but I thought you and Bree should be involved."

"I'll be there. Thanks for letting me know."

They went their separate ways, and as Meg walked
into the lecture hall, she felt pleased that Christopher had
included her in this task. It occurred to her that in fact,
she probably had some legal obligation to know what was
going on. She realized that she had forgotten to ask
Christopher what chemical they were using, but she
would find out in the morning. Maybe she could learn
something about apple scab, just to be prepared.

After class, on a whim she drove to Northampton,
where she knew Hampshire County public records were
kept. She was eager to find more information about her
property. The deeds might be interesting, but since she
already had a good idea of who had owned the property—
generations of the Warren family—Meg figured that
wills might give her some better insight into the actual
people who had occupied the house, what they owned,
how they lived. Wills it was, then.

She made her way through the security screening at
the door, then headed to the Registry of Probate on the
second floor. Posted instructions made it clear that Meg
would have to identify what wills she wanted by official
number, then request those documents from one of the
women behind the long counter. Next to the entrance
there were banks of old-fashioned card files—apparently
the earlier documents hadn't been put into a database yet.
She pulled out the first of the "W" drawers—and quickly
realized how daunting her task would be. There had been
a *lot* of Warrens in Granford over the centuries. Maybe
she should content herself doing a trial run and just re-

quest one. She riffled through the card files again and decided on Eli Warren's will; Eli had been a carpenter, and he'd done the last major remodeling of the house, more than a century earlier. Meg filled out the call slip and presented it to a clerk, who retrieved it in under two minutes, handing Meg a folded bundle of brown paper in a small manila sleeve.

Meg took her prize and went to the lone table, where she sat down and unfolded the brittle document with care. The will was dated 1892, and its handwritten script was easy to read. Eli had left his wife the right to use the house for the rest of her life, and he had divided the carpentry tools between two of his sons. A third son would inherit the house and land after his mother's death. That must have been Lula and Nettie's grandfather. Then as she read further, she came upon a section that made her laugh out loud, much to the surprise of the few other patrons in the office. She followed the lines with a careful finger, incredulous:

> *To my daughter Ellen I give the right to occupy and use during her lifetime two rooms in the dwelling house I now occupy with the right of ingress and egress to and from the same and the right to use the privy and well on the premises in common with the other occupants. She shall have the right to select the rooms for her occupation in case she and the other devisee of the premises or his representatives do not agree as to the rooms suited to her needs.*

Oh my. Father Eli had found it necessary to give his daughter the right to use the privy and water from the well. Which rooms had she chosen? Where had the privy been? And just how dysfunctional had the Warren family been that Ellen could have been banned from the privy without written permission? Alas, nothing else in the document was as interesting, and Meg returned it to the clerk with a smile.

Meg made a list of the other wills to check out when she had more time, and left with regret. Out on the sidewalk again, she found she was still cheered by the silliness of the will. She mused over the details as she drove to the supermarket outside of Granford to stock up on what she needed for her party. Food, obviously. She was going to stick to something safe and easy: spaghetti with homemade sauce, green salad, garlic bread, and for dessert, an apple crisp. She debated with herself for maybe three seconds about baking an apple pie, but she knew that rolling out piecrusts was not her strong suit, and it didn't seem right to buy ready-made crusts. Better to go with simple. She didn't expect to find local apples at this time of year, so long after harvest, so she'd have to make do with imported ones. Still, it was a symbolic gesture, a salute to her own crop to come.

Things to cook in and things to eat from were bigger issues. Big pots she had, although they were of dubious cleanliness, but she could remedy that. But as for the rest . . . Her mother would no doubt have had matched sets of everything on hand in sufficient numbers for a small invading army. Meg, in contrast, had a handful of mismatched plates, glasses, and cutlery inherited from who knew how many tenants who had come and gone—and left their unwanted things behind—and the few things Meg had brought from Boston. She could go with paper plates and plastic cups, but her mother's spirit sat on her shoulder and scolded her at the very idea. *Yes, Mom, you raised me better than that.* In the end she made a quick detour to the closest housewares store and picked up an inexpensive boxed set of china, and threw in a tablecloth, napkins, candles, and a few extra towels. This was her first party in her new home, and she wanted to make it nice. Meg felt the need to set the tone for her tenure in Granford, and paper plates shouted "temporary." That was not the message she wanted to send.

The next morning's weather looked encouraging, and Meg saw the university van approach the house and pull into her driveway. She was ready: she pulled on a warm jacket and headed outside, where she found Christopher supervising the unloading of a piece of apparatus she assumed was some sort of sprayer: a cylindrical tank on wheels.

He waved her over. "Good morning, my dear. The wind bids fair—or do I mean the opposite? We can't spray in a wind."

"Why are you down here, instead of up in the orchard?" Meg watched as Bree scrambled down from the back of the van, carrying a couple of reels of hoses.

Bree announced, "We have to fill the tank down here, where there's a water supply." She turned to Christopher. "You want me to mix?"

"If you would, my dear. You know your proportions?"

Bree snorted. "This isn't the first time I've done this, Professor." Bree turned away and headed toward a spigot on the side of the house that Meg hadn't even noticed before. Bree turned the handle, and nothing happened. "Professor? Looks like it's turned off."

"Of course—we shut it off for the winter. Meg, if you could let me into your house, I know where the shutoff valve is located. Unless you'd like to take care of it?"

"Heavens, no! I've been to the basement maybe twice, and it still creeps me out. You go right ahead." She opened the back door and let him in, and she could hear him tramping down the rickety cellar stairs. A moment later, the spigot started gushing water.

Christopher returned quickly, and Meg asked, "So what are you doing?"

"As I mentioned, today is our first spraying against apple scab. Are you familiar with that?"

"I checked it out on the Internet last night. Sounds nasty."

"It can be, and the best approach is prophylactic spraying, so we'll start today and return at intervals for the next few weeks, depending on how much rain we get that would wash away the spray. But you shouldn't be concerned. You have a good number of scab-resistant trees, we've kept the trash and cuttings cleared out, and there is little history of scab in this orchard. This is a preventive measure."

"What are you using?" Meg asked.

"It's a fungicide called mancozeb, a cholinesterase inhibitor. It's minimally toxic—low on the EPA scale. Doesn't harm birds and dissipates quickly in the soil. We're applying a diluted mixture, which Bree, under my supervision, will administer with the outlet gun. Yours is a small orchard, both in acreage and in tree size. We might save a little time were we to bring in the so-called heavy machinery, but we can manage easily in a few hours with what we've brought, and it's much easier to transport and set up."

Meg heard the sound of a motor starting, and Bree maneuvered the tractor into position and hitched the sprayer, its tank apparently now filled and ready, to the rear of the tractor.

"What about safety issues, Christopher? Respirators? Hazmat suits?"

"You *have* been doing your homework, I see. Even with the mildest chemicals, it is wise to protect oneself. I insist on chemical-resistant gloves, eye and face protection, protective headgear, and a respirator at all times. I'd far rather be safe than sorry, especially when I'm dealing with students."

"Amen. I certainly don't want to be responsible for any work-related injuries. Speaking of which, does the university cover insurance for this, even though it's my land?"

"The university has made provisions for this case. But you're right once more—we should review the documentation. Have you any more questions, or shall we begin?"

"Just one: how long will this take?"

"A couple of hours now, and again in a week or ten days. Come along and let's get ourselves fitted out, then."

A few minutes later, equipped with head and face protection, Meg stood at the border of the orchard and watched as Christopher guided the tractor slowly between the rows of still-bare trees while Bree wielded the spray nozzle. They worked slowly and deliberately to ensure even coverage, and Meg wondered once again if she would ever master all of the diverse tasks involved in getting a crop of apples to maturity. There was so much that could go wrong.

When Christopher and Bree finished their spraying, Bree took the tractor with its trailing sprayer back down toward the barn, while Christopher and Meg followed more slowly on foot.

"Bree seems to like the work."

"That she does. A rare thing, I think, among our women students. She is the exception—and exceptional in more ways than one, if I may make a poor pun."

"I'm impressed with her. And she doesn't treat me like an idiot, although I know I must seem like one."

"My dear Meg, there is a difference between stupidity and ignorance. The latter can be corrected, and you are well on your way to doing so. I must say I admire your perseverance in the face of adversity."

As Christopher turned his attention to loading the equipment back into the van, Meg walked toward the barn, where Bree had stowed the tractor and now stood in the doorway, raking her fingers through her hair where the headgear had matted it down. "Do you think you and I will be able to handle that one of these days?"

Bree smiled. "You mean, without Christopher? No problem. A couple more lessons with the tractor and you'll be good to go. Listen, uh, about Sunday . . ."

"You aren't backing out on me, are you?"

"No, but I hope you don't feel funny about my bringing Michael along. I mean, we haven't really been too public about being together, you know, and we don't get to spend too much time like this."

"Don't worry, Bree, it's fine," Meg said firmly. "The more, the merrier. I'm celebrating, so Michael is more than welcome. I won't even mind if he tries to convert me to the organic side, so he won't have to watch his tongue."

"Thanks. I'll see you Sunday."

Meg watched as Bree and Christopher hoisted the largest piece of equipment, the sprayer drum, into the van. Bree certainly was stronger than she looked.

Shortly after they left, Meg saw an unfamiliar car pull into her driveway—the vet, come to check out her goats, as promised. Meg went out the back door to greet her.

"Hi, Andrea! I didn't expect you this soon."

"I probably should have called, but I was in the neighborhood and I took a chance. Hope you don't mind."

"Of course not. It seems like everybody around here just drops in on me, and I'm beginning to like it. Come on over and meet the goats." The pair was standing side by side at the fence along the driveway, clearly intrigued by the presence of someone new.

"Introduce me, will you?" Andrea said, walking toward the fence.

"I would if they had names. Do they need names?" Meg said, catching up to her.

"Well, it's not required, but don't you want to call them something when you talk to them? Unless, of course, you're planning to eat them. In that case I wouldn't recommend naming them."

"Good heavens, no. I guess I'll have to consider them

pets, so I'll have to think about names. So what else do I need to know?"

Andrea extended a hand, and the goats butted at each other to try to greet her first. "Okay, two females—that's good. Nice pen, good size if you don't plan to add more animals. The shed looks sturdy enough, but keep an eye on it and keep the hay clean."

"What do I need to feed them?"

"Not your garbage, please. They'll keep your grass and brush down for you, but you should give them some hay and grain, and keep a salt block handy. And keep the hay off the ground—goats don't like dirty hay. Maybe some rolled oats, barley, or corn as a treat. But not too much—they tend to overfeed on grain. And that's about it. You planning to milk them?"

Meg laughed. "Doesn't that take breeding them? Right now it's about all I can handle to keep them fed."

"Fair enough. Something to think about, though. Now, you're going to need to keep their hooves trimmed, but otherwise they're pretty low maintenance. Just talk to them once in a while. If they get bored, they tend to get into trouble. They're very curious."

"Great." One more thing to worry about: amusing the goats.

Andrea was looking around the farm. "Your orchard's up that way? I passed it on my way over."

"That's it, all fifteen acres. We were spraying this morning. Oh." An awful thought slammed into Meg. "Should I have kept them in the shed while we were spraying? I mean, could the spray hurt them?"

"I wouldn't worry about it. I think they're fine, unless you decide to go with a helicopter and blast everything, or you spray a tree that they might chew on."

"I guess I'm clear, then. But I feel bad that I didn't think about it sooner."

"Just use common sense and you'll be okay. And don't

store your chemicals where the goats might get into them.
You might think you've locked the door, but then you
forget about that rotten board around the other side, and
before you know it they're inside and chomping away on
whatever you don't want them to. They're smart that way,
but that's what makes them fun."

"If you say so."

Andrea checked her watch. "I'd better run. I've got the
late shift at the clinic. I'm glad I could stop by, though.
Great place you have here. And you'll do fine with the
goats."

"I hope so. What do I owe you?"

"Don't worry about it. I was in the neighborhood anyway."

"Thanks! Good to see you again, Andrea."

Meg watched the vet's car pull out, then wandered
over to lean on her fence and contemplate the goats.
Hoping for a handout, they walked over and stared up at
her, their alien eyes curious. "Hi, guys. How do you like
it here?"

Smaller Goat cocked her head at Meg, then lost interest and wandered after an interesting wisp of hay. Larger
Goat nudged Meg through the fence with her nose.

"You want to talk, goat? Nice weather we're having.
You like that last batch of hay? It looked tasty. I'd better
check out the roof on your shed this summer—looks like
it's lost a few shingles."

The goat continued to stare but in what Meg thought
was an intelligent way. Suddenly Meg laughed: she was
carrying on a conversation with a goat. If her Boston
friends could see her now, they'd think she had lost her
mind. Well, maybe she should invite them out to see for
themselves. Maybe this summer, when the weather was
better and she'd sorted out the bedrooms, but before the
demands of the apple orchard became too hectic. She
could get some nice Adirondack chairs, and they could
all sit out admiring the Great Meadow, sipping fresh-

squeezed lemonade with homegrown mint, and she could regale them with funny stories about "country living," complete with goats.

The thought made her smile, and she carried the feeling back inside with her.

29

Saturday Meg went to the grocery store to shop for the ingredients she had managed to forget the first time around, and then came home and cleaned. She started with the ancient pots she had unearthed in the kitchen cupboards, knowing she would need them for cooking. No way could she handle them all in the sink, so she carried them upstairs and dumped them into the claw-foot tub in the bathroom, along with a lot of dish soap, and turned on the hot water. After a half hour of effort, here and there clean metal gleamed, but it was far outweighed by the black grease, and now there was a slimy ring around the tub. Still, they would probably do to boil water in, and if she was going to feed more than one person, and likely hungry ones, her own modest saucepans wouldn't do. With a sigh she rinsed them one last time and drained the water out of the tub.

Then she moved on to the rest of the house. As she dusted and swept and polished the second- and thirdhand discards of tenants past, and worked to remove the construction debris she had added, she wondered what she was trying to prove. Everyone who was coming to dinner Sunday night knew her situation and couldn't exactly fault her for the inevitable dust and grime that any construction site produced. But still . . . she kept on scrubbing. This was the formal opening of her new home, the first time she had prepared a serious sit-down meal for her new friends, and she wanted the place to look nice. Or as nice as it could. At least it would be dark for most of their time there, and candlelight would be flattering, wouldn't it?

She stopped only long enough to direct the delivery people who arrived with the large cardboard boxes bearing her new refrigerator and stove. She pointed them to the open shed outside the kitchen. She allowed them to haul away the battle-scarred old stove, but she still needed the refrigerator, chugging along in her dining room, and she thought she could probably find a place for it later. One issue at a time.

Sunday morning she was more than a little fidgety, running over to-do lists in her head. Seth arrived at the front door early, as if anticipating her anxiety. "Ready to test the floor?"

She nodded. "I guess. I don't know what I'm going to do if it's not dry. I don't have a Plan B."

"It should be fine—the humidity's been low. You want to do the honors?"

She led the way to the door that separated the dining room and the kitchen, and opened it cautiously. Everything looked fine. Before Meg could bend down to touch the floor, Lolly streaked between her legs and skidded to a stop at the far side of the room, disoriented. Meg tilted her head to catch the light reflecting off the floor: no sign of paw prints. She ran a cautious finger over the surface, and it felt hard and smooth—and definitely dry. She straightened up and turned to Seth. "Feels dry to me. You want to check?"

"Sure." He too knelt down and ran a hand over the surface. Lolly, recovering quickly, ran over to him and pounced on his hand. He laughed. "Feels fine. I think we're good to go. They delivered the appliances yesterday?"

"They did. I had them put out back. I figured that was as close as we'd get to the kitchen door."

"Smart thinking. Let me strip off the boxes, and we can use the cardboard to protect the floor when we move them. Give me a couple of minutes, okay?"

It hadn't occurred to Meg that Seth would need her help to move the appliances. *Right, Meg—he's not Superman, and he can't lift a refrigerator all by himself.* She hoped she was up to it, though she had certainly added a few muscles since moving in.

Luckily their combined strength proved adequate to the task at hand, and within the hour her softly gleaming stainless steel appliances had been jockeyed into their respective niches in the kitchen. Seth plugged them in before pushing them into their final places, fiddled with a few controls, and stood back. "You want to give them a try?"

Meg felt like a child on Christmas morning, only now the toys were bigger than she was. She opened and closed the refrigerator door a few times and marveled at the cool air flowing out. She spun all the dials on the stove, turned on the oven and peered into it until she could feel warmth, then turned everything off again. "It's great. They work!"

"Madame, you insult my honor. Of course they work. I plugged them in, didn't I?"

"Seth, I don't know what I would have done without you. Doesn't it look great in here? And once I get the cabinets cleaned up, and maybe some new countertops, and I could use another light fixture over the sink . . . But this is so much better than it was. Thank you!" Without thinking she gave him a quick hug, which startled him nearly as much as her. She found she was curiously reluctant to let go, but she still had a lot to accomplish before dinner. She looked at his face, which gave away nothing.

He finally spoke. "My pleasure. What do you want to do with the old fridge?"

"Oh, that's right—I need to get it out of the dining room. Should I keep it around?"

"If you don't want it, I can put it in my office."

"Of course. Shall we haul it out there now?"

That last task accomplished, Seth made his farewells on the back stoop. Meg stood in the middle of her new-old kitchen and marveled again. Lolly, who had wisely chosen to avoid the heavy-labor phase, advanced tentatively into the room. She prowled the perimeter, then jumped onto the countertop and from there to the top of the refrigerator. From her elevated vantage point she surveyed the scene and apparently satisfied, washed her face with one paw, then settled herself into a sphinx pose, paws tucked under, and shut her eyes.

At least she won't be underfoot if that's her new favorite place, Meg thought. She turned to the remaining smaller chores, like transferring the microwave from the dining room to the kitchen counter, followed by the china and glassware she had acquired, which she stowed in the cabinets. At last the dining room was cleared for its original purpose—dining—and Meg declared it was time to start cooking.

The spaghetti sauce came first, because she wanted to give that plenty of time to simmer. This was her one foolproof recipe, but the stove was the wild card, and she wanted to allow time for a few false starts. "Well, Lolly, here we go," she said, locating a head of garlic, onions, olive oil, herbs, and a knife and cutting board. Spaghetti was winter food, to her mind, but it really wasn't quite spring yet, and right now she wanted a recipe she trusted, something warm and filling. She sautéed onions and garlic in the oil and contemplated her next ingredient. Sausage? She wasn't sure if Bree or Michael were vegetarians, so maybe she should leave out meat products and go heavy on the herbs. And mushrooms—they'd go in later. Salad and bread were last-minute items, but she could try out the oven on the garlic bread. Oh, and the apple crisp, an old recipe of her grandmother's.

She had to laugh at herself: Farmer Meg, chopping veggies in her rustic kitchen. Maybe she *should* try raising a few chickens? She could use the eggs, although she drew the line at killing the chickens for dinner. The idea of goat's milk was interesting, but she definitely didn't want any baby goats at the moment. Maybe sometime in the future, when she had the orchard routines sorted out. What would fall bring? A good crop, she hoped, although she had no idea what she was going to do to sell it. Christopher would know. And she had plenty of time to figure out a plan.

The afternoon passed pleasantly, as the house filled with the aroma of good cooking. Maybe cinnamon and garlic made an odd combination, or maybe she was just hungry, but it all smelled great to Meg. She set the newly cleared dining table with her new tablecloth and laid out four places, arranging a cluster of candles in the center of the table. She was ready.

Seth arrived first, bearing not one but two bottles of wine, red and white. "I wasn't sure what you wanted so I brought both. Everything still working?"

"Of course. Put the white in my gleaming new refrigerator, unless you'd like to open it first? Oops, corkscrew. I don't know if I can find mine."

Seth reached into his pocket and pulled one out with a flourish. "I came prepared. Can I pour you a glass?"

"Sure, why not? Everything's about done. Let me stick the bread into the oven."

When she had slid the loaf, slathered with butter, garlic, and parsley, onto the oven rack, she turned to find Seth holding out a glass to her. "May I make a toast?" he offered.

She took the glass. "Of course."

He raised his glass. "To all that you've accomplished, and all that you will. Congratulations, Meg—you're doing a great job."

She raised her glass to his, unable to speak for a moment for the lump in her throat.

"I'm not interrupting anything, am I?" Bree's voice startled Meg, who hadn't even heard her car arrive.

Meg smiled at Seth, took a token sip of her wine, and greeted Bree. "No, not at all. Michael isn't with you?"

"No, he had something to finish up at GreenGrow, so he's coming on his own. Uh, I didn't know what you were cooking, so I just brought you some flowers." Bree, looking uncertain, held out a bunch of tulips and irises wrapped in florist's paper.

Meg was touched. "Thank you, Bree. I didn't even think about that. Let's see if I can find something to put them in. I bought most of the necessities for eating, but I didn't think about any fancy touches like vases. I think I saw something in the cupboard in the dining room, though."

"I'll check. Hi, Lolly—you look pleased with yourself." Lavinia was still perched on top of the refrigerator, and Bree gave her head an affectionate rub on her way to the dining room.

Seth was prowling around the kitchen. "You know you can't use a garbage disposal, with your septic system?"

"Yes, sir, you've told me before. Don't worry. Is that another car?"

"Sounds like it. You want me to get the door?"

Meg checked the stove and oven settings. "No, if it's Michael, I should welcome him. I want to do the hostess things right, at least the first time." She dried her hands on a towel and headed for the front door, passing Bree, who was rummaging in the sideboard in the dining room. By the time Michael knocked on the front door, she was there, and she pulled it open. "Hi, Michael . . . and Daphne."

30

Meg's stomach plummeted. What was Daphne doing here? Daphne hung back behind Michael, as if she were trying to hide.

Michael looked distinctly uncomfortable. "Uh, hi, Meg. I hope you don't mind, but I ran into Daphne at the GreenGrow office, and she asked where I was going, and . . ." He looked past Meg, and his expression became even more miserable. Meg turned to see Bree standing in the doorway to the dining room, glaring daggers at him. He turned back to Meg. "If it's a problem, we don't have to stay." Daphne still hadn't said a word.

Meg ran calculations through her head. She didn't want Daphne here, especially since she had more or less invited herself. Bree would be furious, Michael would be defensive, and everyone would have a lousy time. On the other hand, she could hear her mother's voice in her head: *These are guests in your home, and you must make them feel welcome.* At least she had enough food to go around. "Don't worry, Michael. There's plenty for one more mouth. Please come in. Daphne, nice to see you again." Meg wondered how obvious her insincerity was.

"I'm sorry, I didn't mean to just barge in like this, I mean, to your private party and all." Daphne's forward progress stalled in the hallway, while out of the corner of her eye Meg could see Bree drag Michael aside and start talking in a harsh whisper.

Meg shifted to screen their argument from Daphne. "It's all right, Daphne. It's sort of an informal house-warming. I just refinished my kitchen floor and I wanted to celebrate."

Relief was clear on Daphne's face. *What did you expect, Daphne?* Meg wondered. *You weaseled your way into the party, but did you imagine I'd stage a scene and bar the door?*

"Hey, that's cool. Is there anything I can do to help?"

"No, I think everything is good. Why don't we go into the kitchen and I'll get you something to drink. Wine?"

"Oh, no, I don't drink alcohol," Daphne replied. "You have something else maybe?"

Meg sighed inwardly. "Of course. Bree, Michael, can I get you something?"

Michael held the kitchen door for her and Daphne. "Not for me, thanks—I'm driving. Bree, what about you?"

Bree stalked past him into the kitchen. "I'll have some wine, Meg, if that's all right with you."

Seth was leaning against the counter in the kitchen and seemed amused by the whole scene, his mouth quirked in a half smile. He cast a sympathetic glance at Meg before turning to the new arrivals. "You must be Michael." He and Michael shook hands, and then Seth turned to Daphne. "I'm sorry—we haven't met."

"Oh, yeah. I'm Daphne Lydon. I work with Michael. Well, kinda work, because I don't get paid. I mean, I volunteer at GreenGrow. Michael asked if I wanted to come along."

Meg caught Michael's stricken glance and doubted he

had said any such thing. She distributed glasses to everyone. "Daphne, I have some cider—is that okay? Michael, I gave you some, too. Bree, here's your wine. Seth, you're good?" He raised his glass, still half-full. Meg found her own and raised it again. "Welcome to my home, and my first dinner."

Daphne was still staring at her glass. "Is this organic?"

Meg stifled an urge to swat her. "I don't know. You can read the label if you want. Or help yourself to a glass of water."

"Tap water?" At Meg's glare, Daphne shut up, sipping cautiously at the possibly nonorganic apple cider.

"Hey, your floor looks terrific!" That was Michael's desperate bid to change the subject. "Bree said she helped you with it."

"Yes, she did." Meg glanced at Bree, who had finished half her wine already and was apparently sulking. "This was my first try at finishing, and I'm really happy with the way it turned out." Meg could have sworn that Daphne muttered something about toxic fumes, but she ignored her. Now Daphne was wandering around the kitchen. She reached the stove and lifted the lid on the simmering sauce. "Hey, this smells great." She reached for a spoon and poked around in the pot. "What's in here?"

Meg was rapidly losing patience with her unwanted guest. She took the spoon from Daphne and gave the sauce a vigorous stir. "No meat, if that's what you're worried about. Would you mind moving? I have to put the spaghetti on." As Daphne backed away, Meg dumped pasta into the pot of boiling water she had ready, and set the timer on the stove. "Ten minutes, everyone. Bree, could you take the salad to the table, please? And light the candles?"

Bree grabbed the bowl of salad from the counter and stalked away. Seth was struggling to engage an inarticulate Daphne in conversation. Michael drew Meg aside and said, in a low voice, "Look, I really am sorry about this." He nodded toward Daphne. "She kind of cornered me, and I didn't know how to say no."

Meg felt sorry for him, and she knew he'd have a lot more explaining to do with Bree, so she took pity. "I know how that goes, Michael. Don't worry—we'll survive. It's only one evening, right?"

"Thanks. And dinner does smell great."

"Good. Can you take the garlic bread in?" She handed him a plate with foil-wrapped bread on it, and he beat a grateful retreat. She could hear the rumble of his voice coming from the dining room, and Bree's hissed response. Meg sighed: this was not the way she had planned things. But it was too late to do anything about it. "Excuse me, Daphne, I need to get to the stove." How was it that the woman always managed to get in the way? She really was clueless. "Seth, why don't you and Daphne go into the dining room, and I'll bring this out when it's ready?"

Seth got her message. "Sure. I'll take the wine along. Come on, Daphne." He pulled the bottle of white out of the refrigerator, grabbed the bottle of red off the counter, and herded Daphne ahead of him into the dining room.

Blessedly alone in the kitchen, Meg drained the spaghetti into a colander, then poured it into a large bowl. She ladled sauce over it, sprinkled it with grated cheese, and took one last look around. *Main course, salad, bread, wine. Oh, right, dessert.* She had cooked it earlier in the day, so she made sure she had turned the oven off after heating the garlic bread, then slipped the apple crisp in to rewarm. She was as ready as she would ever be.

She bore the bowl of spaghetti triumphantly into the dining room and set it down on the table. The assorted candles in the middle glowed brightly in the gathering dusk, flickering off the faces of her new friends. And Daphne's.

The dinner passed in a blur, with uncomfortable undercurrents. Everyone managed to remain civil, although

Bree tossed in a few catty remarks. Seth contrived to distract the group with amusing tales of the oddities he had unearthed in his plumbing travels, and Meg was grateful. Daphne, the fly in the ointment, sat like a lump and said little, pushing her food around her plate, eating mainly salad and bread. Why had she wanted to come? Meg studied Daphne discreetly. She didn't look desperate to Meg, just morose and angry. Maybe Daphne simply couldn't stand the idea of other people having fun without her.

By nine the wine bottles were empty, the last of the apple crisp was but a memory, and the candles were guttering. Meg felt obscurely exhausted from trying to keep up a neutral conversation with this seething group. Seth once again read her mood and stood up. "Meg, that was great. Let's get these dishes out to the kitchen and clean up."

Meg stood up, too. "Thanks, Seth, but if you all can just put everything in the kitchen, I'll take care of the washing up in the morning. It's been a long day."

Wordlessly Bree joined Seth in collecting plates and glasses and taking them to the kitchen. Daphne didn't move from her seat, instead staring at Michael with a look that Meg couldn't read. If Daphne needed friends, she certainly didn't have a clue about how to make any. Was she hoping to make a move on Michael now that Jason was dead? If so, she was in for an unpleasant surprise when she learned that Bree had beat her to it. But once Meg managed to shoo her out of the house tonight, Daphne would not be her problem.

Michael grabbed a bowl and followed Bree to the kitchen, leaving Daphne alone with Meg. They sat in silence for several seconds, until Daphne said, "Sorry I'm not very good company."

Meg debated seizing the opening that Daphne had presented, and almost asked what she could do to help. But in truth, Meg didn't want to hear the answer. She was responsible for a creaky old house, a needy orchard, a pair of goats, and a cat, and she didn't need to take on Daphne, too. Maybe that was callous, but she knew her own limitations, and she didn't think she had any solutions to offer. Daphne was just going to have to sort out her own life. "Well, we can't all be chatterboxes," she said briskly as she stood up. "I'd better go see what they're up to in the kitchen." She turned on her heel, leaving Daphne alone at the table.

In the kitchen she said, "Look, guys, I mean it. I'll take care of this later."

"I'll stay over tonight. I can help," Bree offered, much to Meg's surprise. "Michael was just leaving. Weren't you? You have to get Daphne home." She leaned against the counter, arms crossed, daring him to contradict her.

Michael cast one more imploring glance at Bree, then nodded and turned to Meg. "Thanks for a nice dinner, Meg. I enjoyed it. If you don't need anything else, we'll be going now."

"Thank you, Michael. It was nice to see you again." *Although I could have done without your companion.* "I'll see you out." She followed him as he rounded up Daphne and headed for the front door, then she stood in the doorway watching them leave.

She returned to the kitchen, where Seth had finished wrapping up the scant leftovers and putting them in the refrigerator. "If that's it, I guess I'll go now. Meg, that really was a great dinner."

"Thanks, Seth. I just wish Daphne hadn't shown up. I know that sounds cold, but I really don't like that woman. I hope she didn't make trouble between you and Michael, Bree."

Bree shook her head. "It's okay. He just couldn't figure out how to say no to her, and she's a real leech. I think he's going to learn pretty fast, after this. You don't mind my staying?"

"Of course not. It's your room, and you can come and go as you like."

"Then I guess I'll turn in, maybe read for a while. 'Night." Bree fled, leaving Meg and Seth alone in the kitchen.

Meg slumped against the stove. "Well, all things considered, I guess that didn't go too badly. And at least all the appliances work! Thanks again, Seth."

"Happy to help. I'll see you sometime this week—I've got a shipment of lumber coming in for the shed build-out. I've got to get moving on that if I'm supposed to be out of my current shop by May."

"And don't forget my apple storage."

"I'm on it. Good night, Meg." He hesitated a moment, and Meg wondered if he was thinking about kissing her good night, and then wondered why she was wondering about it. In any case, he slipped out the back door and was gone.

Meg stood for a moment, debating about doing the dishes despite what she had said earlier. But she was tired, and she had a good book waiting by her bed. She deserved that small treat; the dishes could wait till the morning. She turned off the kitchen light and made her way to the front stairs, turning off lights as she went and checking that the front door was locked. Lolly appeared from wherever she had been hiding and dashed up the stairs, pausing at the top to wait for Meg to catch up.

31

When Meg opened her eyes, it was pitch dark outside, and she wondered what had awakened her. Lolly slept soundly at the foot of her bed, curled up with her nose under her tail, and the house was quiet. She didn't hear anything from the goats. She checked the glowing numerals of her clock: two fourteen. Why was she awake?

The wave of nausea that hit her answered that question. She never got sick. She hated throwing up, and she couldn't remember the last time she had. Years, definitely. What was going on? Couldn't be a hangover—she'd had no more than two glasses of wine at dinner.

The nausea returned, stronger. Unfortunately she wasn't going to be able to ignore it and go back to sleep. Nope, not happening. She stumbled out of bed, not bothering to turn on the light or find her slippers, and reached the bathroom with no time to spare, spewing whatever was left in her stomach into the toilet. When that wave subsided, Meg slumped to the floor, weak and sweating.

She wasn't sure how long she would have sat there, but she was startled to hear a knock on the bathroom door. Meg struggled to her feet and opened it to find Bree doubled over, her dark skin a peculiar ashy color. "Sorry—move!" Bree shoved past Meg and vomited into the toilet. Meg leaned against the bathroom door, confused and dizzy.

If Bree had the same problem as she did, it had to have been the food. *Oh, no*, Meg thought in dismay. *I gave everyone food poisoning!* But how? Those ancient pots, a bad can of tomatoes, something in the salad? She'd cheated and bought a couple of premixed bags of greens. Hadn't she read about contaminated salad mixes? Or had it been spinach? But she had been careful to wash it. That should have helped, shouldn't it?

Bree had rolled around to sit on the floor next to the toilet, and she looked up at Meg. "This sucks."

"Tell me about it." Meg slid down the door to sit, since she wasn't sure her legs would hold her, and she didn't want to move far from the toilet. "Food poisoning?"

Bree shrugged, wrapping her arms around her midsection.

"Stomach cramps?" Meg asked. Bree nodded without speaking.

"Damn—we should call the others and see if they're all right. But I'd hate to wake them if this is limited to the two of us."

Bree hauled herself to her feet. "You'll hear from them soon enough, if they've got this, too. One thing I do know—we need to drink liquids, keep hydrated, flush out whatever's in us. You got juice downstairs?"

"I do." Meg got to her feet. She found she had to cling to the banister on her way downstairs: the dizziness was back and getting worse. The kitchen, when she turned on the light, looked like a battle zone, with dirty dishes and pans everywhere. No wonder her mother had told her not to leave a messy kitchen. It looked surreal, and her stomach lurched at the sight. Bree was rummaging through the refrigerator and pulled out an unopened bottle of cranberry juice. "This should work."

As Meg tried to find two clean glasses, Lolly sauntered into the kitchen and leaped onto the countertop by the sink.

Slowly it occurred to Meg that she should not let the cat eat whatever was left on the plates, but before she could move, Lolly sniffed the remains of the sauce on one plate and backed away, her lips curled. "Bree? Look at the cat. It must be the sauce. But how could it be? I made it myself. I tasted it while I was cooking it, and it was fine."

Lolly gave the dirty plates one last look of disgust, then jumped off the counter and fled the room. With great deliberation Meg shut the door behind her and moved hesitantly toward the sink: her legs were shaky, and it looked very far away. She leaned against the counter and grabbed a tissue from the box she kept there, and blew her nose. And wiped her mouth: she seemed to be drooling. An aftereffect of throwing up?

Then she went very still, clutching the edge of the counter for support. Not food poisoning: that would explain the nausea, but not everything else she was feeling. There was something familiar about all this, something she had read . . . Her mind was working slowly, slowly . . .

Pesticide poisoning. The thought surfaced in her sluggish brain like a bubble of noxious gas in a swamp. She looked up to see Bree swigging juice, but her color was still an ugly gray. "Bree," she whispered, "I think it's pesticide poisoning."

Bree's eyes widened. "What? Can't be. How?"

"I don't know. But it fits: nausea, vomiting, and now I'm drooling and my nose is running. I looked it up online, when Jason died. Those are all symptoms. Oh my God!" Meg stumbled to a chair and sat down heavily, and

Bree followed suit. "And there's worse, a whole lot more symptoms. How are you feeling?"

Bree coughed. "Not so good. What do we do now?"

"I think we should go to the hospital." Although Meg wasn't sure she was in any shape to drive. "What about the others? We have to call them now!"

Bree nodded slowly. "Right. Good. I'll call Michael, and he should have Daphne's number somewhere. You call Seth. Then we call 911, right? Get help?"

"Right," Meg replied absently. What had she done? Poisoned Seth? How could that be? She didn't have any pesticide, certainly not in her kitchen. *Worry about that later.* She picked up the phone, dialed Seth's number. No answer. She dialed again, not trusting her shaky fingers. Still no answer. She wanted to scream, to throw the phone across the room. Instead she sat staring stupidly at it.

"No answer at Michael's," Bree said. "And I don't have Daphne's number."

Meg shook her head, trying to clear it. Somebody should take charge. No, *she* should take charge: this was her house, and she was the boss. "Okay, here's the deal. We need to get to the hospital, and we need to make sure Seth and the others are all right. I'm going to call Art, and let him sort all this out. He lives in town here."

Bree blinked owlishly. "Not 911?"

"No. Art can get here faster, and he can let somebody in Amherst know to look for Michael and Daphne." Meg didn't have a clue whether a single ambulance could transport three sick people to whatever hospital was closest, but she thought Art could figure that out. Her brief stab at authority had left her exhausted.

Meg looked at the phone in her hand and tried to remember how it worked. *Push one button, get a dial tone.* Art would know what to do. But Art wouldn't be in the office at three o'clock in the morning. Did she have Art's home number? No. But it would be in the phone book.

Where was the phone book? She stood up and scrabbled through a pile of papers and magazines she had shoved out of the way. *Aha, phone book.* Skinny little thing, wasn't it? Not like the Boston phone book, nope. *Focus, Meg, focus.* What was Art's last name? Preston, that was it. Meg kept losing her place in the book, but she finally located the "P" pages. Thank God he was listed. Her hand trembling, Meg punched in the numbers.

"Wha?" a sleepy, angry voice answered after five rings.

"Art. Is this Art?"

"Yeah, you got me. Who's this?"

"Meg Corey. I think I've been poisoned."

"What?" The voice on the other end was suddenly more alert. "Why?"

"I had people over for dinner. I'm sick. Bree's here, and she's sick. And the others aren't answering. Art, listen, I think this is more than just food poisoning. I think this is whatever killed Jason."

"Call 911," he said grimly. "I'll be over in five."

"Art, wait—Seth's not picking up his phone. You should get over there."

Art sighed. "Shit. If I have to worry about all of you, it'll be faster if I just collect you all and take you to the hospital myself. Who are the others?"

"Michael Fisher and Daphne Lydon. They live in Amherst somewhere. Bree has Michael's address and number? Bree?"

It took a couple of moments for Bree to focus on her, and then she reeled off Michael's information and Meg repeated it to Art. "But neither of us knows where Daphne lives. Michael might, if you find him, but he's not answering."

"Got it. I'll call it in to Amherst—they'll send someone over. You stay put—I'll swing by your place first, and then we can go to Seth's. Five minutes."

"Hurry." Art hung up, and Meg was left gazing at the phone in her hand. It took her a moment to realize that

Bree hadn't heard the whole conversation. She looked up to find Bree retching into the sink.

When Bree was finished, she turned to Meg. "What?"

"He's going to come by here, and then we're going to Seth's. I guess we don't have time to get dressed, huh?" Meg squashed a bubble of hysteria. Now the police chief was visiting, and she still hadn't washed her dishes, and worse, she was wearing a ratty pair of flannel pajamas. But maybe the plates were evidence now. Maybe that was a good thing she hadn't washed them. *So there, Mom!* She looked at the pile of papers she had dislodged when she was hunting for the phone book. On top of the pile was the printout she had made about the pesticide, the one that had killed Jason. She tried to focus on the words swimming on the page. Those typed in capitals she could make out most easily: HEADACHE, DIZZINESS, WEAKNESS, INCOORDINATION, MUSCLE TWITCHING, TREMOR, NAUSEA, ABDOMINAL CRAMPS, DIARRHEA, SWEATING. She had all of those. *Great.* Knowing what was wrong didn't make it any easier to handle, she thought, as she fought another wave of nausea. She wondered how long these symptoms would go on—and what would happen if they got worse.

Before she could read any further, there was a pounding on her back door. *Art, thank God.* She made her wobbly way over to the door and fumbled with the dead bolt. It took her three tries to make her hands work well enough to get it open, and by the time she had succeeded she was exhausted from the effort.

Art stepped into the room, wearing civvies: jeans and a flannel shirt, which nearly matched Meg's pajamas. He took one look at the scene in the kitchen—Meg wavering on her feet, Bree sitting huddled at the table—and took charge. "Okay, we're getting out of here! Meg, get coats. Can you handle that?"

Meg nodded. "Oh, here." She thrust the printout at

him. "You'd better take this along. Might save time at the hospital."

"Whatever." He folded it roughly and shoved it in his shirt pocket. "Now move!"

Meg laboriously disentangled her coat from the rack by the door, and one for Bree, who was wearing only an oversize T-shirt. "Bree, we're going now. Put on these boots."

Bree looked dully at her, then at the boots Meg shoved across the kitchen floor at her. "Right. Boots."

Meg pulled on another pair. It was getting harder and harder to concentrate on anything, hold anything, do anything at all. *Let Art take care of it. That's his job.* Art was holding Bree up by one arm. "Okay, car, now. Let's go." He grabbed one of Meg's arms and hustled them out of the kitchen, into the night. Meg had already been shaking, but the cold air made it worse. Art pushed Bree into the backseat, and Meg took the front.

She lay back against the headrest. "Seth's house."

Art peeled out of the driveway. "Yes, we're going to Seth's house."

"I don't know where it is."

"I do." He drove fast on the empty roads, one turn, two, then pulled up in front of a small colonial. It looked as though every light in the house had been turned on: every window glowed brightly. "Well, at least he's awake."

Art was out of the car almost before it stopped moving, leaving the engine running. He went to the back door and pounded on it. "Seth, you in there? Seth?"

Nothing. Alarmed, Meg struggled out of the car and shuffled her way to the door. Art was still pounding. Finally, there was an answering bellow from inside. "What the hell you want?"

Seth lurched into view and glared at Art through the glass panel of the door, but he didn't open it. Art said, "Let us in, Seth. We've got a problem."

"No. I don't want you here. Leave me alone, will you?"

Seth seemed to be acting very oddly, Meg thought

dimly. He looked angry. Why would he be angry? She pushed past Art. "Seth, can we come in, please?"

Seth struggled to focus on her. "What do you want? Why can't you leave me alone?" He turned away and disappeared into the house, out of sight.

Meg tugged on Art's arm. "Break in."

Art turned to her. "He says he doesn't want help."

"Art, this pesticide can make you act weird. Do you think he's acting normally?"

Art shook his head. "All right. But if you're wrong, you can pay for the broken window." He pulled his coat sleeve taut, smashed the glass pane nearest the door handle with his elbow, then reached in and turned the dead bolt. "Meg, you wait here. I'll talk to him."

Meg had no desire to argue with him. She wasn't sure how much longer her legs would hold her up. She leaned against the doorjamb, listening as Art made his way through the house, calling Seth's name. *Fine way to see the house for the first time*, she thought irreverently. She'd never been invited, and now she was breaking in. Seth would not be happy about that.

Seth was apparently well beyond unhappy, if the angry shouts coming from the other end of the house were any indication. Without thinking, Meg pushed off the doorframe and lurched from room to room, following the voices. She finally found the two men facing off in a room at the far corner, glaring at each other.

Art was pleading, "Seth, you're sick. You've been poisoned. You've got to come with us, to the hospital."

"I'm not going anywhere with you." Seth rubbed his sleeve across his dripping nose. "Dammit, go away! Just leave me alone."

"Seth," Meg broke in, "you've got to come. This thing could kill you." She stumbled her way toward him, laid a hand on his chest, trying to make him look at her. He shoved her away roughly, and she fell against Art, who caught her.

Reason wasn't working. But as Meg watched, Seth's chest began to heave, and he struggled for breath. He tried to yell something, but he lacked the air to get out more than a few jumbled words. Then he crumpled to his knees on the floor, panting heavily.

Meg grabbed Art's sleeve. "Oh, God, Art—respiratory failure's the worst problem with this stuff. We've got to get him to the hospital, fast."

"I hear you." Art grabbed one of Seth's arms. Seth put up a weak struggle, then finally slumped against Art. "Can you give me a hand?"

Meg wasn't sure she would be much help in her current state, but she had to try. Somehow they managed to drag Seth out the back door to the car. Art dumped him unceremoniously in the front seat. Meg climbed in the back. Bree looked at her vaguely and curled up in the corner.

Art drove fast, but Meg quickly lost track of time. The motion of the car set off another round of nausea, and she rolled down the window and leaned out in time to avoid vomiting in the car, not that there was much left in her stomach. Dimly she heard Bree doing the same on the opposite side. The chill air washed through the car and aggravated her trembling. She reached up to wipe the saliva off her face and stopped briefly, fascinated by the shaking of her hand. She couldn't remember ever feeling this lousy.

Hospital. Lights. People hurrying. Gurney. She didn't resist, because she couldn't. Her legs wouldn't work, and she couldn't stop shaking. There was something important . . . but what? Finally she remembered. "Art, on the paper?" He turned his head to look at her. "The one I gave you. There's an antidote. Tell them."

"Right." He disappeared. So did everything else.

32

Meg peeled her eyes open and looked around her, trying to piece together where she was. What had happened the night before? Her jumbled memories didn't make much sense. She was in a hospital room—that much was clear. Sunlight coming through windows, so it had to be morning. Or afternoon—she wasn't about to guess. Bree was in the room, draped over the stiff-looking plastic chair, wearing a set of mismatched scrubs two sizes too big for her, leafing through a dog-eared magazine. That was good news. "You look perky. What time is it?" Meg managed to croak.

Bree dropped the magazine and pulled the chair closer. "Good, you're awake. I was beginning to worry. It's about eight, so you've been out of it for maybe four hours. The jerks around here wouldn't tell me anything about how you were doing because I'm not related to you, or something like that. They didn't want me to wait in here either, but I just ignored them until they found something else to do. Once they got you stabilized they weren't so worried. How're you feeling?"

Meg tested various body parts. Nothing hurt, although her stomach muscles were sore—all that retching, no doubt. But it took tremendous effort to move anything: she felt as though she had been beaten with baseball bats. "Check with me in an hour or so, when the rest of me wakes up. Maybe you can tell me what happened when we got here? I kind of blacked out."

Bree settled back in the unyielding chair. "Sure, what I remember. We barfed our way into the place, and then they found a couple of doctors who were willing to take a look at us. Since I was the only one still conscious, I had to explain what had happened, about the pesticide and all. And nobody wanted to believe me. Thank goodness that cop buddy of yours was there. He threw his weight around and they had to listen, and then he gave them that paper you handed him. I swear, if they'd had to figure things out for themselves they'd still be scratching their heads and giving us aspirin and ginger ale. So they all argued some more, and then they had to call some bigwig somewhere else to see if they could do what they were supposed to, and then they had to hunt around and see where they'd put the antidote stuff. But they finally got it together. Seems to be working—I feel okay."

Bree obviously felt a lot better than Meg did. It must be nice to be so young and resilient—Meg felt about ninety at the moment. "Did anybody say anything about aftereffects?"

"Nah. They think we got the antidote fast enough."

Meg wasn't sure she was ready to ask the next question, but she had to know. "Seth?"

Bree's expression darkened. "Man, he was acting wild! I figure he got more than we did 'cause he ate a lot, and it seems to affect different people in different ways. He was having trouble breathing, so they clamped some kind of mask on him and took him somewhere else. Like I said, they wouldn't tell me anything. But the chief said to call him when you were awake, because he has lots of questions and he's going to have to call that detective."

"I'll bet he does. Did someone track down Michael and Daphne?"

Bree nodded. "Michael, yes. He said he was already feeling really bad by the time he got back to Amherst, so after he dropped Daphne off at her place, he took himself straight to the free clinic, and they sent him to the hospital because they didn't know what the heck to do with him. He was pissed, because he really doesn't have much money. And I ragged on the chief to keep looking until they tracked him down, or else they wouldn't have known what to give him. But he got off easy, apparently."

Meg hoisted herself up and propped the flimsy pillow behind her. "How do you know all this?"

"Like I said, I just kept pushing. And Michael called me on my cell when he could and gave me his side."

"You brought your cell? Wait—they let you use it here, in the hospital?"

"Grabbed my bag on the way out the door. And yours. Hospitals always worry about all that ID and insurance crap, so I figured we'd need them. And I forgot the phone was on until Michael called."

Meg's estimation of Bree went up a notch. Even sick, she'd kept her head. "And Daphne?"

Bree looked concerned. "Nobody's seen her. Michael says he took her home, but she wasn't there when the cops checked. They broke in the door and all, just to be sure. No sign of her."

"Oh no." Meg tried to find a more comfortable position. "Where on earth could she have gone in the middle of the night? She doesn't have a car. Did the police check the clinics and the hospitals? Student health? They have to find her before it's too late for the antidote."

Bree nodded, her eyes grave. Meg wrestled with a mixture of guilt and frustration: just because she didn't particularly *like* Daphne didn't mean that she wished her harm—but why had she managed to disappear just when the police went looking for her? And Meg didn't want to think about what it would mean if Daphne died after eating Meg's food . . .

She pushed the dark thoughts away; she had to know if Seth was all right. "Listen, Bree, can you do me a favor? Find out where Seth is? Oh, and maybe find me some clothes?"

"I'm on it. I'll bring you some scrubs or something and snoop around till I find Seth. Give me five."

Bree bounded out into the hallway, leaving Meg feeling ridiculously old. There were only ten years between them, but at the moment it felt more like fifty.

From the flashes she remembered, Seth had been ranting, out of his head. And then gasping for breath. That was bad. But they'd gotten here quickly, hadn't they? He had to be all right. As soon as Bree found out where he was, she'd go make sure. A fine plan, except that she wasn't even sure she could stand.

Better find out. She threw off the thin blanket and swung her legs over the edge of the bed. So far, so good. She slid down until her feet touched the cold linoleum floor—and almost kept sliding. She waited until she steadied, then took a few tentative steps toward the bathroom. Okay, the parts seemed to be working. She was almost sorry when she reached the bathroom and saw herself in the mirror: pale, bags under her eyes, hair lank and stringy. *What did you expect, Meg? You were poisoned. Bet that never happened at your dinner parties, Mom.*

Meg splashed water on her face, ran her fingers through her sweat-matted hair, and rinsed out her mouth. She wished she could remember more specifics about the pesticide. She did remember that the pesticide was extremely toxic—and obviously, it had killed Jason. How long had it taken him to die?

Not Seth. No, please, not Seth. He didn't deserve to die just because he was a nice guy who had helped her out. Or because he'd liked her spaghetti sauce. That would be so wrong.

Meg walked back to her bed, feeling steadier, and sank back onto the mattress, exhausted by her efforts. Still no sign of Bree. *All right, Meg, think!* She had tasted the sauce throughout the afternoon and had suffered no ill effects. Then the others had arrived: Seth, Bree, then Michael and Daphne together. One of them must have added pesticide to the sauce. But who? Not Seth: he had no reason to poison anyone. Which left Bree, Michael, and Daphne, any one of whom could have brought the pesticide and known how to use it.

But had that person meant to kill or only to make them sick? Obviously someone knew what a fatal dose would be, because that person had killed Jason. But why would anyone want to make them sick? Who stood to gain by poisoning, or even killing, any of the others? It made no sense.

Bree reappeared and tossed a sweatshirt, some scrub pants, and a pair of disposable booties onto the bed. "There you go. Best I could do, but you'll be covered. Seth's one floor down, room 217, but that's all I could find out. They wouldn't tell me about his condition."

"Thanks, Bree." Meg stripped off the gown, thankful that at least the hospital had left her her underwear, and pulled on the clothes—too large, but clean. "I'm going to go find him. Can you call Art and tell him what's going on? And wait for me here—I'll be back as soon as I know that Seth is all right."

"I hear you. No problem. If you're not back, I'll tell him where to look. And take the stairs—that way you don't have to go past the nurses' station and they won't hassle you. Stairs are on the left, down the hall."

"Got it." Meg looked up and down the hall. There was no one in sight, so she left the room, trying to act normal, and found the door to the stairwell and slid through it. Down one flight, she opened the door and peered out. Same layout. She scanned the numbers on the doors. Room 217 should be at the opposite end of the corridor. She strode down the hall, pretending she belonged there. Pretending she wasn't terrified about what she might find when she reached Seth's room.

She arrived without attracting notice from the nursing staff but stopped before opening the door, her heart pounding. If he wasn't all right, she'd never forgive herself. *Only one way to find out, Meg.* She pushed open the door.

A room much like hers. One bed. Seth. He didn't notice her immediately: his eyes were closed. He was pale, but he was breathing. Was he conscious?

Meg stepped cautiously into the room. "Seth?" she said tentatively, but it came out as a whisper.

It was enough. His eyes opened; he turned his head. "Meg? You look good. You're okay?"

He was worried about *her*? She moved quickly to the bed and perched on it, grabbing his hand. "I look like crap, but thanks. You really had me scared last night."

"Good thing you knew what was going on. I don't remember a lot of it, but . . . did I hit you?"

"No. Maybe kind of pushed. But that's okay—I know you didn't mean it. How're you doing?"

"Not bad. I think they want to keep me around, give me another round of the antidote, make sure I'm still breathing. They going to let you go?"

"I don't know. I haven't asked yet." *I wanted to see you first.* "Art's on his way, and I assume he'll call Marcus."

Seth grimaced. "Just the person I want to see. Can I play possum?"

"I don't see why not."

"How's everyone else?"

"Bree is fine—she's upstairs. Must be great to bounce back so fast. The local police tracked down Michael, and it sounds like he'll be all right—Bree talked to him. I'm worried about Daphne, though. There's been no sign of her. Michael said he took her home, but the police haven't found her yet."

"So what happened?"

Meg studied her hand, entwined with his. "I've been trying to work that out. I'm betting somebody slipped pesticide into my dinner, and if I rule you and me out, it leaves either Bree, Michael, or Daphne. But why would any of them do something like that?"

Seth shut his eyes, and Meg felt a stab of anxiety. "Seth?"

"Oh, sorry. I was trying to think, but it's not easy with a headache like this. I'm pretty sure we don't know the big picture. Why would any of them want us dead?"

"You're the sickest one, but you ate more than anyone else. Let's take them one at a time. I think if someone wanted to kill us, they would have used a bigger dose." *Like the one that killed Jason.* "So they wanted to scare us? Or point the finger at someone?"

"You mean at Jason's killer?" Seth grimaced as he hauled himself up to lean against the pillows. "Doesn't make sense—then there would be *two* people running around with the poison."

"But that might be true. What if Michael and Daphne, or Michael and Bree, were working together to kill Jason, and they wanted to throw suspicion on whoever wasn't involved?"

"Meg, this is just too complicated. Daphne told you she loved Jason, and Michael was his friend."

"But Jason used Daphne, and Michael gets to take over GreenGrow now. So either of them might have a motive."

"What about Bree? Why would she kill Jason?"

"I don't know—an ex-lovers' quarrel? Do *you* think Bree had anything to do with this?"

Seth hesitated before responding. "No, I don't. She's

young, and she's got a chip on her shoulder, but I think she's a good kid, and I can't see her plotting anything like this. She'd be more likely to confront someone to his or her face."

"I agree. Which leaves Daphne and Michael, either one of them or working together. Seth, what am I supposed to tell Art? Or Marcus?"

"Art will probably come to the same conclusions we have. I can't guess what Marcus is going to make of this."

"I bet he'll find a way to blame me for all this," Meg said bitterly. She stood up, relinquishing Seth's hand reluctantly. "Then I'd better go now, because Art's on his way. Are you sure you're all right?"

"I will be."

"Seth, I'm so sorry. I seem to be some sort of magnet for disaster. And you could have died . . ."

"Meg, you are not responsible for this—any of it. And I'll be fine, really."

Before she could find anything else to say, a nurse bustled in, surprised to see her. "No visitors. Who are you?"

"I'm a friend, and I was just leaving. Oh, Seth, I'm so glad you're okay."

"So am I."

The nurse had watched the exchange with exasperated amusement. "Do this on your own time. I've got to check his vitals. Now shoo." She smiled to soften her statement.

Meg fled. And she realized that she was angry. Someone had poisoned them, had almost killed Seth. Marcus had been dragging his feet, and look at what had happened. Meg was going to talk to Bree and then see what Michael and Daphne had to say.

33

She made her way back to her room, but by the time she arrived she was exhausted again. Bree was still there, and there was no sign of Art. Meg collapsed on the bed with relief.

"Seth okay?" Bree asked.

"I think so. He says he is. Look, Bree, before Art gets here, we have to talk."

"Yeah?" she said cautiously.

Meg struggled to find the words and finally opted for the simplest. "The police are probably going to ask you if you had anything to do with this. That is, if they don't decide to go after me first, just for being there both times." When Bree started to protest, Meg stopped her. "No, I don't think you had anything to do with this, but maybe you had a motive to kill Jason that I don't know about. You might even have eaten some of the stuff yourself, just to throw everybody off. You have to be prepared for the questions."

Bree stood up and leaned over the bed, glaring into

Meg's eyes. "Meg Corey, what kind of a motive would I have? Jason and me, we were over, period. And I would never do harm to another living being, even a piece of trash like Jason. Why do you think I do what I do? I want to make things grow, not kill them. And if you don't believe me, you can find yourself another employee. Let the goddamn cops ask. I'm not hiding anything."

Meg stopped for a moment to muster her strength. "Bree, I believe you. But *somebody* poisoned the spaghetti sauce. So if you didn't, and I didn't, and I can't see any reason why Seth would, that leaves only two choices: Michael or Daphne."

Bree spoke quickly. "I cannot believe Michael would do such a thing."

"How well do you really know him? You haven't been together all that long. The police could think he had reason to want Jason out of the way, so he could run Green-Grow the way he wanted."

"But why go after us then?" Bree protested.

"I don't know. Maybe he thought he could shift blame to one of us. Odds are it was the same batch of poison that killed Jason. Michael certainly had opportunity to slip something into the sauce last night."

Bree was shaking her head vigorously. "No, no, no. He's a good man. He was Jason's friend, and it made him sad to see Jason go off the rails the way he did, but he wouldn't have killed him. He didn't want Jason dead. Michael doesn't like to be in the spotlight. He hates speaking to groups and promoting the organization. That's why he let Jason go on as long as he did—he didn't want to have to take over that side of things."

"Okay, okay. So that leaves Daphne."

Bree threw herself back in the chair and contemplated the ceiling. "Then tell me why she would kill Jason. She worshipped him, followed him around like a dog. She took all kinds of crap from him, hoping he'd toss her a crumb. It was pathetic."

"Maybe she finally had enough? Or she thought, if she couldn't have him, nobody else would."

Bree looked unconvinced. "I don't see it."

Meg had to admit she had trouble casting sad-sack Daphne as a villain, but *someone* had killed Jason and had tried to poison all of them. "But, Bree, it has to be one of us. And why else did Daphne invite herself along? Michael didn't want her there." *Or so he said*, Meg amended. Maybe they *were* working together and covering for each other? Maybe Michael was the brains behind this, and Daphne was carrying out his orders? She'd already demonstrated her talent for playing a doormat; maybe she'd switched allegiance from Jason to Michael.

Lost in thought, Meg was startled by a rap on her door. Expecting Art, she looked up to see Michael. Bree jumped up and went to him, and then stopped. Meg wondered if she was shy about showing him affection with an audience present—or whether she had taken Meg's comments to heart and suddenly had doubts about him.

Then Michael wrapped an arm around Bree, and she didn't protest.

"Michael, I'm glad to see you're up and around," Meg said. "You feeling okay?"

"I'm all right. Listen, Meg, I really wanted to apologize for bringing Daphne last night."

"I think we have more important things to worry about. Somebody tried to poison us, all of us, and Daphne is still missing." And she'd eaten mainly bread and salad, Meg recalled. Had she known about what was in the sauce? "Do you think Daphne did this?"

Michael stared at her. "I hadn't . . . Wait, you don't think I had anything to do with this?" Bree's grip on his arm tightened.

Meg met his look. "Michael, Bree believes in you, but I hardly know you. If you had anything to do with this, I'll make sure you pay."

Michael looked sheepish. "Meg, I swear I had nothing

to do with this. Bree's already read me the riot act." His expression sobered. "And Jason was my friend. I want to see whoever killed him punished. If it *was* Daphne, I don't like that she used me. I'll tell whoever asks whatever they want to know."

"Good, because the police are going to ask."

"Damn straight they are," Art said, coming up behind Michael. "I'm getting tired of people trying to kill people in Granford. I have to say, Meg, and you, too, Bree, you're looking a hell of a lot better than the last time I saw you. Damn good thing you had that information handy, Meg—it made a difference. Although it wouldn't surprise me if that gets twisted around on you. You all doing all right?"

Meg smiled at him. "More or less. Anyway, I had good reason to look up the pesticide in the first place, and the only reason I kept the printout was because I'm such a lousy housekeeper. Or maybe my karma is finally improving. What now?"

Art took charge. "Technically I should wait until Marcus gets here, and I should be talking to each of you alone, but screw that. We need to find Daphne, make sure she's okay. Marcus has got men out looking for her. Oh, by the way, Meg, I went back to your place and rounded up your dirty dishes and your leftovers for evidence."

"Great—now I don't have to wash the dishes." Meg realized she was feeling giddy—a remarkable improvement over dizzy. "Okay, what do you want to know, Art?"

"Let me rustle up some more chairs, so you invalid types don't have to stand up for this." He went out into the hall and returned with more chairs.

Since it was her room, Meg remained on the bed, sitting cross-legged against the pillows. "What first?" she asked Art once everyone else was seated.

"Give me the outline of what happened last night, up until you called me," Art said.

Meg took Art through the events of the previous day.

When she mentioned that Seth had brought wine, Art interrupted. "Hang on. Did everyone drink the wine?"

"No—Michael didn't, because he said he was driving, and Daphne didn't, because she said she didn't drink."

"Okay. Who showed up next, after Seth?"

"Then Bree arrived, in her car, and then Michael and Daphne together, in his car." Meg grimaced. "I hadn't expected Daphne."

"So how did she end up there?" Art asked.

"That's my fault," Michael said. "I had some stuff to do at GreenGrow headquarters, and she was there, dinking around at something. She's there a lot. I thought maybe she'd stop, after Jason . . . Anyway, I couldn't *not* talk to her, if you know what I mean." Michael sighed. "She started talking about how lonely she was without Jason, and how she wished we were better friends. Heck, I was worried she'd latch on to me next, so that's why I invited her along."

"Michael, what were you thinking?" Bree swatted his arm.

He turned to her. "I thought that maybe if she saw you and me together, she'd get the idea and back off."

Art put up a hand. "Hold it. You and Bree?"

Michael nodded. "Yeah, for a while now. But Bree didn't come around to the office, so Daphne wouldn't have had any reason to notice or know about us."

"Did you two get together before or after Jason died?"

"Before, a few months, maybe. That was the main reason Bree stayed away from GreenGrow—she didn't want to cross paths with Jason. You guys went through all that when he died, right? About him and Bree?"

"Yes. But Bree, you told Marcus you were at the GreenGrow dinner the night Jason died, right?"

"Yeah. I got tired of hiding, and Michael asked me to come."

Bree and Michael exchanged a glance, and then Bree nudged Michael and nodded toward Art. "Tell him."

Michael straightened up and faced Art. "We kind of left something out the last time we talked to the police. Bree and I were at the dinner, and we left together, and Jason left with Daphne. But Bree and I were together the whole night. I didn't want to say anything until she did."

Chivalry lives, Meg thought—and then realized the implications of what Michael had said. "But that means you couldn't have been hauling Jason around in the middle of the night! That's an alibi, you idiots!" Unless they were co-conspirators, but no way was Meg going to believe that.

Art struggled to suppress a smile, and Meg wondered if he was thinking the same thing. "Can we get back to last night? So there you all were, at Meg's. What were you doing?"

"I was putting the finishing touches on dinner—boiling spaghetti, heating the garlic bread," Meg answered.

"Who was in the kitchen?"

"Everyone, at one time or another."

"So anyone could have slipped something into the food."

"More or less. But nothing tasted off."

Art smiled openly this time. "Turns out the stuff tastes like garlic. Handy, wasn't it? Who knew what your menu was?"

"Nobody! Except me. Next you're going to be telling me I did it."

"Calm down, Meg. I'm not accusing anybody of anything at the moment. I'm just trying to work out the timeline. Let's move on. You all ate. And everybody seemed fine after dinner?"

Three heads nodded in unison.

"What order did people leave in?"

"Michael left with Daphne. Bree decided to stay over— she has a room at the house. Seth left last, and I decided not to bother cleaning up the kitchen and just went to bed."

"When did you start feeling sick?"

"I woke up a little after two, and I threw up. And then Bree did. And then we went downstairs looking for some juice or something. Anyway, Art, you know the rest. We felt sick, we were getting worse fast, and we called you. And here we are."

Art stood up, then leaned against the wall so he could look at all of them at once. "So any one of you could have done it. Most of you have the expertise to calculate dosage of this pesticide."

"What a minute!" Bree exploded. "It's not that simple. How could anybody know how much one person would eat? Or how it would affect them? You saw yourself, different people showed different symptoms. And everyone ate everything, more or less."

"Daphne didn't eat much of the spaghetti," Meg said slowly. "I thought she just didn't like my cooking, but maybe she knew what was in it. But then, she watched Seth eat seconds, and I don't know of any reason she'd have to hurt him. Maybe she just wanted to stir up trouble?"

"Or, if she killed Jason, she was trying to set up someone else. Anyone else—you, Michael, Bree. Whoever killed Jason knew what the right fatal dose was," Art said grimly.

A thick silence fell. To her surprise, Meg felt tears behind her eyes. She saw Bree lean toward Michael, and he put an arm around her.

Art finally broke the silence. "We need to find Daphne. Any ideas? Michael, you know her best."

"Hey, I don't know her well," Michael protested. "Other than her place and the GreenGrow office, I have no clue where else she might go."

"She doesn't have a car, she told me," Meg added. "So she couldn't go far. But where would she go? Does she have family around here?"

"We're looking into that."

The looming figure of Detective Marcus filled the doorway. "Cozy little gathering we have here. Getting your stories straight?"

Did he deliberately try to antagonize people? Meg wondered. "Nice to see you again, too, Detective. Please join us."

Marcus looked momentarily nonplused by Meg's remark and decided to ignore what he probably suspected was sarcasm. "I need to ask you some questions."

"And we'd be delighted to answer them. Where would you like us to start?"

"To begin with, I want to talk to you separately, although it's probably too late. Preston, you should have kept out of this."

"Marcus, I was part of the scene, so I was already involved. But you go right ahead, and we'll wait outside. Or maybe we'll go find the cafeteria. Michael, Bree?"

Michael and Bree silently filed out in Art's wake, leaving Meg alone with Detective Marcus. Marcus sat down in a vacated chair, pulled out a pad, and said, "Okay, from the top."

Meg repeated her story, sticking to the facts. Marcus jotted a note or two. "So, anybody there could have done it, and almost everybody had a motive."

"What was my motive? Or Seth's?" Meg said indignantly.

"Would you rather it was your little employee? Or her new boyfriend?"

"I'd rather think it was Daphne. Is she still missing?"

"We have only Michael's word for it that he took her home. Maybe he killed her, too, and dumped her somewhere on the way home."

Meg stifled hysterical laughter. Her head hurt, she was dizzy again, and Marcus kept coming up with increasingly improbable scenarios. "Just find Daphne, will you? Ask her what her side of the story is. Then you can start assigning blame."

Detective Marcus gave her a stony glare. "Ms. Corey, one man is dead, and more people could have been, last night. Someone has to answer for it. I'm just doing my job."

He did have a point. "I know, Detective," Meg said, contrite. "I'm sorry if I was out of line. As you pointed out, somebody tried to kill me, too, and I take that seriously. Please find whoever is doing this."

"That's what I aim to do. Thank you for your cooperation, Ms. Corey. I'll go find the others now."

"Oh, wait," she called out after his retreating back. "When I go home, can I use my kitchen, or is it still considered a crime scene?"

"I have all I need," he said and stalked out, leaving Meg feeling steamrolled again. He was right: he had only Michael's word about what had happened after he and Daphne had left her house. Could Michael have killed Daphne? She just didn't know. She trusted Bree, and Bree trusted Michael, so by some transitive property, she had to trust Michael. And that was the best she could do at the moment.

Where was Daphne?

34

 Meg and Bree were cleared to leave before noon, although Meg was told that the hospital wanted to keep Seth around a while longer. Meg was happy to be liberated, and thanked her lucky stars that she still had insurance coverage. Right now she just wanted to get home.

Michael had hung around and volunteered to drive them back to Meg's place. When they pulled into the driveway, Meg felt as though she had been gone for days, not for less than twelve hours. "I'm going in the front door," she announced when Michael turned off the engine. "I can't face the kitchen just yet."

"Um, I can help you clean up, if you want," Bree volunteered. Michael looked uncertain.

Meg took pity on them. "Michael, are you sticking around? You're welcome to stay. Bree, I think the first thing I want is a nap, and then we can figure out what to do next." She led the way to the front door and dug around for her keys. When she opened the door, she was greeted by Lolly, protesting loudly.

Meg laughed. "That's right, you haven't been fed, you little pig. Hey, you had dry food, so don't try and go all pitiful on me." Lolly continued to complain, but when she saw three humans, she retreated up the stairs in a huff. "Bree, I meant what I said. I'm going to crash for a while and then see how I feel. I'll see you later."

"Deal." Bree and Michael looked like a pair of kids waiting for Mom to go away so they could do whatever they wanted. Meg had a pretty good idea what that was, so she beat a retreat to her bedroom. The unmade bed looked very welcoming. Meg crawled in, pulled the covers over her head, and was out in seconds.

When she awoke again, the sun cast slanted rays across the floor. She checked her clock: nearly five. She felt alert, but she also didn't want to move, not just yet. She listened for a moment. No sound from the rest of the house, and she wondered if Bree and Michael were still there.

Bree and Michael. An interesting and unexpected combination. Most of the time Bree defended her independence fiercely, so to let down her guard with Michael would be a big step for her. And from what Meg had seen, Michael apparently did care for Bree, which was good.

Seth.

Why had he popped into her head? She'd been thinking about Bree and Michael and . . . young love. They seemed so young to her, so untried; in contrast, she felt old. Had her past relationships shut down something in her? Eroded her confidence in herself, in her judgment about other people? There had never been anything like what she would call love in her life, although she had dated her share of men, but she didn't want to jump into anything with Seth, either. For one thing, if things went wrong, it would be hard to avoid him, since he'd be running his business out of her property.

What Seth needed was a stable, long-term relationship and a houseful of kids and dogs and gerbils, and Meg wasn't sure whether that was what she wanted, or if it was anything she could offer. But still . . . when he'd been in danger, she'd been terrified. Maybe she wasn't ready to "have" him, but she didn't want to lose him, either. She wanted a chance to find out if there might be anything between them.

She stretched and sat up. Time to get up, get back to her life. But as she walked past the window facing the orchard, Meg saw a flicker of movement. She stopped and looked out. Yes, there, at the springhouse. She felt a pang of irrational fear: had Jason come back to haunt her? No, she thought she recognized the dumpy outline, the slump of the shoulders. *Daphne.*

What should she do? First, call Art. And then see if she could talk to Daphne without spooking her.

Meg picked up the phone and dialed the number for the police station, now engraved on her memory, and was put through quickly. "Art, it's Meg."

"Not again." He chuckled. "What's wrong this time?"

"I think Daphne's up at the springhouse in the orchard."

Suddenly Art was all business. "I'll be there in five. Don't do anything. Who else is there at the house?"

"Bree, and Michael, I think. They may be asleep."

"Just sit tight, and I'll be right there." He hung up.

Right, like she was going to do nothing. Meg pulled on jeans, sweatshirt, shoes. She opened the hall door cautiously and listened. There was no sound from Bree's room at the far end of the hall. Meg tiptoed down the stairs, found her coat and keys, and set off for the orchard.

She was panting by the time she reached the top of the hill. *Being poisoned takes something out of you*, she reflected wryly. She slowed as she approached the springhouse. She had been right: Daphne was sitting where

Jason's body had been, staring into space. She turned to watch Meg approach but made no other move.

Meg stopped about ten feet away from her, then dropped to the ground, leaning against the trunk of one of her apple trees. "What are you doing here, Daphne? The police have been looking for you."

"This is where Jason died. I had to come here."

"How'd you get here?"

"Walked. Took a while."

"Why?"

Daphne ignored her question, wrapping her arms around herself and rocking back and forth. "Have you ever been in love? I mean, sick in love, so much that you'd do anything for the guy, even though you knew it was stupid and pointless?"

"Is that how you felt about Jason?"

"I did. For a long, long time. I dropped out of school so I could be with him, and my parents stopped talking to me. I stopped seeing any of my friends, so I could help him at GreenGrow. But he was so wonderful, at least at the beginning. He was smart and sure of himself, and he could talk to people, make them see what he saw, and he really believed in what he was doing, in GreenGrow. And I kept hoping and hoping that he'd see—I mean, really *see* me. And when we started sleeping together, I thought maybe it was happening, maybe things would work out. But I never meant anything to him." Tears started running down her cheeks, and she ignored them. "Whenever he wanted a quickie, there was Daphne, always willing." Her voice was tinged with bitterness. "Whenever he wanted any stupid job done, there was Daphne, again. God, I was a fool. But I loved him. And now he's dead."

Meg had a lot of questions she wanted to ask, but as she took a hard look at Daphne, she realized something was very wrong. "Daphne, did you take something? Are you trying to kill yourself?"

Daphne smiled sadly. "I had some left."

Daphne had come here to die, Meg realized. And then suddenly she was boiling mad. "Damn it, Daphne, you're not going to die here. I'm not going to let you. I'll get you to the hospital."

Daphne's only response was to lean over and throw up. Meg waited until that bout had passed, then reached down and grabbed Daphne's arms, hauling her to her feet. She had to get her down the hill, to her car, or Art's if he showed up in time. Daphne felt like a large mass of dough, sloppy and boneless. *Come on, you silly cow. I am not going to let you die on my property.*

And Daphne had to be all right, Meg thought selfishly—otherwise she'd never know what had been going on. Somehow she wrestled her down the hill, lurching and stumbling. Art pulled into the driveway just as she reached it.

He jumped out of the car. "What's going on?"

"She took the same damn stuff. I don't know how much or when. Get her to the hospital and tell them that."

Art wasted no time. "Right." He shoved semiconscious Daphne into the backseat.

"I'll call you when I know anything." He started his car and pulled out in a spray of gravel, and then was gone, leaving Meg standing in the driveway, trembling. Poor obsessed Jason, poor foolish Daphne. What a mess.

When she got back to the house, she heard noise from the kitchen, and laughter. Meg followed the sounds.

When Bree spotted her, she said, "Hey, where'd you go? I checked your room but you weren't there."

Might as well get it out of the way. "Daphne was up at the orchard."

Bree turned off the water in the sink and turned to face her. "What? What happened?"

"I called Art, then I went up there to talk to her. She tried to kill herself—with the same pesticide."

Michael took a step closer to Bree. "What the hell was she thinking? Why? What did she say?"

"Not much. She loved Jason, but she realized he was using her. So she was going to kill herself on the spot where he died. Art is taking her to the hospital." Meg sat down heavily at the kitchen table. "Maybe it sounds callous, but I suppose we should eat something. Though I don't feel like cooking, that's for sure."

"I could go get a pizza?" Michael offered, probably eager to get out of the way.

Meg considered. No nausea, no stomach pains—and she was suddenly very, very hungry. "Sounds good to me, Michael. That work for you, Bree?"

"Yeah, sure, fine." Bree slammed pots in the sink with more force than was necessary.

"Great." Michael grabbed his coat and was out the door before anyone could say anything else.

Bree rinsed the last pot and stacked it in the dish drainer, then turned to Meg. "So did Daphne kill Jason?"

"That's my guess, although she didn't say so outright. I wonder how long it would have taken Detective Marcus to figure it out."

Bree snorted. "Try never. That man doesn't get people at all."

"You're right about that. So, you and Michael are okay?"

"Looks like it. There's no rush. If it works, it works. How about you?"

"Me?"

"You and Seth."

"What are you talking about?"

"Meg, you wake up in a hospital bed after someone nearly kills you and the first thing you want to do is find Seth Chapin?"

"Well, he was hit harder by this stuff than the rest of us. I was worried."

"Yeah, right. Whatever you say. You don't have to talk about it with me." Bree grinned.

Meg had to smile. "Fine. You mind your business, and

I'll mind mine. Except where they overlap. We've still got an orchard to run, right?"

"That we do."

Art called as they were finishing the last of the pizza. "She's going to be all right, but they want to keep her overnight. I persuaded Marcus that he could wait until morning to interview her. She wants you to be there."

"Me?" Meg sputtered. "Why?"

"She didn't explain. Can you come by about ten?"

"I guess. I really would like some answers."

"So would we all. See you tomorrow."

35

Tuesday morning Meg woke and wondered if maybe her life was finally going to go back to normal: no one trying to kill her, no outstanding murders, and no more bodies. Things with Bree were good, after a rocky start. She was learning to drive a tractor. She had a cat and a pair of goats. What more could she ask for?

As she was dressing, she heard Bree's car start up, and Meg watched her leave from the window. It was going to take some getting used to, having a roommate again, much less one who worked for her. Still, maybe having Bree here would be a good thing. At least she'd have someone else around to assure that the cat—and the goats—got fed, and there would be a second set of eyes and hands to keep things on track. Meg still had no idea how time-consuming the orchard might be, but she was prepared to be very busy. And that was good.

She wandered downstairs, reveling in the silence, fed

the cat, made herself some breakfast. The kitchen spar-
kled, thanks to Bree's and Michael's efforts, and the
morning sun gleamed on the glossy golden boards of the
floor. It looked great, even if she did say so herself. And
she had christened it with a memorable party, even if the
party hadn't turned out quite the way she had expected.
What was on the calendar for today? She had a class in
the morning, and was woefully behind on the required
reading, but that seemed kind of irrelevant at the moment. Murder was more important than academics.

She arrived at the hospital shortly before ten and spent
a few minutes convincing the receptionist that, despite
the fact that visiting hours hadn't started, yes, her presence was required in Daphne Lydon's room for an interview with a state police officer. When she finally made it,
she was surprised to find not only Detective Marcus and
Art but also Seth clustered in the hallway outside of
Daphne's room.

"Gentlemen? Seth, I thought you'd be home by now."
To her he still looked pale.

"They just turned me loose, and Art volunteered to
give me a ride home. He thought I should hear this first."

Meg noted smugly that Marcus didn't look very happy.
"Ms. Corey, Ms. Lydon insisted that you be here, or she
wouldn't say anything. I don't want this to turn into a
three-ring circus, so I hope you will all keep your mouths
shut and let me conduct my interview."

"I have no problem with that, Detective," Meg said.
"How is she?"

"Recovering nicely, or so I'm told. Let's get started."

They trooped into the room, with the detective in the
lead. "Ms. Lydon, I am going to read you your rights and
remind you that you have the right to have an attorney
present."

Daphne lay against a stack of pillows, but she didn't
look particularly ill. She did, however, look peevish. Meg
thought irreverently that this was probably the most con-

centrated attention she had received in years and she probably wanted to draw it out and enjoy it for as long as possible.

Marcus recited the familiar words, while Daphne watched him, unblinking. When he was done she said, "Sure, fine. I get it. And I don't want a lawyer. Can I start now?"

Meg stepped forward and claimed the sole guest chair, while Marcus checked a small recorder he had pulled from a pocket; Seth and Art leaned against the walls. Before Marcus could begin, Meg said, "Daphne, why did you want me here?"

"I feel kinda bad that you got mixed up in this. I mean, I didn't even know you, and Jason didn't, either. But he knew the orchard and he wanted to take it back."

"Ms. Lydon," Marcus broke in, "can you please state your full name and residence for the record?" Formalities completed, he asked, "Were you responsible for the death of Jason Miller?"

"Kinda. Look, can I tell this in my own words? It's kind of hard to explain."

"Go ahead."

"Jason had this brilliant idea that he was going to kill himself, like a political protest or something, you know? Like he'd done all he could with GreenGrow, and people still wouldn't listen to him, and this chemical company was moving in on the university at the same time the university was throwing him out, see? So he was going to make a statement and get some attention, maybe some good press. Only he never meant to die. I was supposed to come along and find him and save him."

Well, that was a new twist. Jason had trusted Daphne enough to help him stage a phony suicide? But obviously, something had gone wrong.

"Were you delayed?" Marcus asked.

Daphne glared at him for interrupting, but Meg thought she saw a glint of sly triumph in her expression. "No, I was not delayed. I was there, at his apartment, right on time. He had this suicide note written—ha, book was more like it, full of political stuff. And he mixed up some of this pesticide stuff and he drank it down, and then he checked the time and looked at me and said, 'Let's give it a couple of hours and then you can call for help, okay?' So we waited, and he started getting nauseous and sweaty." Daphne stopped.

"We found no note," Marcus said grimly.

"Well, duh. I got rid of it—the printed copy, anyway. But he probably wrote it on the GreenGrow computer."

Marcus sighed, almost imperceptibly. "And then what did you do?" he said.

"Nothing. Not. A. Thing. I watched him get sicker and sicker, and all I felt was empty. And then I figured, somebody would find him dead and they'd just think he'd killed himself. Which he did, right? I mean, he was the one who took the stuff."

Meg was chilled by the image of Daphne watching Jason die, but she had to know: "Daphne, why was he in the orchard?"

"Figured you'd wonder about that. Well, he started getting kind of crazy, and loud, and he decided that to make his point, he ought to make it look like he picked the orchard to die in. So I went along with the idea."

"He knew the property?"

"Sure. Professor Ramsdell's been teaching classes out there for years, and Jason took one of them a while back."

"Was that where he found the poison?" Marcus asked.

"Yup. He'd seen it there, one time, when he was snooping around, and he kind of helped himself to some. You never know when things like that will come in handy. Problem was, it turned out to be kind of unstable—which he found out the hard way. It acted a lot faster than he thought it would. Hurt more, too." Daphne looked ghoulishly pleased at that idea.

Meg felt a pang: so it *had* been the pesticide from her barn. Her carelessness was going to haunt her—she should have known what she had on her property.

"How did you transport him?" Marcus asked.

"His car. I can drive, you know—I just can't afford a car."

"But," Meg interrupted again, "his car was found in Amherst. You just left him here and went home? Without telling anyone?"

Daphne settled herself more comfortably on her pillows. "Well, you know, I had plenty of time to think, sitting out there in the dark with him, waiting. Good thing he'd quieted down by then, or the whole neighborhood would have been awake. Anyway, I guess it was the first time I felt like I was in control, you know? I mean, it was always like, Daphne, do this. Daphne, come over when I want you. He never cared what *I* wanted. So now I had the power, and I started thinking: what did I care about GreenGrow or all this organic crap? I was only there because Jason cared. Okay, maybe his death would help them, but then I had a better idea. I figured I'd make it look like it was Bree's fault."

The men in the room looked blank, but Meg had an inkling of Daphne's intentions. "Because she rejected Jason?"

"That was part of it. She didn't want him, and he was really pissed about that. But then she started sniffing around Michael, and she started coming back to Green-Grow. Jason wasn't too happy about that. Him and Michael, they started arguing a lot more. Everybody knew it. Why should Miss High-and-Mighty get everything she wants? And why did she have to horn in on the only thing I had? Jason and GreenGrow? So I thought, let's see if the cops will think maybe she had something to do with it."

Not a bad plan, Meg thought. It might have worked, or

the whole thing might have blown away for lack of evidence and Jason's death would have gone down as unsolved. "Then why did you try to poison us last night?"

"Because you jerks just weren't getting it! I mean, Jason had been dead for two weeks, and nobody had a clue! I figured I'd better give the police a shove in the right direction."

"And you could have killed all of us, if that pesticide was as unstable as you say."

"Yeah, well, sorry. I guess I didn't plan it very well."

"So when you saw that your plan had failed, you decided to kill yourself?" Marcus said.

"Yeah, I guess. I couldn't think of anything better. I mean, I have no education, no money, the only guy I loved didn't care about me, and now he's dead. It just seemed like the easiest way out."

Meg felt nauseated again, but this time it was due to the horror she felt at Daphne's words. Daphne had watched someone she claimed to love die, and had let it happen; worse, she'd come close to killing more people, just because she was jealous of Bree. Poor Daphne—the killer.

Seth moved to her side. "Had enough?" he whispered in her ear.

Meg nodded. "Get me out of here."

He turned to face Detective Marcus. "Do you need her for anything else?"

"I think we have enough."

"Talk to you later, Art. Meg, let's go home."

36

"Did the hospital clear you to go?" Meg asked Seth on the way down to the lobby.

"No problem. You all right?"

"Sad, I guess. Daphne's such a mess, and Jason was a jerk. If he'd just been a little nicer to Daphne, maybe none of this would have happened. And how pathetic is that?"

"I'm sorry it had to involve you, and your orchard."

"So am I."

"Are you okay to drive?"

"Sure. I come from tough Yankee stock. And I've got work to do."

They drove back in silence, but somehow Meg didn't turn off toward Seth's house, going straight home instead, without asking Seth. It was a lovely sunny day, and she wanted to check on the orchard. Thank God she had managed to get Daphne out of there alive—she didn't need any more ghosts in her orchard.

Things happened quickly during this uncertain season, didn't they? She got out of the car, stuck her keys in her pocket, and set off up the hill, toward air and sunshine. Seth followed without a word.

When she reached the edge of the orchard, she stopped. Superstitiously her eyes were drawn to the springhouse, but there was no one there, dead or alive. The rows of trees stretched in all directions, and—she did a double take—some of them appeared to be blooming. Wasn't it early for that? But here and there were hints of pink as new blossoms sought the sun. Baby apples in the making, and—bees, weather, pests, and time willing—they would be full grown by the fall.

"Seth, look! I've got flowers. Or blooms, or whatever you call them." The orchard had gone on, with or without their attention.

"You do. Looks good." He came up behind her. "Listen, Meg, I don't want you to let what happened with Daphne and Jason get to you."

She turned to him. "Seth, why shouldn't it? They were living out their own little tragedy, right here under our noses. Sure, it wasn't my fault, but I still feel bad about it. What a waste."

A minute or two drifted by as Meg moved away, looking at more individual trees. Then she said without turning, "Seth, I'm glad you're not dead."

He laughed. "Yeah, I'm kind of glad about that, too."

She took a deep breath. "You know, I have a lousy romantic track record, and I'm not sure I trust my judgment right now, but if there's a chance of something happening between us . . . I think I'd like to know."

"Meg, you've got to know that I think of you as a lot more than a friend."

It wasn't easy for her to turn around and look at him. Same Seth, solid and warm, watching her. She reached out, grabbed his shirt, and pulled him into the shelter of an apple tree's low branches. "Good," she breathed.

She wasn't sure who kissed who, but it didn't matter. It felt right. She leaned back against the rough bark of the tree and pulled him closer. He was alive, she was alive, and it was spring . . .

"Ahem."

Meg jumped a foot at the sound of a discreet cough.

"Is that you, Meg? And Seth Chapin?"

Meg could feel herself blushing. "Tell me it isn't Ruth Ferry," she said into Seth's chest.

Seth backed up—all of an inch—without letting her go. "I won't, but Rachel will."

Meg giggled. "Not Rachel, too. Can we get back to this later?"

"Definitely."

Seth backed out of the branches cautiously, and Meg followed after running her fingers through her hair, releasing a shower of pink petals. "Hi, Rachel. Were you looking for me?"

Rachel struggled to hide her smile. "I was. It was such a nice day, I thought Ruth might enjoy a drive, and here we are. I hope I haven't disturbed you."

The expression on her face made it clear that she hoped no such thing. Seth intervened quickly. "Rachel, behave yourself. Ruth, it's great to see you—how long has it been?"

"Long enough, my dear boy. Do you know, I believe I came upon your grandfather under the same circumstances, when I was about twelve. It must be the spring. If you can spare the time, however, I'd love to see the orchard."

Meg beamed at her. "Of course! It looks like the bloom is just beginning. Seth, you want to come, too?"

"There's nowhere else I'd rather be."

Cooking with Apples

While almost all apples taste good when cooked, their texture varies widely, so you have to choose carefully when you're using apples in cooking. Some cook down into mush, others become leathery and tough, and some are "just right."

Old cookbooks may recommend apple varieties, but they're not always available these days. In your local stores today, the best cooking apples are: Braeburn, Cortland, Granny Smith, Jonathan, Mutsu, and Stayman. Golden Delicious is a dependable variety, but don't try to cook with Red Delicious! And keep in mind that a good eating apple is not always a good cooking apple.

1 pound of apples = 2 large, 3 medium, or 4 small

Apple Recipes

Grandmother's Apple Crisp

Apple desserts come with all sorts of wonderful names—cobblers, buckles, betties, pandowdies, crisps, crumbles, slumps, and grunts. They're all related, but with complicated genealogies. For her ill-fated dinner party, Meg chooses a recipe she remembers her grandmother making—it's hard to go wrong with it.

Serves eight

Topping

2⅓ cups all-purpose flour
¾ cup packed dark brown sugar
¼ cup granulated sugar
½ tsp. cinnamon
¼ tsp. salt

2 sticks (1 cup) unsalted butter, cut into
    tablespoon-size pieces and softened
1⅓ cups toasted, chopped pecans

Filling

½ cup granulated sugar
½ tsp. cinnamon
5 lbs. apples
2 tbsp. fresh lemon juice
grated lemon rind

Preheat oven to 375°.

Blend the flour, sugars, cinnamon, and salt in a food processor. Add the butter and blend until mixture forms large clumps. Place the mixture in a bowl and work in chopped nuts with your fingers (quickly—you don't want the butter to melt).

Peel, core, and slice the apples (slices should be about a half-inch thick). Blend the sugar and cinnamon in a large bowl. Combine the sliced apples, sugar-cinnamon mix, lemon juice, and zest and toss well.

Butter a 4-quart shallow baking dish and spread the apples in it. Crumble the topping evenly over the apples. Bake in the middle of the preheated oven until the topping is golden brown, about an hour.